BLOOD BOND
ARIZONA
AMBUSH

BLOOD BOND
ARIZONA
AMBUSH

William W. Johnstone
with J. A. Johnstone

PINNACLE BOOKS
Kensington Publishing Corp.
www.kensingtonbooks.com

PINNACLE BOOKS are published by

Kensington Publishing Corp.
119 West 40th Street
New York, NY 10018

PUBLISHER'S NOTE
Following the death of William W. Johnstone, the Johnstone family is working with a carefully selected writer to organize and complete Mr. Johnstone's outlines and many unfinished manuscripts to create additional novels in all of his series like The Last Gunfighter, Mountain Man, and Eagles, among others. This novel was inspired by Mr. Johnstone's superb storytelling.

All Kensington titles, imprints, and distributed lines are available at special quantity discounts for bulk purchases for sales promotions, premiums, fund-raising, educational, or institutional use. Special book excerpts or customized printings can also be created to fit specific needs. For details, write or phone the office of the Kensington special sales manager: Kensington Publishing Corp., 119 West 40th Street, New York, NY 10018, attn: Special Sales Department; phone 1-800-221-2647.

ISBN-13: 978-0-7860-2345-5
ISBN-10: 0-7860-2345-7

First printing: November 2011

10 9 8 7 6 5 4 3 2 1

Printed in the United States of America

Chapter 1

"Are we in Arizona or New Mexico?" Matt Bodine asked with a puzzled frown.

Sam Two Wolves shook his head.

"I don't know. We might've even strayed over the line into Colorado or Utah. That's why they call this area the Four Corners."

Matt frowned.

"You don't know exactly where you are? You're an Indian, aren't you? Shouldn't you know these things?"

"I'm half Cheyenne, as you well know."

"Well, then, shouldn't you be at least half-sure where we are?"

"The Indians who live around here are not Cheyenne," Sam pointed out with the tolerant air of someone explaining things to a small child. "I believe most of them in these parts are Navajo."

Matt shook his head.

"Sounds like an excuse to me."

"What about you?" Sam asked. "You're blood brother to the Cheyenne. Shouldn't *you* know?"

"I'm blood brother to *one* Cheyenne—you. And since you're half Cheyenne, that makes me . . ." Matt squinted as he thought. "I never was that good at ciphering. You're the one with the college education. You figure it out."

"Maybe we should just admit that we're lost."

"*I'm* not lost." Matt pointed south over the mostly flat, dry terrain through which the two young men rode. "That way's Mexico." He turned in the saddle and waved a hand northward. "And Montana and Canada are up yonder a ways. California's in front of us, and the Mississippi River's behind us. See? I'm not the least bit lost."

Sam just shook his head as Matt grinned.

The companionable relationship between them came naturally. Matt Bodine and Samuel August Webster Two Wolves had ridden together for a number of years, drifting across the frontier, and before that they had been childhood friends in Montana. That was where they had become blood brothers.

The link between them was even stronger than that. They were *onihomihan*, brothers of the wolf. The adventurous lives they had led made them brothers of the gun, as well. Theirs was the unbreakable bond of men who had fought side by side and saved each other's lives on numerous occasions.

At first glance they might have been mistaken

for actual brothers. Both young men were tall, broad-shouldered, and powerfully built. The differences between them were apparent on a second look, however.

Matt's close-cropped brown hair was lighter than Sam's shaggy black hair, which was as dark as a raven's wing.

Sam also had the slight reddish tint to his skin which was also part of his legacy from his father Medicine Horse, as were the high cheekbones.

Matt wore jeans and a faded blue bib-front shirt. His battered brown Stetson was thumbed back on his head most of the time, as was the case now.

Sam wore jeans and a fringed buckskin shirt, although the fringe was strictly utilitarian, not gaudy like that on the outfits of Wild West Show performers. His black hat had a wide brim and a slightly rounded crown.

Another difference was in the way they were armed. Sam wore only one holstered revolver while Matt sported a pair of Colts. Sam was fast on the draw and accurate in his aim, but Matt was in a whole other league when it came to lead-slinging. His speed rivaled that of famous gunfighters such as Smoke Jensen, John Wesley Hardin, and Frank Morgan. Matt's name wasn't quite as well known as those others, perhaps because of his relative youth.

Matt and Sam both owned lucrative ranches in Montana, but except for brief visits, they hadn't been home in years. The ranches were run by top-notch managers, and that allowed Matt and Sam to do the thing they loved best—drift. Both were fiddle-footed hombres, always eager to see what was on the other side of a river or over the next hill.

The fact that they didn't know exactly where they were wasn't going to stop them from riding on. The destination mattered less than the getting there, and as long as they were moving, Matt and Sam were happy.

But that didn't mean they weren't alert. Matt suddenly stiffened in the saddle and said, "I just saw the sun reflect off something on that bluff over yonder."

He nodded toward an upthrust of rocky ground several hundred yards northwest of them.

"So did I," Sam agreed. He looked around in case they needed to find some cover. The reflection could be nothing . . .

But it could also be the sun glinting off a pair of field glasses, or worse, a rifle barrel.

"There's an arroyo off to our left," Sam began. "Maybe we'd better—"

A buzzing sound, like a giant bee that had just flown between them, interrupted him. Both young men recognized the sound, having heard similar ones all too many times in the past. That buzz was a heavy-caliber slug cutting through the air, and it was followed an instant later by a distant boom.

"Head for the arroyo!" Sam finished as he and Matt kicked their mounts into a gallop. The horses, big, strong animals with plenty of sand, raced toward the gully that twisted its way across the arid landscape.

Matt saw dust fly in the air as another bullet struck the ground to their right. The arroyo was about fifty yards away, and it wouldn't take the racing horses long to cover that much ground.

Even so, several more slugs whipped past the heads of Matt and Sam as they leaned forward in their saddles to make themselves smaller targets. There had to be more than one rifleman up there on the bluff shooting at them.

Why they were being bushwhacked like this was a whole other question, one that didn't really matter at the moment. They could worry about who the would-be killers were and why they wanted Matt Bodine and Sam Two Wolves dead once they were safely behind some cover.

The arroyo was only about twenty yards away when Matt was hit by what felt like a giant fist punching him in the right side. The terrible impact drove him so far to the left that he couldn't stay in the saddle.

He was stunned, but a part of his brain continued working. He had been shot before, so he knew one of the rifle bullets had hit him and reacted accordingly.

When he felt himself slipping off the horse, he kicked his feet free of the stirrups so neither of them would catch and hang up when he fell. If that happened, he would wind up being dragged over the rough ground, and probably that would be just as bad or worse than being shot.

Suddenly there was nothing under him but air, and a split second later he crashed into the ground, landing on his left shoulder. Momentum tumbled him over and over as more bullets kicked up dust and gravel around him.

Chapter 2

Zack Jardine was down by the wagon, keeping an eye on the unloading, when rifle shots began to crash from the top of the nearby bluff.

Jardine's head jerked up and he grated out a curse. He saw powder smoke spurting from the places in the rocks where he had posted guards to keep an eye on the semi-arid landscape around them.

The men seemed to be shooting at something southeast of the spot where the guns were being unloaded. Jardine swung around, looked in that direction, and saw two men riding hellbent-for-leather, several hundred yards away.

Rifle in hand, Jardine broke into a run toward the trail leading to the top of the bluff. He was a big man, heavily muscled and handsome in a rugged, cruel way, and he didn't like running in the hot sun.

He glanced toward the men on horseback when he was halfway up the trail and saw one of them tumble off his horse, probably hit. The other one was still mounted, though.

Jardine reached the top. Angus Braverman was one of the riflemen, Doyle Hilliard the other. Jardine figured Braverman was the one who'd started shooting. He was impulsive, reckless . . . a damned fool, some might say.

"You opened the ball," he shouted at Braverman and Hilliard. "You'd better kill both of them. I don't want either of them getting away!"

To help ensure that, Jardine lifted his own rifle to his shoulder. He sighted at the distant figures and started cranking off rounds as fast as he could work the repeater's lever.

He paused only long enough to wave an arm at the men he'd left below and yell, "Kill them!"

Everybody forgot about the crate of rifles they had just lifted down from the wagon and got busy trying to ventilate those two unlucky hombres who had wound up somewhere they shouldn't have been.

From the corner of his eye, Sam saw his blood brother go down. He hauled back on the reins as hard as he could, but by the time his horse skidded to a halt, he was already a good ten yards past the spot where Matt had fallen.

Sam threw himself out of the saddle and ran toward Matt, holding the reins and pulling the horse with him. Bullets thudded into the ground and kicked up dust.

As he ran, Sam felt a hot streak on the side of his neck and gritted his teeth. He knew a slug had just come within an inch or so of ending his life.

But the thought of abandoning Matt to his fate never entered Sam's mind. Not even when Matt lifted his head and bellowed, "Blast it, Sam, get out of here!"

Sam ignored that and stooped to get an arm around Matt. He had been blessed with great strength, so he was able to lift Matt without much trouble.

"Can you run?" he asked.

By way of answer, Matt lurched toward the arroyo.

Sam ran alongside him, still leading the horse. Matt's mount had bolted off somewhere. They could find the horse later—if they were still alive.

Sam's horse let out a shrill cry and leaped ahead, pulling loose from Sam's grip on the reins. As the horse galloped down the arroyo's bank, Sam spotted the bloody streak on its rump where a bullet had creased it.

He'd been using the horse as makeshift cover. Now he and Matt were left out completely in the open. Sam slipped his arm around Matt's waist and half-carried, half-dragged him toward the shelter of the arroyo.

Sam felt a bullet tug at his buckskin shirt as he and Matt reached the bank and tumbled over it. The slope wasn't too steep, about a forty-five-degree angle.

When they reached the bottom, Sam lifted his head and looked to make sure the bank cut them off from the view of the riflemen on the bluff. He couldn't see the bluff at all anymore, so that meant they were out of the line of fire.

Sam turned to Matt and asked, "How bad are you hit?"

Matt's face was pale under the permanent tan. He had his hand pressed to his right side. A dark stain had spread beyond it on his shirt.

"Think the slug caught me at an angle . . . and went on through without penetrating too deep," he answered in a voice taut with pain. "I'm bleedin' like a stuck pig, though."

The booming of the rifles on the bluff had stopped. The men hidden up there must have realized they'd just be wasting bullets if they kept shooting. They couldn't hit Matt or Sam from where they were.

Sam pulled up Matt's shirt and saw the two puckered, bloody holes in his friend's torso. The smaller hole was in Matt's side, the slightly larger one that marked an exit wound on Matt's back only a few inches away and a little lower.

Matt was right about the bullet going all the way through. The angle of its flight had been shallow enough that Sam hoped the slug had missed any vital organs.

Even if that were true, the bullet had still done plenty of damage. And Matt could easily bleed to death if Sam didn't get those crimson streams stopped—soon.

* * *

Up on the bluff, Zack Jardine cursed bitterly again as over the barrel of his rifle he saw the two strangers disappear. From this height, Jardine could see the dark line of the arroyo zigzagging its way across the ground, and knew they had taken cover in it.

Jardine lowered his rifle.

"Get down there," he told Braverman and Hilliard. "We're gonna have to go after those two."

"One of 'em's hit bad, Zack," Braverman said as he straightened from behind the rocks where he had been crouched. "Did you see the way he fell? He's bound to be dyin'."

Braverman was a short, quick man with red hair who never tanned in the desert sun, just blistered. He looked harmless, but Jardine had seen him kill more than one man in cold blood without batting an eye.

Hilliard was bulkier, with a drooping mustache and what seemed like a permanent week's worth of beard stubble. "Those fellas ain't worth gettin' killed over, Zack," he rumbled.

"Well, then, you shouldn't have opened fire on them in the first place!" Jardine's words lashed at the two men. "Why the hell didn't you just let them ride on past? They probably didn't even notice us over here."

A number of boulders littered the ground along the base of the bluff, huge chunks of sandstone that had broken off and rolled down the slope in ages past.

The wagon and the horses were down there among those big rocks, easy to miss if somebody wasn't looking for them. That was the main reason Jardine had picked this isolated place to deliver the rifles.

"They was actin' funny, Zack," Braverman said. "Lookin' this way and all. I think one of 'em pointed. I was watchin' 'em through my spyglass."

Jardine's jaw clenched in frustration. It was all he could do not to walk over there and stove in Braverman's stupid skull with the butt of his rifle.

It wouldn't do any good, he told himself. Braverman was too dumb to realize that a reflection off the lens of the telescope was probably what had alerted the two strangers that somebody was over here.

"Come on," he ordered as he started down the trail.

Braverman and Hilliard fell in behind him, thumbing fresh cartridges into their rifles as they followed their boss.

When Jardine reached the parked vehicle, he snapped at the other men, "Put that crate back in the wagon with the others."

"But we haven't got the money yet, Zack," Dave Snyder protested.

"And we're not going to today. We're calling off the swap." The men didn't look happy about that, so Jardine went on, "Don't worry, we'll get our payoff, and it'll be just the first of many. But I don't like the way this is playing out, so we'll set up another meeting."

The other men exchanged glances. They knew that Zack Jardine was something of a superstitious man by nature. If a deal didn't *feel* right to him, he wouldn't go through with it until it did.

So there was no point arguing with him. Anyway,

arguing with Jardine was dangerous, and they knew it. They were a hard-bitten bunch, but Jardine was the worst of the lot.

He knew that, too.

As several of the men gathered around the long, heavy crate to lift it back into the wagon bed with its brothers, Jardine leveled an arm and pointed toward the arroyo he had spotted from the top of the bluff.

"Those two hombres are over there in a gully, on foot, and at least one of them is wounded. I want them both dead. That shouldn't be too hard. I'm going back to Flat Rock with the wagon. The rest of you go take care of those two . . . and don't come back until they're buzzard bait."

Chapter 3

"Give me your bandanna," Sam said.

Matt reached up to the blue-checked bandanna tied around his neck.

"This is my favorite bandanna!" he protested. "You remember that girl who gave it to me—"

"Yes, and she seemed quite taken with you, at least at the time, so I doubt that she'd want you to lie there and bleed to death. Hand it over."

With a sigh, Matt took off the bandanna and gave it to Sam, who used the Bowie knife he carried in a sheath on his left hip to cut it into two pieces. He wadded up each piece and shoved them into the bullet holes.

Matt grunted in pain.

"Take it easy," he said. "I just got shot, you know."

Sam lifted his head as he heard the swift rataplan of hoofbeats somewhere on the prairie not far away.

"And you're liable to be again," he said, "because unless I'm mistaken, those bushwhackers are about to pay us a visit and try to finish us off."

Sam looked both ways along the arroyo, at least as far as he could see. That wasn't very far, because of the way the gully twisted and turned, less than a hundred yards in either direction. But he spotted his horse a short distance away and whistled for the animal. He wanted the Winchester in the saddleboot.

As the horse trotted toward him, Sam stood up and got both hands under Matt's arms from behind.

"I can stand up!" Matt said.

"Faster this way."

Sam dragged Matt along the floor of the arroyo toward a pile of brush that had washed up against a rocky outcropping during some past flash flood.

In this part of the country, these arroyos were bone-dry nearly all the time, except for the one or two occasions every year when a rare desert thunderstorm would send walls of water gushing through them.

The brush and the rock would provide a little cover for Matt. Sam propped him up against the outcropping.

"Think you're strong enough to handle your guns?"

Both of Matt's Colts were still in the holsters attached to the crossed gunbelts. He drew the revolvers and said, "You bet I am. Just give me something to shoot at."

"You ought to have some targets soon enough." Sam's horse had come in respose to the whistle. Sam hurried over to the animal and drew the Winchester from its sheath.

Then he took off his hat and slapped it against the horse's bullet-creased rump. That sent the horse galloping off along the arroyo where Sam hoped it would be safer.

Sam went to the far side of the arroyo and waited there with the rifle in his hands. The banks were steeper here. The bushwhackers would have to descend into the arroyo and come along the bottom of it to get at their intended victims.

"Keep your eyes on the rim above me," Sam called to Matt. He pointed up with a thumb. "They might cross over somewhere else and try to get above us. I'll watch the rim on your side."

Matt nodded and lifted his gaze to the top of the bank about six feet above Sam's head. The bushwhackers might try to sneak up and fire down directly on them from up there.

The hoofbeats had stopped. That meant whichever way the bushwhackers planned to proceed, they were approaching on foot now.

Matt and Sam both listened intently for the scrape of boot leather on the ground or anything else that might give away the location of the would-be killers.

They didn't hear anything except the faint sighing of the wind across the plains. Then a shadow moved on the rim above Sam's head. Matt knew that a man on his side of the arroyo cast it, and he jerked a gun barrel up to alert Sam to the lurker.

Sam had already realized the man was up there. He lifted the Winchester to his shoulder as the crown of a sweat-stained, pearl-gray Stetson came into view.

Sam held his fire, well aware that this could be a trick. One of the bushwhackers could have put his hat on a stick and lifted it up there, trying to draw a shot that would tell him and his companions where Matt and Sam were.

A few seconds later, the man stepped into sight. He held a rifle, and as he spotted Sam, he tried to lift the weapon.

He was too late. Sam's Winchester was already lined up. The rifle cracked and sent a .44-40 slug drilling through the bushwhacker's shoulder. With a yell of pain, the man twisted and flopped backward out of sight.

But as if that had been a signal, more shots erupted from farther along the arroyo as several more gunmen charged toward Matt and Sam.

Matt twisted and pressed himself against the out-cropping, grimacing as the movement made pain from his bullet wound jolt through him. Flames stabbed from the muzzles of his Colts as he opened fire on the darting, shooting figures.

On the other side of the gully, Sam dropped to one knee and triggered several rounds from the Winchester. Fire spat from the rifle's muzzle as a storm of lead howled back and forth along the arroyo.

Bullets sizzled through the air and whined off rocks. One of the slugs hit the bank just above Matt's head and sent dirt and gravel spraying over his face. He jerked back and blinked as the grit stung his eyes and blurred his vision for a moment. The barrels of his Colts drooped.

Sam kept up his deadly fire. Through the haze of gunsmoke that floated in the arroyo, he had seen several of the attackers stagger and a couple of them had fallen. He wasn't surprised when he heard a man bellow out a curse and then order, "Come on! Let's get out of here!"

Sam knew that might be a trick, a tactic to make him and Matt think their enemies were giving up.

But when he stopped firing, he could tell that the other guns had fallen silent, too. Echoes of the thunderous blasts still bounced back and forth between the walls, but as they faded, Sam heard swift hoofbeats again. It certainly sounded like the bushwhackers were pulling out.

"You all right?" he called over to Matt.

"No new bullet holes, if that's what you mean," Matt replied. He had blinked most of the dirt out of his eyes and could see fairly clearly again. "Reckon they're really gone?"

"I don't know. We'd better wait and see."

"I don't want to cause a problem for you, Sam, but these holes in my side are still leaking."

"Just hang on," Sam said. "I'll get you out of here and find some help for you."

"Where do you figure on doing that? We're out in the big middle of nowhere. There's probably not a settlement within thirty miles. Maybe not even that close. Might find a ranch house somewhere, but that'd just be a matter of dumb luck."

Sam flashed a grin at his blood brother.

"Well, then, you've got that going for you."

"I'm gonna keep track of all these mean things

you're sayin' to me while I'm hurt, so when I get to feeling better . . ."

Sam motioned for Matt to be quiet.

"I'm going to go take a look."

"Be careful," Matt said, and the joking tone was gone from his voice now.

Sam came up from his kneeling position and stalked along the floor of the arroyo, turning his head constantly from side to side as he looked for any sign of the attackers.

He reached the area where the bank's slope was gentler, and his keen eyes spotted several indications that the gunmen had fled this way. Carefully, he ventured up.

The plains on both sides of the arroyo were empty as far as the eye could see, which was pretty far in this flat terrain. The bushwhackers were gone, all right.

Sam hurried back to the place where he had left Matt. As he approached, he saw that his friend's head hung forward limply, as if in death.

Chapter 4

Sam's breath seemed to freeze in his throat. His heart slugged heavily in his chest. Fearing that Matt had died from the loss of blood, Sam ran forward and dropped to his knees beside his friend.

Sam put his hand to Matt's throat and searched for a pulse. Relief flooded through him when he found one. Matt's heart was beating fast but steadily. He had just passed out.

There was no time to lose, Sam sensed.

He checked the pieces of bandanna he had wadded into the bullet holes. Both of them were soaked, and more blood was leaking out around them.

Sam threw the sodden bits of cloth aside and cut replacements from Matt's shirttail. When he had them in place, he fastened Matt's belt around them to hold them there.

A whistle brought Sam's horse back. The animal shied a little at the smell of fresh blood, but Sam calmed it with a quiet word.

He lifted Matt into the saddle. It wasn't easy, since Matt was so much dead weight in his unconscious state, but Sam managed, then climbed on behind him.

Sam rode out of the arroyo, holding Matt in front of him with one arm and using the other hand to hold the reins.

They had been headed west when the bushwhackers opened fire on them, so he started off in that direction again. He didn't know of anyplace he could get help that was within reach back the other way.

They had ridden about two miles when Sam spotted something up ahead. A moment later, he recognized it as Matt's horse. The animal had bolted this far after Matt was shot out of the saddle, then stopped to graze on the sparse clumps of hardy grass that dotted the desert.

Finding the horse didn't really help matters right now. With Matt out cold, they had to ride double so Sam could keep him in the saddle. But Sam whistled for the horse to follow them, anyway. They would need the animal later, he told himself, when Matt recovered from his injury.

Sam wasn't going to allow himself to consider any other possibility.

They had covered another mile or so when Sam saw something else in front of them. A haze of dust rose into the hot air. Sam figured it was being kicked up by the hooves of several horses moving quickly over the plains.

He thought at first the dust came from the bushwhackers' mounts as they put this area behind them, but after a moment he realized the cloud was moving toward him and Matt.

Of course, it could still be the bushwhackers doubling back to look for them, Sam reminded himself.

But it could also be a group of cowboys from one of the isolated ranches that could be found in this region, or even a cavalry patrol. In that case, it would be good to meet up with them. They could help him patch up Matt's wounds.

Until he knew for sure, it might be wise to err on the side of caution. He turned the horse to the south, thinking he would move out of the path of the oncoming riders.

There was a cloud of dust rising into the blue sky from that direction, too.

Sam's mouth tightened into a grim line as he turned back to the north. Somehow, he wasn't surprised to see more dust that way.

Whoever the riders were, they were closing in around him and Matt. The only possible way to escape would be to turn completely around and gallop eastward.

Even that would be futile, Sam realized. His horse was big and strong, but carrying double this way, it would only be a matter of time until the pursuit caught up. They couldn't possibly outrun it.

Instead, Sam slid down from the saddle, caught hold of Matt, and lowered him gently to the ground. Then he drew the Winchester again and thumbed cartridges into it until the magazine was full and a round was in the chamber.

He forced his horse to lie down. Sam stretched out behind the animal and laid the rifle over the horse's flank.

He had sixteen bullets in the rifle and six more in his Colt. He would sell their lives at the cost of every one of those slugs if he had to.

The dust clouds came nearer. Sam saw the dark shapes of the riders at the base of those clouds as they closed in. When they came in range of the Winchester, he held his fire because he couldn't be sure who they were.

A moment later he was able to make out buckskin leggings, red and blue shirts, bandannas bound around black hair, and ponies being ridden without saddles. The three groups of riders converged around him and Matt and then came to a halt about fifty yards away.

One man urged his pony forward. His dark face was set in a grim expression, and he carried an old single-shot rifle.

Sam had a hunch that he was looking at a Navajo chief.

The rider called out a challenge in his native tongue, demanding to know who Sam was. Sam wasn't fluent in the language, but he understood enough to know what was being asked of him.

He kept his rifle trained on the chief as he replied in Spanish, "Two Wolves, son of Medicine Horse!" A lot of the tribes in this part of the country spoke that language in addition to their own.

The chief scowled—although it was hard to discern much change in what was evidently his natural expression—and turned to say something to one of the other warriors.

This man, who also carried an old rifle, rode forward past the leader and came closer to Sam.

"Caballo Rojo says you look like a white man, not a Mexican," the warrior said in English. "Are you?"

"My father was Medicine Horse of the Cheyenne," Sam insisted, also speaking English this time.

"And your mother was white," the Navajo said. He spoke the white man's language well, which led Sam to believe that he had spent some time on the reservation, around missionaries and the Bureau of Indian Affairs functionaries.

"My mother was white," Sam admitted. Most Indians were fairly tolerant of people with mixed blood, although like any other group, some looked down on the so-called half-breeds.

The warrior who was talking to him sneered.

"You travel with a white man, you dress like a white man, you use a saddle like a white man. You might as well be white."

Sam felt a surge of anger and didn't try to suppress it.

"The Cheyenne blood is strong in me!" he called. "My people have fought and defeated the whites many times!"

Unlike the Navajo, he thought, who had a history

of losing more battles than they had won against the invaders of their land.

More than likely, however, pointing out that fact to a proud Navajo warrior wouldn't be the smartest thing in the world to do. But Sam was proud, too, and the impulse was strong in him.

Proud, but not a blasted fool. He was surrounded, outnumbered, and Matt needed better medical attention. Sam went on, "My friend is hurt. I ask hospitality for him."

"And for you?"

"I go where he goes," Sam declared, even though he couldn't really enforce that position.

The chief—Caballo Rojo, or Red Horse, Sam recalled—spoke again, and the Navajo who had been talking to Sam turned and answered him.

The discussion went back and forth quickly for a couple of minutes. Sam understood enough of it to know the two Indians were talking about what to do with him and Matt, but he couldn't tell what conclusion they came to.

When the spokesman turned back to him, every fiber of Sam's being was tense with the knowledge that he might be fighting for his life, and Matt's life, in a few seconds.

"Caballo Rojo says that you and your friend are welcome among the people of our clan," the warrior said. Judging by the sullen expression on his face, he didn't agree completely with that decision. "You will not be harmed, and we will help your friend if we can. This is the word of Caballo Rojo."

Relief went through Sam. Being given the word of the chief like that meant that he and Matt were safe, at least for the time being.

Of course, a man could ride into almost any Indian village on the frontier and be safe at first.

They wouldn't kill him until he tried to leave.

Chapter 5

Sam slid the Winchester back in the saddleboot. He stood up and tugged on the horse's reins. The animal struggled upright and shook itself.

Sam went over to Matt and once again lifted his unconscious friend. The Navajo didn't make a move to help, but Sam didn't expect them to.

As soon as he was mounted behind Matt, the riders closed in around them. There would be no getting away now, even if Sam wanted to, which he didn't.

As the group started off, heading west, the man he'd been talking to fell in alongside him.

"What is your white man name?" the Navajo asked, and he seemed genuinely curious now.

"Sam. Samuel August Webster Two Wolves."

The Navajo made a face.

"A mouthful of words," he said disdainfully. "A waste of time and breath." He thumped his bare chest lightly with a clenched fist. "Juan Pablo, but sometimes I am called Corazón de Piedra."

Heart of stone, Sam translated.

"Because your heart is hard like a stone?"

"Toward my enemies it is."

"I'm not your enemy, so I think I'll call you Juan Pablo."

The Navajo looked like he wasn't sure about that.

The group rode in silence for several minutes before Sam said, "Your people are Diné?"

That was the Navajo name for themselves.

Juan Pablo nodded.

"Yes. The true rulers of this land, and someday those who try to take it will be sorry that they did."

Nobody was trying to take this rugged, arid land in the Four Corners region, at least not that Sam had heard of. Much of it had been set aside by the government for the Navajo.

But it was true that there were white settlements in the area, as well as wagon trails, stagecoach routes, and the like, not to mention the ranchers who moved in and tried to graze cattle or sheep on the hardscrabble land. Most of them laid claim to waterholes the Navajo might consider theirs.

Sam didn't recall hearing anything recently about Indian raids in this part of the country, so he asked, "Do you and your people make war against the whites?"

"We want only to be left alone," Juan Pablo snapped. "But if that does not happen . . . then there may be war."

It would be a short one, Sam thought. The only guns these warriors had were practically antiques, old

single-shot rifles that probably jammed as often as
they fired.

The Navajo might be able to raid an isolated ranch
house or something like that, but against a company
of cavalry they wouldn't last fifteen minutes.

To change the subject, Sam said, "How did you
happen to find my friend and me? From the looks of
the dust clouds, it seemed like you were searching for
us."

"We were," Juan Pablo said. "I was hunting when
I heard much shooting. I went back to my people and
told Caballo Rojo, and he gathered the men and came
to see what it was about."

Sam nodded.

"Well, I'm glad you found us," he said. "My friend
Matt needs help."

"What happened to the two of you?" Juan Pablo
asked with grudging interest.

"Some bushwhackers opened fire on us from the
top of a bluff," Sam explained. "We were taking cover
in an arroyo when Matt was wounded. The men came
after us, but we were able to fight them off."

"Who were these . . . bushwhackers?"

Sam shook his head.

"I don't have any idea, and I don't know why they
started shooting at us."

"Did you see them?"

"They were white," Sam said. "Or maybe a few
were Mexican, I don't know. I was too busy shooting

at them to get a good look at them, if you know what I mean."

Juan Pablo grunted to indicate that he did.

"Will you try to find these men and seek vengeance for what they did to your friend?"

"Matt's more than my friend," Sam said. "We're blood brothers. And the only thing I'm interested in right now is making sure that he's all right. But if he doesn't make it—or even if he does . . ." Sam's voice hardened as he went on, "Yes, I'd like to know who they were and why they tried to kill us."

"I would feel the same way," Juan Pablo admitted.

The flat terrain had become more rugged as they rode, until now they were in a region of bluffs, ridges, and mesas, cut with deeper arroyos. A line of low cliffs appeared in front of the riders.

Sam saw a canyon cutting into the cliffs and had a hunch that was where they were headed. The members of Caballo Rojo's clan probably lived in there. The place could be defended by putting men at the narrow mouth of the canyon.

His guess turned out to be correct. They rode past a couple of sentries armed with bows and into the canyon itself, which had steep walls that would be difficult, if not impossible, to scale.

After a few hundred yards the canyon widened out and ran for more than a mile into the plateau formed by the cliffs. Sam spotted a number of squat, mound-like hogans built of earth and wood scattered along the banks of a little stream, none of them too close together, because the Navajo liked their privacy.

A few scrubby trees grew on those banks, as well as some grass. A flock of sheep cropped at the grass.

Dogs ran out to bark greetings at the newcomers, followed by quite a few children and some women.

Caballo Rojo looked over his shoulder and called something back to Juan Pablo, who nodded and answered in the Navajo tongue.

"We will take your friend—your blood brother—to my hogan," Juan Pablo told Sam. "My wife will care for him."

"Thank you," Sam said. "I appreciate your hospitality."

"It is the way Caballo Rojo wishes it," Juan Pablo said, making sure that Sam knew it wasn't his idea.

The warriors dispersed. Juan Pablo led Sam to one of the hogans, where a short, stocky Navajo woman waited. He spoke to her, obviously seeking her approval.

Sam recalled that women wielded quite a bit of power in the Navajo society. Juan Pablo's wife might refuse to go along with Caballo Rojo's decision.

After a moment the woman replied at length to Juan Pablo, who then turned and nodded to Sam.

"I can carry him inside," Sam said as he slid down to the ground next to the horse.

"I will help," Juan Pablo said, still grudgingly. He and Sam lifted Matt down from the horse, then put their arms around him to help him into the hogan.

Another woman stepped through the dwelling's door as Sam and Juan Pablo approached with Matt between them.

This woman glanced at Sam, and he felt a shock go through him as he saw her long, curly red hair and brilliant green eyes. Despite the green shirt and long calico skirt she wore, like the Navajo women, she was white, and from the looks of her, as Irish as she could be.

Chapter 6

Sam tore his eyes away from the young woman. He didn't want to offend Juan Pablo by staring at her. He wasn't afraid of the Navajo warrior, but since Juan Pablo and his wife were going to take care of Matt, it wouldn't be polite to stare.

Juan Pablo motioned for Sam to enter the hogan. He did so, stepping past the redheaded woman, who held the entrance flap open.

A small fire smoldered in the rock-lined pit in the center of the hogan. The smoke curled up and out the opening at the top of the shelter. That opening let in a shaft of afternoon sunlight that revealed a thick pile of blankets.

Sam and Juan Pablo lowered Matt onto the blankets and rolled him onto his left side. The woman knelt beside him and pulled up his shirt so she could examine his wounds. She plucked the blood-soaked wads of cloth from the bullet holes and tossed them into the fire.

"My wife will tend to his wounds," Juan Pablo told Sam. "Come with me."

Sam hesitated.

"I'd rather stay here with my blood brother."

"You do not trust us?" Juan Pablo snapped.

"Of course I trust you," Sam replied, although if he had been honest, his answer would have been *No, I don't trust you. Not completely.*

But that would be an insult, and Sam knew it would be a mistake to push this proddy Navajo warrior too far. He went on, "Where are we going?"

"To see Caballo Rojo."

Sam nodded.

"Good. I want to thank him again for his hospitality. And you, too, of course."

Juan Pablo just gave one of his skeptical grunts.

The redheaded woman had followed them into the hogan. As the two men turned to leave, she stepped aside from the entrance. Juan Pablo went past her without even a glance.

Sam tried to do the same, but it was difficult. He hadn't expected to find someone like her in this Navajo camp.

The canyon was still in a mild state of excitement as Juan Pablo led Sam through it. The people who lived here probably didn't see visitors very often.

Juan Pablo took Sam to the largest hogan along the stream, which evidently belonged to Caballo Rojo, or rather to his wife, given the matriarchal nature of these people. He went to the entrance and spoke, and

Caballo Rojo answered from inside. Juan Pablo jerked his head at Sam, who went first.

Caballo Rojo sat cross-legged on a buffalo robe near the fire. Several women, ranging in age from their teens to their late thirties, bustled around the hogan, engaged in various chores. The younger ones would be Caballo Rojo's daughters, the older ones his wife and possibly her sisters.

Several men who appeared to be about Caballo Rojo's age sat around the fire with him. They would be the chief's inner circle, his most trusted advisers. One of them was probably a shaman.

Caballo Rojo spoke respectfully to the women, who stopped what they were doing and left the hogan. Whatever would be said in here was for the men.

With a brusque gesture, Juan Pablo motioned for Sam to sit down. They took their seats on blankets.

Having grown up in a Cheyenne village, Sam found all this familiar despite the significant differences in the Navajo culture. He knew that if he stayed in surroundings like this for very long, he would start thinking and acting like an Indian again. That part of his heritage was never far from the surface.

Now that Sam had a better look at Caballo Rojo, he saw why the man had been given that name. Sam had assumed at first that Caballo Rojo had ridden a red horse at some time or another, but instead the man's long, narrow face had a definite horse-like shape to it.

Caballo Rojo spoke, and Juan Pablo translated for him.

"Did you and your friend come to this land in search of the Navajo?"

Sam shook his head.

"We were simply riding through the area. We bear your people no ill will."

Juan Pablo translated again, then said, "Caballo Rojo has promised you the hospitality of our people. You and your friend will be safe as long as you remain here. We will do our best to nurse your friend back to health, and then you will be free to leave."

"Tell Caballo Rojo I am very grateful to him. I promise on behalf of myself and my friend to repay his kindness."

Sam finally began to relax. It looked like he and Matt might live through the day after all, he thought.

Matt had no idea where he was when he opened his eyes, but he was glad to be there for a couple of reasons.

One was that he was still alive.

The other was that he was looking into the prettiest pair of green eyes he had seen in a long time.

Sam must have found a town, Matt thought. He remembered the fight in the arroyo but nothing after that. Now he was lying on a featherbed and had a good-looking redheaded nurse leaning over him.

Then he realized that the bed wasn't soft at all, but hard instead, as if he were lying on the ground. As his vision cleared even more, he realized that wasn't a roof over his head but rather the curving roof of an Indian hogan. And as for the "nurse" . . .

Well, she was a green-eyed redhead, no doubt about that, but she was dressed like an Indian woman and when she spoke the words made no sense to him.

Matt figured whatever she had said to him was in an Indian language. Navajo, probably, given the area through which he and Sam had been traveling when they were ambushed.

Matt was fluent in Cheyenne and could get by in several other tongues spoken by the tribes on the northern plains, but Navajo was mostly a mystery to him.

His side hurt where he'd been shot, but not as much as he expected it to. He heard someone else moving around in the hogan and turned his head slightly to see another woman. She was older than the redhead and obviously an Indian. Matt figured the two of them had patched up his wounds.

He wasn't sure how he'd ended up in a Navajo hogan or what in blazes that good-looking redhead was doing here. The Navajo didn't take white captives like some tribes did.

But those questions could wait. Right now he wanted to make sure his blood brother was still all right.

"Do you know where Sam is?" he asked the redhead. "Sam Two Wolves?" Matt made a guess. "The man who brought me here?"

The redhead replied in whatever language she'd been speaking before. Matt tried to pick up some of it, but he couldn't figure out what she was saying. After a moment, though, she repeated, "Sam?"

Matt nodded.

"Yeah. Sam. Big fella." He tried to gesture to indicate what he meant. "Half Cheyenne."

The young woman just stared at him for a second and then abruptly burst out laughing.

"Your friend Sam is fine," she told Matt in perfect English. "And I'm sorry. I shouldn't have teased you like that. You just looked so puzzled and confused I couldn't resist."

Suddenly angry, he tried to sit up, but she put a hand on his shoulder and held him down. That made him aware that he was no longer wearing his shirt. No great loss, since it had a couple of bullet holes in it and had been soaked with his blood. The lightheadedness he felt now was probably a result of all the blood that had leaked out of him.

He was able to prop himself up on an elbow and look down at his side. He couldn't see the wound on his back, but the one in his side was covered with a poultice of some sort. He figured the hole in his back was being treated the same way.

Matt let himself relax on the thick pile of blankets. They weren't a featherbed after all, he thought, but they were fairly comfortable.

"Who are you?" he asked the redhead. He wanted to express his gratitude for their help, but he was a mite peeved at the moment.

Also, his uncertainty about Sam's fate, regardless of what the redhead had said, plagued him, but he was too weak to get up, and chances were the young woman wouldn't let him, anyway. She wore a determined look on her face.

"My name is Elizabeth Fleming," she said. "You should lie back down. You lost a lot of blood."

Matt nodded and said, "All right. Don't reckon I've got much choice in the matter. I'm about as weak right now as a newborn kitten."

"You're probably wondering what I'm doing here."

"The thought crossed my mind," Matt admitted as he stretched out again on the blankets.

"I'm a teacher. I've come to help educate these people."

The Navajo had been living in this part of the country for hundreds of years, Matt thought. He wasn't sure how much educating they needed.

Folks back East didn't think of it that way, however. They had the idea that everybody ought to live like them . . . whether the people to be "educated" wanted it or not. "Lo, the poor Indian!" they said, leading the cavalry to adopt Mister Lo as a scornful nickname for all Indians.

Some good things came from that Eastern attitude, misguided though it was most of the time. Sam's mother had been a white teacher who had come west to educate the so-called savages.

In the process she had won the heart of Sam's father Medicine Horse.

"I reckon I'm pleased to make your acquaintance, Miss Fleming," Matt said. "I'm Matt Bodine."

"I'm pleased to meet you as well, Mr. Bodine . . .

although the circumstances are somewhat lacking in, ah, propriety."

Such as the fact that he wasn't wearing a shirt, Matt realized. He wondered if he ought to try to cover up with one of the blankets he was lying on.

The older woman knelt by the fire, where a pot was sitting at the edge of the flames. Matt didn't know what was in it, but the hogan began to fill with a good smell that made him realize he was hungry in spite of his weakened condition. Or maybe because of it.

Before he had a chance to think any more about that, somebody stepped into the hogan. Matt looked up and saw a fierce-looking Navajo warrior standing there. The man looked at Elizabeth Fleming, then at Matt.

And as he glowered down at Matt, his hand dropped to the hilt of a knife tucked behind the scarlet sash around his waist. The look in his eyes was unmistakable.

He wanted to pull that knife and plunge it into the white man's chest.

Chapter 7

Matt tensed himself to roll out of the way if the warrior lunged at him, but a second later Sam stepped into the hogan, too. Sam didn't appear concerned, so Matt figured he was safe after all.

"You're awake," Sam said, sounding happy about it. He came over and hunkered on his heels next to the pile of blankets where Matt lay. "How do you feel?"

"Those bullet holes hurt like blazes, and I'm a mite lightheaded," Matt replied, "but on the whole I reckon it's a heap better than being dead."

Sam nodded.

"You had me pretty worried for a while, Matt. You lost so much blood, you looked like you were about to run dry."

"Yeah, I can feel it, too," Matt said with a feeble nod. He glanced toward the unfriendly-looking warrior. "Who's your pard there?"

"That's Juan Pablo. He's the one who heard the shots when those bushwhackers opened up on us. He came back here to the canyon, got Chief Caballo Rojo and the rest of the men, and rode out to see what had happened."

"They're Navajo?" Matt guessed.

Sam nodded.

"That's right."

Even though he was weak, Matt lifted a hand and rested it on Sam's arm. Quietly, he asked, "Are they going to—"

"Kill both of you?" Juan Pablo broke in. Obviously, Matt's question hadn't been quiet enough to keep the warrior from overhearing what he said. Juan Pablo went on, "Caballo Rojo has promised that the two of you will be safe."

Sam inclined his head toward the warrior and told Matt, "Juan Pablo speaks English."

"Of course he does," Elizabeth said. "Quite a few of his people have been to mission schools." She stood up and held out a hand to Sam. "I'm Elizabeth Fleming."

"Sam Two Wolves," he told her. "I was wondering what a, uh . . ."

"—Redhead who looks like she's straight from Killarney was doing in a Navajo clan?" Her green eyes twinkled as she smiled. "I'm a teacher, Mr. Two Wolves."

"So was my mother," Sam said, unknowingly echoing Matt's thoughts earlier.

From the blankets, Matt said, "Help me sit up."

Sam frowned.

"I don't know if that's a good idea."

"I've got something to say, and I'd rather be upright while I'm doing it."

"You're going to be stubborn about this, aren't you?"

"You ever know me *not* to be stubborn when I thought something was right?"

"All right," Sam said. "Just take it easy. I'll give you a hand."

He got his arm around Matt's shoulders and lifted him into a sitting position. Matt's head spun crazily for a few seconds before settling down.

The wounds in his side and back throbbed, too, but he ignored the pain. The bleeding had stopped, thanks to the poultices, and as long as it didn't start again, he was confident that he would be all right.

"Juan Pablo, thank you for helping me," Matt said. "I owe you a debt."

Juan Pablo looked skeptical, but he gave Matt a curt nod. Without saying anything, he went over to the fire and hunkered next to the pot where the stew was simmering. He took a wooden bowl from his wife, dipped it into the pot, and began eating with his fingers, picking out chunks of meat and wild onions from the savory broth.

Elizabeth brought bowls of stew to Matt and Sam. Earlier, when Matt smelled the stuff cooking, he had thought he was hungry. But now his stomach suddenly rebelled against the idea of eating. He grimaced and pushed the bowl away, saying, "I'm sorry, but I can't."

Sam said, "Drink the juice, anyway, even if you

can't eat the rest of it right now. After losing all that blood, your body needs the nourishment."

Matt could see the logic in that argument. Sam held the bowl to his mouth and tipped it up, and Matt forced himself to swallow the thick liquid, sip by sip. When he was finished, Sam helped him lie down on the blankets again.

"For some reason . . . I just got . . . mighty tired," Matt managed to say as his heavy eyelids drooped and exhaustion washed over him.

"Go ahead and get some sleep," Sam urged. "It'll be good for you."

Matt nodded, or at least thought he did. He couldn't be sure. He closed his eyes to let sleep overtake him.

Just before he dozed off, a thought occurred to him and he tried to open his eyes again. He wanted to tell Sam he had seen that green-eyed, redheaded young woman in the Navajo getup first.

But that probably wasn't true, he realized, since he'd been unconscious when they got here, so it was just as well that oblivion claimed him before he could say anything.

Sam didn't sleep much that night, because Matt developed a fever and would have tossed and turned restlessly all night if Sam hadn't sat beside him and tried to keep him calm.

As it was, Matt muttered incoherently most of the time and jerked his head back and forth. Elizabeth

Fleming, who seemed to have appointed herself a nurse as well as a teacher, and Juan Pablo's wife took turns wiping Matt's forehead with a wet cloth in an attempt to cool his fever.

Juan Pablo himself left the hogan, muttering disgustedly to himself as he went to look for somewhere more peaceful to sleep.

Sometime during the long ordeal, a rustle of movement close by made Sam's head come up sharply. He had dozed off sitting up, without realizing it. He saw Elizabeth on her knees on Matt's other side. She had taken over the job of bathing his feverish forehead.

Sam started to smile and nod at her. He was in mid-nod, though, when the urge to yawn gripped him. He couldn't hold it back. His mouth opened wide before he could stop it. All he could do was cover the yawn sheepishly with his hand.

Elizabeth laughed.

The soft sound didn't waken the older woman, who now snored on the other side of the hogan. Sam chuckled, too, and grinned at the redhead.

"I can tell by your accent you're not really fresh from Killarney," he said. "Where are you from?"

"Bennington, Vermont, actually," she told him. "What about you?"

"Montana. Like I said, my mother was a teacher. My father was Medicine Horse of the Cheyenne."

"I don't think I'll be marrying one of my students here in Arizona."

"Then we *are* in Arizona?" Sam asked. "Matt and

I were talking about that earlier today . . . before the shooting started."

Elizabeth nodded.

"Yes, in Sweetwater Valley, about twenty miles west of Flat Rock."

"I didn't think there was any sweet water in these parts."

"You should know that Indians are capable of irony," Elizabeth said with a smile.

"What's this Flat Rock you mentioned? I don't reckon I've heard of it. Some natural landmark?"

"No, it's a town," she said. "The closest town to this spot. I took the stagecoach there from Chinle."

Sam shook his head.

"Must not have been there for very long. It's been a few years since Matt and I rode through this area."

"All I know is that it has a rather rough reputation. The stage line ends there, and the driver said he would be glad to turn around and start back to civilization."

Calling anywhere in this region "civilization" was stretching things a mite, Sam thought. A lot of it had been unchanged for hundreds of years.

Matt stirred and let out a low moan. Elizabeth leaned over him with a frown for a moment, then got the cloth wet again in the basin of water on the ground beside her and wiped it over his forehead.

"He needs proper medical care," she said, "but I'm afraid this is about all we can do for him."

Sam nodded.

"Matt's strong. He'll pull through this all right."

His voice was confident. He just wished his heart was.

But Elizabeth was right. All they could do was try to keep Matt comfortable and wait for his fever to break.

Chapter 8

Two days later, it did. Big drops of greasy sweat formed on Matt's face as his temperature went down. As the sun came up that morning, he was groggy but awake again.

"Sam . . . ?" he whispered as he saw his blood brother sitting beside him and looking down at him anxiously.

"Just take it easy," Sam told him. "You were real sick for a while, but I think you're better now."

Juan Pablo's wife knelt beside Matt and removed the poultices from the wounds. Those poultices had been changed several times while Matt was in the grip of the fever.

Each time Sam had seen the bullet holes, his worry had deepened. The wounds were angry-looking, and streaks of red radiated out away from them. He knew that the festering threatened to spread all through Matt's body.

But now the redness had faded so much it was

almost invisible. The poultices had drawn the corruption out of Matt's flesh. The wounds were beginning to pucker a little, too. Soon they would close up and start to heal.

The woman covered the holes with pieces of clean cloth and bound the bandages in place with long strips of rawhide. Sam hadn't seen her smile even once since he and Matt had been here, but now she as she looked at him and nodded, her expression wasn't as severe as it had been. He took that as a good sign.

"We're still in the Navajo canyon?" Matt asked.

"That's right. You've been too sick to move you. Juan Pablo's wife has been taking care of you, along with Miss Fleming."

"That's mighty nice of 'em. Hasn't been . . . any trouble?"

"Nope."

"No sign of those . . . bushwhackers?"

"No, but I've been thinking about what happened. Either we almost stumbled into something they didn't want us to see . . . or somebody sent them after us because they wanted us dead."

"Who would . . . send hired killers after us?"

"I don't know, but I'd like to find out for sure one way or the other."

"Yeah," Matt agreed, "if somebody's after us . . . it'd come in handy to know who and why." He sighed. "Soon as I . . . get some of my strength back . . . we'll see if we can pick up their trail."

Sam shook his head.

"You're not going to be in any shape to travel for a

while. Right now, though, since it looks like you're going to be all right, I need to find Juan Pablo and go talk to Caballo Rojo. I want to make sure it's all right with him before I try to leave the canyon."

"Leave the canyon? I told you, I'm gonna have to rest up some first . . ."

"It'll be at least a week before you're on your feet again, Matt. The trail's already several days old. If we wait until you're strong enough to travel, it'll be so cold there's a good chance we'll never be able to find those varmints. Unless they ambush us again, and we won't have any warning of that coming if we don't know who they are."

"Yeah, but you can't track them down by yourself," Matt protested.

"Why not? I know we make a good team, but I can take care of myself, you know. And I'm a better tracker than you are, too."

"Durned well ought to be, since you're half-Indian," Matt muttered. "But that still won't stop you from going off and gettin' yourself killed."

"Have a little faith," Sam said as he got to his feet.

"You're just gonna leave me here?"

"You'll be well taken care of, and Caballo Rojo has given his word that you'll be safe. Anyway, I don't think the ladies would let anything happen to you. They've worked too hard pulling you through to lose you now."

"Where is that . . . pretty little redhead?"

"Miss Fleming, you mean?"

"I don't reckon there are too many other redheads around here," Matt said.

"She's around. She's got to get some rest sometime, you know. Taking care of you will wear a person out." Sam grinned. "I ought to know."

"Do I remember her sayin' . . . she's a school-teacher? My memory's a mite fuzzy right now."

"That's right. From Vermont."

"And we run into her in the middle of nowhere," Matt muttered. "If that don't beat all."

Sam found Juan Pablo sitting on a rock beside the creek, restringing a bow. The warrior glanced up and grunted, but didn't say anything.

"Matt's fever finally broke," Sam reported. "He's feeling a lot better."

"Good. We will not have to trouble ourselves dragging his body away from the canyon for the coyotes and the buzzards to feast upon."

Sam swallowed the angry retort that almost sprang to his lips. He and Matt were guests of the Navajo, after all. Anyway, he should be used to Juan Pablo's surly nature by now, he told himself.

"I'd like to speak with Caballo Rojo."

That drew some interest from Juan Pablo. He looked up with a frown and asked, "Why?"

"Because I want to find those men who bush-whacked us and make them tell me what it was all about."

Juan Pablo grunted again.

"Probably they were thieves who wanted to rob you. All white men are thieves."

"I suppose they could have been, but Matt and I didn't look like very tempting targets for a robbery."

That was true. Despite the fact that neither of the young men had to worry about money because of the ranches they owned in Montana, nobody could tell that by looking at them. They had good horses, and their guns were relatively new and well-cared-for, but other than that they appeared to be typical, down-on-their-luck drifters and grub-line riders.

"Those men could be far away by now," Juan Pablo pointed out.

"That's true. And that's all the more reason to try to pick up their trail now, before they get even farther away."

"You are set on doing this thing?"

"I am."

"Caballo Rojo said that you may leave the canyon whenever you wish."

Sam nodded.

"I know. But I want to tell him where I'm going and why, and make sure it's all right with him if Matt stays here while he recovers from his wounds."

"You are going to leave your friend?" Juan Pablo didn't sound happy about that.

"He's not going to be fit to travel for a week or more," Sam explained. "I don't want to wait that long to go after the bushwhackers."

A put-upon sigh came from Juan Pablo. He set the bow aside.

"Come," he said as he stood up. "We will talk to Caballo Rojo."

They walked through the canyon to the large hogan that belonged to the chief. Sam had been here long enough now that the novelty of having him around had worn off for the most part. Some of the children still followed him wherever he went, and some of the young, unmarried women eyed him with open interest and speculation that he was careful not to return. Making some warrior jealous was one of the last things he needed.

Caballo Rojo was sitting outside his hogan enjoying the morning sun. He greeted Juan Pablo in Navajo, then gave Sam a solemn nod and said, "Two Wolves."

Sam was pleased that the chief used his Cheyenne name. He considered that a good omen.

"Good morning, Caballo Rojo," he said. "My friend Matt Bodine is better this morning. The fever no longer consumes him."

Juan Pablo repeated that in Navajo. Caballo Rojo nodded again and spoke. Juan Pablo translated, "Caballo Rojo says this is a good thing and that your heart must be lightened."

"It is," Sam replied. "Tell him that it's due to his great mercy and generosity that Matt survived at all, and that we are indebted to him."

Juan Pablo complied.

Sam went on, "But now I must ask him for even more of that mercy and generosity, because I want to leave Matt here to recover while I search for the men responsible for hurting him."

Juan Pablo spoke the words, and Caballo Rojo considered them gravely. For a long moment he didn't reply, and when he did, it was at great length. Sam knew not to read too much into that. The Navajo could be as wordy and obsessed with formality as any other tribe.

Finally Juan Pablo turned back to him, and the warrior's translation was predictably brief.

"Caballo Rojo says that this is agreeable to him, and he promises that your friend will continue to be cared for and kept safe."

"Please express my deepest gratitude to the chief."

Juan Pablo did so. Caballo Rojo acknowledged that with another grave nod and a slight wave of his hand.

Juan Pablo asked, "When will you go?"

"As soon as I can," Sam said. "Now that Matt appears to be out of danger, I don't see any reason to wait. I want to pick up the trail before much more time goes by."

"Can you find the place where you were attacked?"

"I think so," Sam said with a smile. "I kept my eyes open while we were on our way here, and I'm pretty good at remembering landmarks."

"I can take you back to the place where we found you."

Sam was a little surprised by the offer. He hadn't expected Juan Pablo to be so cooperative.

"I appreciate that, but it's not really necessary."

Juan Pablo shrugged.

"If you change your mind . . ."

"I don't reckon I will."

The familiar sneer appeared on the warrior's face.

"Now you sound like a white man," he said. "Always convinced you are right."

Sam shrugged and turned to head back to the hogan where he'd left Matt. That was where he'd been staying, too.

Sam gathered his gear, checked the place where the bullet crease was healing on the animal, and then saddled his horse, which was picketed on a grassy stretch beside the creek with the Navajo ponies. When he was ready to go, he returned to the hogan and found Matt sitting up, eating a bowl of stew.

Matt's face was a little thinner from his ordeal and pale under his permanent tan. But he seemed to have a healthy appetite, and that was a good sign. He finished the stew, set the empty bowl aside, and said, "You look like you're ready to ride."

"I am," Sam said with a nod.

"You're really gonna leave me here?"

"Caballo Rojo has given me his word personally that you'll be taken care of."

Matt made a face.

"I don't much cotton to being taken care of." He glanced across the hogan, where Elizabeth Fleming sat with Juan Pablo's wife, each of them weaving a blanket. Elizabeth wasn't the only one doing the teaching during her stay with the Navajo. "Even when the surroundings are pleasant most of the time."

A worried frown creased Sam's forehead.

"I trust Caballo Rojo," he said as he folded his arms across his chest and gave Matt a stern look. "Can I trust you?"

"Trust me to what?" Matt asked in apparent innocence.

"Behave yourself."

"Me? Why, I always behave myself, Sam, you know that."

Sam grunted.

"I'm not joking here, Matt," he said. "You'd better take care of yourself and let those wounds heal up."

"I have a strong constitution," Matt said with a smile.

"You've got a strong something." Sam held out his hand. "I'll be back as soon as I can."

"You'd better be back in a week or less," Matt said as he clasped Sam's hand.

"Why's that?"

"Because by then I'll be strong enough to come after you, and that's exactly what I plan to do if you haven't shown up by then."

So that was a new worry, Sam thought. But Matt had a point. In a week's time, he probably *would* be strong enough to leave. Matt had always healed quickly and had a vast core of inner strength. He might joke on the outside, but on the inside he was steel and whang leather.

"Fine. If I'm not back in a week, you can come pick up *my* trail."

Matt nodded.

"Darn right I will."

"So long."

Matt started to get up.

"I can come outside—"

Sam waved him back down onto the blankets.

"Just sit there and rest, blast it. The more you do that, the sooner you'll get well."

Sam started to duck out through the hogan's door. Matt stopped him by saying, "I suppose it'd be too much to ask for you to save a couple varmints for me."

"I reckon that'll be up to them," Sam said.

Chapter 9

Juan Pablo was waiting next to Sam's horse.

"You are certain you do not want me to come with you?" he asked.

Sam thought quickly. He remembered the looks of dislike that Juan Pablo had given both of them. He didn't think Matt would do anything to cause trouble while he was gone, but it might be better to have Juan Pablo where he could keep an eye on him.

Sam considered the situation, then said, "Juan Pablo, I've changed my mind. I appreciate your offer, and I accept."

Juan Pablo's expression was as flinty as ever, but Sam thought he saw a flash of satisfaction in the man's eyes. Juan Pablo nodded and said, "I will tell my woman and get my pony."

"I'll be waiting right here," Sam told him.

Navajo warriors traveled light. Less than ten minutes later, Sam and Juan Pablo rode away from the hogans. Several barking dogs followed them for a while before turning back.

It would take them until the middle of the day to reach the place where Caballo Rojo and his men had found the blood brothers. Sam didn't want to pass all that time in silence, so after they had ridden for a while, he said, "You speak pretty good English. Did Miss Fleming teach you?"

Juan Pablo didn't look over at his companion. He kept his eyes turned straight ahead in a haughty glare, and for a moment Sam thought he wasn't going to answer.

"I learned at one of the missions, years ago, when the white man thought he could keep the Diné penned up like wild animals. Life at the agency was no way for my people to live."

Sam knew that in many ways, Juan Pablo was right. Reservations and Indian agencies were often badly run, either through greed and corruption or just sheer incompetence. Too many of the people in charge came from back East and had no real idea of how the tribes lived. Their intentions might be good, but their zeal was misguided.

"Lo, the poor Indian!" Sam thought again, not without a trace of bitterness at the way his own people had been treated. The reformers tried to turn their charges into white men, when all that was really needed was a place where the Indians could be left alone without constant encroachment by the whites. It seemed simple to Sam.

But of course, the simple, effective answers were

never good enough for government. Not when there could be hordes of rules and regulations and bureaucrats to enforce them.

Once the Indians moved to the reservations, the government tried to run everything about their lives. Someday, it might come to the point where the government tried to do the same to all the country's citizens. And that day would be the true end of liberty and freedom.

Sam was just thankful that he would be long dead before that ever happened.

"But there were teachers at the agency," Juan Pablo went on. "Like Miss Fleming, though none of them had hair like flame. They taught us. Or tried to. Most of my people could not or would not learn. Somehow . . . the words stuck in my head. I could not get them out, even though I did not really want them."

Sam thought there was something odd in Juan Pablo's voice when the man talked about Elizabeth Fleming. The Navajo seemed to despise almost everything about the white men . . .

But maybe not Elizabeth.

Sam didn't let his companion see the frown that creased his forehead. If Juan Pablo had feelings for Elizabeth Fleming, that could lead to trouble sooner or later.

Especially since Matt was back there alone with her now. Sam was confident that Elizabeth wouldn't return any affection Juan Pablo felt for her, but that might not stop the Navajo from being angry if she got mixed up with Matt.

Before leaving the canyon, Sam had told his blood brother to behave himself.

Now he hoped Matt was doing that in more ways than one.

The knowledge that Sam had gone off on an adventure without him gnawed at Matt's guts. Sure, he knew he was too weak to stay in the saddle right now, and ten minutes on horseback would probably start blood running from those bullet holes again, but still, it was annoying.

Matt didn't know what to hope for: that Sam would find those bushwhackers without any trouble and settle their hash for them, or that he'd have to come back here and get Matt to help out like he should have in the first place.

While he was pondering that, he supposed he might as well distract himself in other ways.

Luckily, he had a mighty nice distraction in the person of Miss Elizabeth Fleming.

She spent hours in the hogan, talking to him about growing up as the pampered daughter of a wealthy family that controlled a highly successful shipping line.

"I suppose it was having everything handed to me like that that made me want to do something for people who weren't so fortunate," she told him.

"Don't feel too sorry for the Navajo," Matt said. "They had it pretty bad when the army rounded them up and forced them all to live down at Bosque Redondo and other agencies like that, but once they were allowed to come back up here to their traditional homeland, they were a lot better off."

"But they live in . . . well, in dirt huts," Elizabeth said, lowering her voice so Juan Pablo's wife wouldn't hear her. "And they raise sheep."

"Well, I might agree with you about the sheep," Matt said with the cattleman's natural disdain for those woolly, bleating creatures. "But as for the rest of it, this is the way the Navajo have always lived. It's all they know."

"I suppose you're right. I can't help but think they would want to better themselves, though."

Matt didn't waste his time arguing with her. Like every professional do-gooder, Elizabeth was convinced she knew what was best for everybody and nothing would shake her from that almost religious conviction.

Anyway, he had a long-standing policy of not arguing too much with pretty, green-eyed redheads, and he didn't see any reason to change it now.

Elizabeth couldn't spend all of her time with him, though, and when she wasn't there he had nothing to do except recuperate from that bullet wound.

Sitting and resting was as boring as all get-out, but Matt forced himself to do it. Any time he heard something going on outside the hogan, he wanted to get up and go see what it was, but he made himself sit quietly.

He slept for a while during the afternoon, then woke up and ate supper with Elizabeth and Juan

Pablo's wife. Juan Pablo hadn't gotten back yet, or if he had, he hadn't put in an appearance at the hogan.

Matt dozed off again, gradually settling down into a deep sleep as night closed in around the encampment. He didn't know how long he had been asleep when something woke him.

His eyes opened. Even wounded, he was fully awake and alert instantly. He couldn't see anything, but he sensed movement somewhere close by.

"Matt."

The voice was a whisper. He propped himself up on an elbow and looked around.

Elizabeth was on her knees beside his pile of buffalo robes. The fire had burned down, but it still gave off a faint glow that he could make out behind her, silhouetting her hair and her slender form, which was now clothed in a long nightgown. Juan Pablo's wife was asleep on the other side of the fire.

"Matt," she said again, "I . . . I know I shouldn't be here. It's very improper."

"Yeah," Matt said. "It is."

"And I know that you're . . . well . . . injured and need your rest, but I . . . I've been lonely here. I know I'm doing good work with these people and all, but still . . . one gets lonely for the company of one's own kind after a while. I thought perhaps . . . if I could simply lie here with you for a while . . ."

Matt took a deep breath. He couldn't believe he was about to do this, but he said, "I don't reckon that would be a good idea, Miss Fleming."

"I think you can call me Elizabeth. And I wasn't

proposing anything, well, indecent, Mr. Bodine, just some companionship."

She might believe what she was saying, and it might actually start out that way, Matt thought, but it wouldn't stay that way and he didn't figure that was a good idea.

For one thing, he really was injured, and he wasn't sure he was up to any romping. For another, that stolid-faced Navajo woman was snoring on the other side of the hogan, and he didn't know how sound a sleeper she was.

And for another, he just flat didn't need the complication of a romance with this Vermont schoolteacher, no matter how pretty she was. He had to concentrate on getting better, so he could catch up with Sam and help him settle the hash of those bushwhackers.

"I'm sorry—" he began.

"No, that's perfectly all right," Elizabeth said, and now her voice was stiff and formal again. "There's absolutely no need to apologize. Of course it would be a bad idea. I'll go back to my own hogan now and leave you alone."

Now you've gone and done it, Matt thought. He had insulted her.

As she stood up, he lifted a hand toward her and said, "Elizabeth . . ."

"You should go back to sleep now," she said firmly. "I'm sorry I disturbed your rest, Mr. Bodine."

Before he could say anything else, she turned and left the hogan. As Matt looked through the open doorway, he saw the white shape of her nightgown for a moment, floating through the dark night like a ghost.

Then she was gone.

Matt sighed and stretched out on the blankets again. Under different circumstances, he would have been pleased to have Elizabeth pay him a nighttime visit like that, but not here and not now.

He didn't know what things would be like between them when the sun came up in the morning. If she was so mad at him that she didn't come to visit him anymore, he didn't know how he was going to get through the long, empty hours while he regained his strength.

What it amounted to was that Sam didn't need to waste any time getting back here, so they could go after those blasted bushwhackers together.

Chapter 10

By the middle of the day, Sam and Juan Pablo had reached the place where the Navajo warriors had found the blood brothers. They stopped there to eat some of the dried, jerked venison they had brought with them.

"I suppose you'll be going back to your home now," Sam said when they finished with the meal, such as it was.

Juan Pablo said, "No, I will come with you to the place where you and your friend fought those men. I can help you find their trail."

"I appreciate the offer, but that's not necessary."

"The sooner you find them and deal with them, the sooner you can return to the canyon, get the one called Matt, and leave my people alone."

"Well, if that's the way you want to look at it . . ." Sam shrugged. "I reckon you're welcome to come along."

Juan Pablo just grunted and turned away to tend to his pony.

They rode on, backtracking the trail Matt and Sam had left after their encounter with the bushwhackers several days earlier. The terrain had flattened out to the point that there weren't many landmarks, so it didn't really look all that familiar to Sam.

After they had gone several miles, though, he spotted a bluff that he recognized in the distance.

"That's where they were when they started shooting at us," he told Juan Pablo as he pointed to the bluff that jutted up from the flats. Sam swept his hand back to the south. "The arroyo where they caught up to us is over that way."

"These men outnumbered you," Juan Pablo said. "If they wanted you dead, why did they not keep fighting until they had killed you?"

"We'd already ventilated several of them, maybe fatally. I don't think they had the stomach to keep fighting. They decided to cut their losses and leave us alone instead. Anyway, they knew Matt was wounded, and they may have thought I was, too. Maybe they hoped we'd just crawl off somewhere and die."

"No man worthy of the name *hopes* that his enemy dies. He makes certain of it."

"Well, it's lucky for Matt and me that they didn't."

Sam rode over to the arroyo. He dismounted to study the welter of hoofprints nearby where the bushwhackers had left their horses. He was looking for prints with distinctive horseshoe markings and found a few he might be able to recognize if he ever saw them again.

He saw bootprints as well, but there was nothing

remarkable about them. He studied them anyway and tried to commit them to memory.

Sam also found a number of spent cartridges that had been left behind by the would-be killers. Standard .44-40 rounds used in most Winchesters and some handguns, he decided. Nothing there that would lead him to the bushwhackers.

But some scouting around turned up more hoofprints that led southeastward.

"Is there a settlement in that direction?" Sam asked.

Juan Pablo made a face and spat.

"A place the white men call Flat Rock."

Sam had never heard of the place. When he said as much, Juan Pablo went on, "The first white man to settle there had a trading post. He sold whiskey and women. The town grew around it. Miners and men who raise cattle go there to indulge their lusts."

"Then I'm not surprised a bunch of bushwhackers would head for there," Sam said. "How far away is it?"

"A day's ride. Maybe less."

Sam glanced at the sun.

"I probably can't get there today . . . but I can sometime tomorrow. Maybe I'll find some answers there." He pointed toward the bluff. "I think I'll ride over there and have a look around."

"But the trail is here," Juan Pablo said as he nodded at the tracks on the ground.

"Yeah, but I want to see if I can figure out what those fellas were up to."

Sam swung up into the saddle. Juan Pablo mounted the pony and rode with him toward the bluff.

As they came closer, Sam saw that it was a fairly common upthrust of rocky ground, probably formed sometime in the dim ages past by an earthquake.

He didn't know exactly where the bushwhackers were when they opened fire on him and Matt, so the first thing he did was ride along the base of the bluff, keeping a close eye on the ground as he weaved around the big sandstone boulders that littered the area.

After a few minutes he reined in and pointed as he spoke to Juan Pablo.

"Look there. Wagon tracks."

Sure enough, the iron-rimmed wheels of a wagon had cut parallel ruts into the ground, until the vehicle had stopped right here where Sam had spotted the tracks among the rocks.

It appeared the wagon had been pulled by a four-horse team and accompanied by a number of riders. Sam could tell where the driver had swung the vehicle around and started back in the direction it came from.

Sam rubbed his chin as he frowned in thought.

"Who'd drive a wagon out here into the big middle of nowhere, then turn around and go back?"

"There is no understanding the madness of the white man," Juan Pablo said. "Even a mixed-blood like you should know that."

Sam ignored the veiled insult and continued studying the ground.

"Looks like there were about a dozen riders with the wagon. It had an escort. An army wagon, maybe?"

"Did you and your friend see a wagon when you rode by here the other day?"

"No. At least I didn't. I'd have to ask Matt to be sure, but I think he would have said something about it if he had. You have to remember, though, we weren't really paying any attention to this bluff until the shooting started, and once the lead was flying, we lit a shuck for that arroyo as fast as we could. The wagon could have been here, and we just didn't notice it among these rocks. We were several hundred yards away."

"Or maybe it was here some other time and had nothing to do with the men who tried to kill you. There has been no rain and not much wind to disturb the sign."

Sam nodded.

"That's true. My hunch is that this bluff's not that popular a place, though. I think it's all connected. Let's take a look and see if there's a trail to the top of the bluff anywhere around here."

As it turned out, there was a narrow trail that angled up the bluff about fifty yards away. It was only wide enough for one man at a time, but Sam found several marks on the rock where boot heels had scraped it recently.

He put everything he had seen together in his mind to form a theory and tried it out on Juan Pablo.

"That wagon and about a dozen outriders came here for some reason. The man or men in the wagon stayed below, along with some of the riders, and the rest of the bunch went up to the top of the bluff to keep an eye on all the country hereabouts. As flat as it is, they could probably see a long way. Then Matt and I came riding along, and for some reason the men on the bluff didn't want to take a chance on us noticing what's going on. So they tried to kill us."

"That makes no sense," Juan Pablo insisted. "What could they have been doing to make them feel that way?"

"I don't know, but it had to be something pretty bad, probably illegal."

"Madness," Juan Pablo muttered.

Sam turned his horse.

"I want to take a closer look at the place where those wagon tracks stop."

He rode back to the spot and dismounted, being careful not to disturb any marks he might find on the ground. As he walked slowly back and forth, his keen eyes searched for anything out of the ordinary.

After a few moments, he hunkered on his heels to get an even closer look at an area a short distance off to the side of the wagon tracks.

"Did you find something?" Juan Pablo asked.

"Maybe." Sam pointed a finger. "Right here, the corner of something has gouged a little place in the dirt. There's a line leading away from it." His finger traced the faint mark on the ground. "There's another corner mark, about eight feet away." Sam moved around. "And another line in the dirt where the sharp edge of something was sitting. It goes to a third corner . . . and back along there to a fourth one . . ."

Sam looked up at Juan Pablo, who hadn't dismounted.

"Somebody brought a crate of some sort out here on that wagon, unloaded it, and set it on the ground here. The crate, or what was inside it, was heavy enough to leave those marks."

"A crate," Juan Pablo repeated. He sounded skeptical. "What sort of crate?"

"Well, there's no way of knowing how deep it was, but we can tell that it was about two feet wide and eight feet long."

Juan Pablo shook his head.

"Is that supposed to mean something?"

"Not to you, maybe," Sam said. "But to me that sounds an awful lot like a coffin."

Chapter 11

"The box you white men bury your dead in?" Juan Pablo asked. He sounded slightly disgusted. The Navajo did not enclose the bodies of their dead in boxes.

"That's right."

"There is no grave here." Juan Pablo pointed at the ground. "No one has dug in this dirt. We would be able to tell."

"You're right. Maybe it wasn't a coffin. But it was sure shaped like one."

"None of this makes sense," the warrior said.

"It will, sooner or later. Once I find the men who tried to kill me and Matt."

"You thought that some enemy might have sent them after you. Now, according to what we have found, that is not what happened. You and your friend were shot at simply because you rode along here at the wrong time."

"That's the way it looks," Sam admitted.

"Then why seek them out?" Juan Pablo wanted to know. "It had nothing to do with you. You and the one called Matt still live. Why not return to the canyon, wait until he is fit to travel, and ride on? Why search for the men who shot at you?"

"Because I don't like it when somebody tries to kill me," Sam said. "Besides, if they were that worried about somebody seeing them, they were up to no good. They need to be stopped."

"Why?" Juan Pablo sounded genuinely puzzled.

"Because they might hurt somebody else."

From the warrior's expression, it was obvious he thought Sam was completely loco.

"Look, you can go back," Sam went on. "I never expected you to come this far with me. I'll handle things from here on out."

"You are being foolish."

"Maybe, but it's my choice to make, isn't it?"

Juan Pablo scowled.

"If you die, what will happen to the man in my hogan?"

"If I don't come back, as soon as Matt has recovered he'll come looking for me. And if they've put me under, he'll avenge my death. You don't have to worry about being stuck with Matt."

"Do what you want," Juan Pablo snapped. "I am going back."

He stalked over to his pony, leaped on the animal's back, and galloped off, soon vanishing except for a thin pillar of dust that rose in the west.

Sam was glad to see him go. He was glad for Juan

Pablo's help, but the warrior wasn't the best company in the world.

Several hours of daylight were left. That was enough time for Sam to cover some of the ground between here and Flat Rock.

He rode back to the arroyo and picked up the trail there. He could have followed the wagon tracks, but there was still a slim possibility that the wagon and its escort weren't the same bunch that had jumped him and Matt.

He hadn't gone more than half a mile, though, when the two trails merged. The men who had fled from the battle at the arroyo had rejoined the wagon, and all of them had headed southeast toward the settlement called Flat Rock.

Sam's eyes constantly searched the barren landscape around him as he followed the tracks. He didn't expect to run into an ambush . . . but he and Matt hadn't been expecting the one several days earlier, either. Out here on the frontier, it was always a good idea to be alert.

From time to time, Sam even checked behind him to make sure Juan Pablo hadn't changed his mind and started following him. He didn't know of any reason the Navajo warrior would do that, other than sheer contrariness, which Juan Pablo seemed to have in abundance.

The trail didn't deviate much from its southeastward course, just enough now and then to avoid natural obstacles, like the scattered red rock mesas and stone chimneys that thrust up from the plains around them.

From time to time Sam came to narrow creeks that were little more than trickles, but in this dry, dusty land, that was enough water to cause lines of green where mesquites and stunted cottonwoods grew on the banks. The countryside wasn't what anybody would call pretty, but Sam had been in worse places.

When the sun was touching the western horizon behind him, he began looking for a place to make camp. He settled for a place beside one of those narrow streams, so he and his horse would have water and he could refill his canteens.

Quickly, he picketed and unsaddled his horse, then gathered buffalo chips and used them to fuel a small fire just big enough to boil some coffee.

As soon as he'd done that, he scooped sand on the flames to extinguish them and sat back to make a meager supper on the venison and dried corn he'd brought from the Navajo canyon.

When Sam had finished eating, he stood up and plucked a large handful of bean pods from the mesquites. He scattered them around the area where he intended to spread his blankets.

If anyone approached those blankets in the darkness, they would either step on the pods, causing them to crunch under the skulker's boots, or kick them and set the beans to rattling. Either way, the noise would serve as a warning.

He spread the blankets and set his saddle where he could use it as a pillow, then placed his hat on the saddle. Then he took his Winchester and stepped across the creek. It was narrow enough that he didn't even get his boots wet.

He walked along the stream for about fifty yards to a place where the bank had caved in some and formed a little hollow. After poking in that space with the rifle barrel to make sure no rattlers were lurking in it, Sam settled down with his back in the hollow. He could sleep sitting up when he had to, and tonight his gut told him that might be a good idea.

The heat of the day lingered as night fell, although it would cool off some before morning. Sam's eyelids grew heavy as he sat there with the Winchester across his lap. He let himself doze off. He knew there was probably no need for so much caution, but better to be careful than dead.

When he woke up, sometime far in the night, at first he didn't hear anything and wondered what had roused him from slumber. A couple of seconds later, mesquite pods rattled. There was no wind, so he knew they weren't swaying on the trees.

That was confirmed an instant later when a man's voice ripped out a curse and ordered, "Ventilate him!"

Six-guns began to roar. Sam leaned forward as he saw orange flashes stab from the muzzles of two revolvers. He knew they were pouring lead into his blankets, saddle, and hat, and he wasn't happy about the damage they'd be doing to those items.

Better than putting holes in his hide, though.

He brought the Winchester to his shoulder, levering a round into the chamber as he did so. The rifle cracked as he aimed just above one set of muzzle flashes.

Sam triggered half a dozen swift rounds, shifting his aim to the other bushwhacker in the middle of the volley.

He heard yells of pain that told him some of his bullets had scored, but the gunmen didn't stop firing. They just shifted their aim to his sanctuary along the creek.

Sam pulled back as far into the hollow as he could as slugs smacked into the dirt wall next to him. He waited for a lull, then cranked off another four rounds, spraying the shots along the opposite side of the creek bank where the men had believed him to be camped.

That was enough for them. They held their fire and retreated. Sam heard them running, followed a moment later by the clatter of hoofbeats as the bushwhackers galloped away.

Wary of a trick, he stayed where he was and took advantage of the opportunity to reload the Winchester, thumbing cartridges through the loading gate until the magazine was full again. Once he had done that, he waited some more, until finally he stood up and made his way cautiously toward the campsite.

He had picketed his horse a short distance away, hoping the animal would be out of the line of fire if any trouble broke out. That was the first thing he checked, and he was relieved to see that the horse appeared to be fine, other than being a little spooked by the racket and the stench of powder smoke in the air.

When Sam approached the spot where he had spread his blankets, he saw several dark splashes on the ground. Kneeling, he touched a finger to one of those splashes, then rubbed it against his thumb.

Blood, he was pretty sure. So he had winged at least one of the men, no doubt about that. Not fatally, though, and possibly not even seriously, because both of the bushwhackers had been able to flee like they had wings on their feet.

He straightened and went over to his bedroll. His hat lay off to one side where it had been thrown by the bullets that hit it.

Sam picked it up and held it over his head. Stars shone through the holes ripped in the hat. He grunted. He could always buy another hat, but not another head.

The leather on his saddle had been torn, too, and slugs had gouged grooves in the wood underneath it. That damage could be repaired, and his blankets could be patched and mended.

He gathered his gear, stuffed the ruined hat in one of his saddlebags, and saddled his horse. He was moving his camp in case the bushwhackers came back with reinforcements.

Sam followed the creek for a couple of miles before he found another place to settle down for the rest of the night. In the morning it would be easy enough to come back to the site of the ambush and pick up the trail again.

In other ways, though, the situation had become much more complicated. As he lay looking up at the stars, he asked himself how the bushwhackers had known where to look for him. He supposed it was possible the leaders of the bunch, whoever they were, could have posted men to watch the trail and ambush anyone who seemed to be searching for them.

It was also possible that the two men who'd snuck up on his camp tonight had nothing to do with what had happened several days earlier. They could have been a pair of drifting outlaws bent on murder and robbery.

But if they *weren't* . . . if they were connected to the men who had tried before to kill Sam and Matt . . . now they knew one of their intended victims was on their trail.

That meant if they were in Flat Rock, they would be on the lookout for him when he rode into town. This was going to make his job even more difficult and dangerous.

But that was nothing new, Sam told himself. He and Matt didn't go looking for trouble, but it seemed to find them anyway. This was just one more instance of that happening.

He would deal with whatever was waiting for him in Flat Rock when he got there, Sam told himself. He rolled over and went to sleep.

Chapter 12

Zack Jardine was in a bad mood when the pounding on the door woke him. He sat up in the tangle of grimy sheets and muttered a curse.

The woman who lay beside him shifted a little and muttered in her sleep. Jardine couldn't remember her name. Dolly, Dotty, something like that.

It didn't matter. She was a whore, and that was more important than what her name was.

Somebody was still hammering on the door with a fist. Dolly had taken a nip of laudanum when she and Jardine were through with their business, so it wasn't likely she was going to wake up anytime soon.

That racket was liable to rouse anybody else who was sleeping, though, so Jardine swung his legs off the bed and stood up.

If that was one of his men at the door, drunk as a skunk, Jardine intended to whip him within an inch of his life.

Wearing only the bottom half of a pair of longjohns,

Jardine fumbled around on the little table beside the bed until he found a match. He snapped the lucifer to life and held it to the wick of the candle that sat on the table as well.

Then he turned to the ladderback chair where he had hung his gunbelt. He pulled the Colt from its holster and looped his thumb over the hammer.

With the candlelight shining on the heavy slabs of muscle on his chest and shoulders, he went to the door.

"What the hell is it?"

As soon as the question was out of his mouth, Jardine took a quick step to the side, just in case whoever was in the hall fired a slug through the door.

Of course, if somebody wanted to kill him, the varmint might figure he would do that. In that case it would be a matter of the man guessing whether Jardine moved left or right.

Fifty-fifty odds. Jardine could live with that. He'd faced worse odds before and was still alive.

No shot sounded in the hallway. Instead a man called through the thin panel, "Zack, Joe Hutto just rode in with Three-Finger Smith. Three-Finger caught a bullet."

Jardine jerked the door open. He had recognized Dave Snyder's voice.

"How bad is he hurt?"

Snyder shook his head.

"I don't know. That Englisher woman's takin' a look at him now. She claims to know somethin' about doctorin'. I think he'll live, though."

"Joe's still downstairs?"

"Yeah."

"I'll be down in a minute to talk to him. I want to know what happened."

"I got a pretty good idea what happened, Zack," Snyder said. "Somebody's on our trail."

"That's what I think, too," Jardine said. "Tell Joe not to go anywhere."

"You bet," Snyder said as Jardine swung the door closed.

Jardine went to pull his clothes and boots on. The night was warm, and Dolly—if that was her name—had thrown the covers aside. Jardine glanced at her naked body.

She was young and still relatively pretty, with a lot of curly blond hair, and under other circumstances he might have tried to wake her up enough to have another go with her . . . or maybe not even bothered waking her.

But he had more important things to worry about now, such as the potential threat to the deal for those stolen rifles.

Jardine buckled on his gunbelt and left Dolly sleeping there. He clattered downstairs to the main room of the Buckingham Palace, the saloon and whorehouse that was the biggest building in the relatively new town of Flat Rock.

According to the banjo clock on the wall behind the bar, it was nearly two o'clock in the morning. The place was still open but not very busy at that hour.

Only about a dozen men were in the barroom, and more than half of them were Jardine's men.

Including the one stretched out on the bar, bleeding onto the hardwood from the bullet hole in his side.

The auburn-haired woman who called herself Lady Augusta Winslow looked up from examining the wound and said coolly, "I charge extra for medical services, Mr. Jardine. I assume you'll cover the expenses incurred for the care of your man here."

"Yeah, yeah," Jardine replied, not bothering to try to keep the irritation out of his voice. "How's Three-Finger doing?"

"With the proper treatment, he should survive. The bullet's still inside him, so it will have to be removed. If he lives through the surgery, he'll be fine."

Jardine gave the woman a curt nod.

"Go ahead. But be careful. He's a good man."

That was one of the rare occasions when someone had used the term "good man" to refer to Three-Finger Smith, so called because he had only three fingers on his left hand.

A lot of hombres on the frontier were missing fingers, but usually the loss was the result of an accident, like getting a finger caught in a rope while taking a dally around the saddlehorn.

Three-Finger had lost his index and middle fingers when the husband of a married woman caught him with those fingers where they shouldn't have been. Faced with the choice of getting a bullet in the head or laying his hand out flat on a table, the man previously known as plain Hal Smith had chosen the table, whereupon the offended husband had promptly chopped off the offending digits with a Bowie knife.

The man would have been smarter to chop fingers off Smith's gun hand, because as soon as Three-Finger, as he was newly dubbed, had the injury wrapped up, he returned and shot the luckless cuckold in the back.

The man was on top of his wife at the time, trying to mend the fences of her straying, and the bullet went all the way through him and killed her, too.

Jardine had heard Three-Finger tell that story numerous times, and it always provoked Three-Finger to such laughter that he had to slap his thigh with his mutilated hand.

Snyder, Joe Hutto, Angus Braverman, and Doyle Hilliard were among the man clustered around the wounded Three-Finger now. Lady Augusta reached behind her to the backbar, picked up a bottle of whiskey, and handed it to Snyder.

"Pour as much of that as you can down his throat," she instructed. "It'll be a lot easier to operate on him if he's soused to the gills."

Snyder nodded.

"Angus, you and Joe grab on to him. Doyle, pry open his mouth."

Jardine countermanded that order.

"Just give him the bottle. Nobody ever had a problem getting Three-Finger to drink. Joe, come with me."

Hutto nodded. He followed Jardine to a table in the corner while Smith grabbed the bottle away from Snyder, tilted it to his mouth while Braverman and

Hilliard helped him sit up, and let the who-hit-John start gurgling down his throat.

"What happened?" Jardine asked when he and Hutto were seated at the table. "I left you out there to make sure nobody picked up our trail after that foul-up the other day. I'm guessing somebody did."

Hutto nodded. On the gang's way back to Flat Rock, Jardine had dropped off him and Smith at one of the little buttes that overlooked the trail about fifteen miles from the settlement, ordering them to stay there until he told them otherwise.

The next day, he had sent a rider out there with enough supplies to last the two sentinels a week. A few days had passed since then, long enough so that Jardine had become convinced the two men they had bushwhacked had crawled off and died or moved on somewhere else.

Either way, he didn't think they were a threat anymore.

Judging by the way Three-Finger was bleeding on the bar, he'd been wrong about that.

"We spotted one of those hombres ridin' toward town," Hutto explained.

"You're sure it was one of the men we had that run-in with the other day?"

Hutto nodded.

"Yeah. I got a good look at him through the spyglass. It was that big fella in the buckskin shirt, looks sort of like a redskin."

"What did you do?"

Hutto rubbed a hand over his angular, beard-stubbled jaw.

"We saw where the son of a buck made camp, so we figured if we snuck up and killed him, there wouldn't be anything to worry about. But he pulled a fast one on us and was holed up waiting for somebody to jump him. Three-Finger caught a slug while we were tradin' shots with the varmint."

Jardine said wearily, "You were supposed to light a shuck back here to town and warn me if you saw anybody like that following our tracks."

"Yeah, I know, but we thought—"

"And that was your mistake right there," Jardine cut in as he leaned forward. His face was dark with anger. "You're not supposed to think, damn it! I handle that!"

He flung a hand toward the bar, where Three-Finger had polished off the whiskey and now lay there with a cherubic smile on his face, cradling the empty bottle against his chest.

"Now I've got another man with a bullet hole in him, and that fella you ambushed may be smart enough to figure out why somebody tried to kill him . . . again."

Lady Augusta poured more whiskey over a knife with a keen blade that glittered in the lamplight.

"Now you'll have to hold him down, gentlemen," she told Jardine's men who were still gathered on the other side of the bar. "Hold him tightly. I won't be responsible for what happens if you don't."

At the table, Joe Hutto shook his head.

"I'm sorry, boss. We thought we were doin' the right thing. What happens now?"

Three-Finger screamed as the knife cut into him, but the strong hands on him kept him from moving.

"Now we wait to see if that son of a bitch shows up in Flat Rock," Jardine said. "If he does, I guess we'll just have to kill him here."

Chapter 13

Sam wasn't familiar with Flat Rock's history, but he knew the settlement couldn't have been in existence for too many years.

As he approached the next day, he saw that it had sprung up at a spot where one of the little creeks in the area flowed across a large, flat rock, spreading out to form a shallow pool.

That much water was rare in these parts. There were a few mines in the Carrizos to the north and some ranches in the basin that spread south toward Black Mesa and Canyon del Muerto.

Officially, this was all Navajo land, but when there was money to be made, "civilized" men never worried too much about things like reservations and treaties. There were ways around any obstacle, routes usually paved with discreet payoffs.

Those mines and ranches needed supplies, and the men who worked on them needed a place to blow their wages on loose women, watered-down whiskey, and marked cards.

Flat Rock filled those needs, and as a result the settlement had more saloons than any other sort of business establishment, by a large margin.

When Sam rode into town, the main street was mostly empty in the blistering Arizona sun. A few wagons were parked in front of buildings, and a handful of saddle horses were tied at hitch rails. Less than half a dozen pedestrians were making their way along the boardwalks or trying to avoid the piles of horse droppings that littered the broad, dusty avenue.

No one seemed to pay much attention to Sam, despite his buckskin shirt and copper-hued features. Many frontiersmen had such deep, permanent tans that they appeared almost to have Indian blood.

Anyway, Indians were nothing out of the ordinary around here.

Sam had followed the wagon and horse tracks to within a couple of miles of Flat Rock. When the trail got that close, it was lost in the welter of tracks left by other riders and vehicles coming and going from the settlement.

Since he didn't know anyone here in Flat Rock, he couldn't trust anyone, either. He couldn't even go to the law, if there was any, because it was possible the authorities were connected to the bushwhackers. He and Matt had run into plenty of crooked lawmen in the past.

While he was trying to figure out how to proceed,

he might as well get something to eat besides the dried venison and corn he'd been subsisting on for the past day, he decided. He angled his horse toward the hitch rail in front of a squat adobe building with a sign on it that read simply CAFÉ.

Sam dismounted and wrapped his horse's reins around the rail. As he stepped toward the open door, two men in dusty, well-worn range garb came out of the building. Heavy revolvers rode in holsters on their hips.

One of the men was tall and thin, with a hawk-like face and a drooping black mustache. He had an open-clasp knife in his hand and was using the point of the blade to worry at a piece of food stuck in his teeth. That seemed to Sam like a fairly dangerous method for a man to pick his teeth.

The other hombre was shorter and considerably stockier than his companion, though not actually fat. His battered old brown Stetson was thumbed back on a thatch of rusty red hair. He had an open, honest face with a slight scattering of freckles across his nose and cheeks.

The tall man folded his knife and slipped it into a pocket as he gave Sam a smile and a friendly nod.

"Howdy," he said.

"Good morning," Sam replied. "Or good afternoon. I'm not sure exactly which it is."

The short man pulled a big railroad watch attached to a thick chain from his pocket and flipped it open.

"Seventeen minutes after twelve," he announced. "So it's afternoon."

"Well, then, good afternoon," Sam said.

"Are you new in town?" the tall man asked. "Don't recollect seein' you around Flat Rock before."

"This is the first time I've been here," Sam replied.

"Just passin' through?" the shorter man asked.

Sam was puzzled by the questions, but then he remembered how much interest strangers sometimes drew in frontier towns. Anything to break the monotony of a sometimes drab existence was welcome.

And surrounded by such a rugged, arid landscape, life in Flat Rock would certainly be drab.

Sam had no real idea what the men he was searching for looked like, but the bushwhackers might have studied him and Matt through field glasses before they opened fire.

So for all he knew, these two apparent grub-line riders could be part of the gang.

Which meant they could know who he was, too.

But without any way of being sure about that, all he could do for the moment was play along.

"That's right, just passing through," he said.

"If you're lookin' for a ridin' job, there ain't many to be had hereabouts," the tall cowboy told him. "We ain't lookin', in particular, 'cause our dinero ain't run out yet. But Flat Rock's a good place to be if you're aimin' to make some money. It just looks like a sleepy little burg. Lots of excitin' things goin' on in this town, yes, sir."

"Well, that's good to know," Sam said. He was about to decide that these two men were just the pair of harmless cowpokes they appeared to be, although he couldn't rule out anything else. He nodded toward the door of the café. "If you'll excuse me, I'm a mite hungry . . ."

"Then you've come to the right place," the shorter man said. "Best chow in town."

"I'm obliged," Sam said. He took a step toward the door.

"Say," the tall man spoke up, "I don't mean no offense, but you look like you got some Injun blood in you."

Sam stopped.

"I'm half Cheyenne," he said. He had never denied or been ashamed of his heritage.

The tall man grinned.

"I'm an eighth Cherokee, myself. Like I said, no offense meant, just curious. Only way a fella really finds out anything is by askin' questions."

"I suppose that's true." Sam grasped the doorknob and nodded to the two men. "So long."

He opened the door and went inside before the talkative cowboys could say anything else.

Sleepy little burg or not, the café was doing good business in this noon hour. Half a dozen tables covered with blue-checked tablecloths were occupied, and the stools along the counter were almost all full.

Sam took one that wasn't and sat down between a

burly man who looked like a freighter and a smaller gent in a suit and rimless spectacles.

The freighter, if that's what he was, ignored Sam, but the other man nodded and said, "Hello." His formerly stiff collar had wilted in the heat.

Sam returned the nod.

"Afternoon."

The man held out his hand.

"Noah Reilly."

Sam shook the townsman's hand and introduced himself.

"I'm Sam Two Wolves."

"That's certainly a colorful and unusual name."

Sam shrugged.

"Not where I come from."

"Where's that?"

"Montana," Sam said without going into any more details. Folks in Flat Rock seemed to be a friendly, inquisitive bunch.

"I've never been to Montana. From everything I've heard, I'm sure it's beautiful up there. More beautiful than this part of Arizona, anyway."

A middle-aged counterman with gray hair and a white apron came over and said, "Noah, quit yammerin' at this fella. He probably came in for something to eat, not a lot of talk."

"No, that's all right, really," Sam said as he saw the contrite expression that appeared on the bespectacled man's face. "I don't mind talking. But I would like something to eat."

"Lunch special's chicken and dumplin's," the counterman told him.

Sam nodded and said, "That'll be fine, thanks."

"Comin' up."

As the counterman turned to the pass-through window that led to the kitchen, Noah Reilly pointed to the empty bowl in front of him and told Sam, "I had the chicken and dumplings. Delicious. You'll enjoy it."

"I'm sure I will. What do you do for a living, Mr. Reilly?"

"You can call me Noah. I work at the general store."

Sam had taken the man for a clerk of some sort, so he wasn't surprised by Reilly's answer.

"I'll bet you know everybody in town, then."

Reilly grinned.

"All the ones who have any money to spend, anyway." He laughed at his own mild wit.

"You probably don't get a lot of strangers riding through Flat Rock."

"No, not as out of the way as we are here. Most people have to have a good reason to come to Flat Rock, or they'd never even hear of it. But people always need supplies, and this is the only place in fifty or sixty miles to get them."

"That's true," Sam admitted. He didn't see how talking to Noah Reilly was going to help him find the men who tried to kill him and Matt, but he didn't have anything better to do at the moment, he supposed.

"Are you a full-blooded Indian, Sam?" Reilly went on.

The blunt question made Sam raise his eyebrows a little.

"Half Cheyenne," he explained, just as he had told the tall cowboy outside.

"Most of the Indians in these parts were Navajo. This is part of their reservation, you know."

Sam nodded and said, "So I've heard. They're peaceful, though, aren't they?"

"For the most part. Some of the people around here still get nervous about the Navajo, even though all the trouble with them seems to have been over for fifteen years. But for all we know, some of them may have long memories."

"Could be," Sam said. Caballo Rojo was old enough to have taken part in the Navajo wars back in the Sixties.

"Well, no standing in the way of progress, eh?" Reilly scraped his stool back. "Here comes Harvey with your food, and I have to get back to work. It was a pleasure to meet you, Sam."

"Likewise," Sam said with a nod.

Reilly reached down to the floor, picked up a black hat, and put it on. He placed some coins on the counter to pay for his meal and left the café as the counterman put a big bowl of chicken and dumplings in front of Sam.

"Want some coffee or a cup of buttermilk?"

"Coffee will be fine," Sam said.

"Comin' up," the man replied. That seemed to be a habitual response with him.

Sam took a bite of the food while the counterman poured coffee in a cup for him.

"That *is* good," he said. "Mr. Reilly told me it would be. He was right."

The counterman chuckled.

"Ol' Noah likes to talk, that's for sure. Hope he didn't bend your ear too much."

"Not at all," Sam said. "Everybody in town seems pretty friendly. I ran into a couple of cowboys just outside who talked to me, too."

"Tall, skinny fella and a little redheaded gink?" When Sam nodded, the counterman went on, "Yeah, they've been hangin' around town for a week or so. Don't know where they get their money, but they seem pretty flush. Maybe they've been lucky at the tables over in Lady Augusta's place."

Sam's interest had perked up at the counterman's mention of how the two cowboys had been in Flat Rock only for a week or so. Of course, that timing didn't have to mean a thing . . .

But it was an indication that the two men had shown up in this area about the same time as he and Matt had been ambushed. The fact that they had money but didn't seem to be working for it was intriguing, too.

But before Sam pursued that angle, he satisfied his curiosity on another matter.

"Lady Augusta?" he repeated.

"You haven't heard of the Buckingham Palace Saloon?"

Sam shook his head.

"Woman came into town about a year ago," the counterman explained. "Said her name was Lady Augusta Winslow. She let it be known that she was some sort of English nobility. I couldn't say one way or the other about that. Whole thing could be just a crock of buffalo chips. But she talks like an Englisher, I'll give her that. And she had enough money to start the Buckingham, which is what most folks around here call the place. Biggest and best saloon and poker parlor in Flat Rock, which means it's the biggest and best in the whole Four Corners. You should check it out."

"They let half-breeds in there?" Sam asked.

"Mister, they'd let a dang Rooshian cossack in if he had money to buy booze or gamble."

"I just thought since Mr. Reilly said folks around here are still a little nervous about the Navajo . . ."

"Well, that's true," Harvey said with a nod. "But you look as much like a white man as an Indian, so I don't reckon you'd have any problems." He rubbed his jaw and frowned in thought. "Except maybe with John Henry Boyd."

"Who's that?"

Before Harvey could answer, the teamster sitting next to Sam suddenly turned toward him and said, "By God, mister, are you gonna sit there flappin' your gums all day? Your food's gettin' cold!"

"Take it easy, Jase," the counterman said. "Nothin' wrong with a little conversation."

"There is when it's gettin' on my nerves!"

Sam said, "Take it easy, friend. No one meant to cause a problem here."

The teamster muttered something under his breath, shoved his stool back, and stood up. He tossed a coin on the counter and stalked out of the café.

"Don't mind him," Harvey said as he scooped up the coin. "He's like a surly old bull buffalo pawin' the ground. He don't mean nothin' by it."

"I'll keep that in mind," Sam said. "Now, you were sayin' about this John Henry Boyd fella . . ."

"He owns the Devil's Pitchfork ranch, south of here," the counterman explained. "Has a powerful hate for Indians of all kinds. I don't know for sure why he feels that way, but I've heard it said that his whole family, except for him, was wiped out when Indians attacked the wagon train they were traveling with, twenty years or more ago."

Sam nodded. It was an old, familiar story. There had been plenty of senseless bloodshed on both sides during the long clash between red men and white on the frontier, and it had left a lot of hatred behind it. He wished things could have been otherwise, but no one could change history.

"If you're just passin' through, though, you shouldn't have to worry about John Henry," the counterman went on. "He don't come into town much. He's almost always out at the ranch." He lowered his voice. "Which, to hear some folks tell it, is as much of a way station for hombres on the dodge as it is a real ranch."

That was interesting, too, Sam thought. If outlaws frequented Boyd's ranch, that could have some connection to the attack on him and Matt.

"I'm obliged to you for telling me."

Harvey grinned.

"Just lookin' out for my customers. It ain't like I've got all that many of 'em. Tell you what, Jase was right about one thing . . . that food's gettin' cold."

"Wouldn't want that," Sam said. He dug into the chicken and dumplings.

As he ate, he mulled over everything he had learned so far, which on the surface didn't amount to a blasted thing. He had some minor suspicions about the two garrulous cowboys he had met outside but nothing really to tie them to the bushwhackers, and what he had heard about the Devil's Pitchfork Ranch was intriguing.

Other than that, nothing.

Or maybe not quite nothing, he corrected himself. He had learned that the Buckingham Palace was the biggest and most popular saloon in Flat Rock, so that meant most of the people around here would pass through its batwings at one time or another.

If the bushwhackers were still around and on the lookout for him, that would be a good place for them to spot him.

And he *wanted* them to spot him, no doubt about that. The odds of him being able to find the men he was looking for were slim, so it made more sense to let *them* find *him*. Maybe then he could figure out what it was all about.

That amounted to just about the same thing as painting a target on his back, Sam realized . . . but this wouldn't be the first time he had done that.

Usually, though, he had Matt with him. This time he was alone in a strange town that might be full of enemies, for all he knew.

Didn't matter. When he got through here, he told himself as he ate the chicken and dumplings, it would be time to pay a visit to Buckingham Palace.

The one in Flat Rock, Arizona Territory, not London.

Chapter 14

When he had finished the food and downed the last of the coffee, Sam paid Harvey for the meal, said so long, and left the café.

He looked along the street and spotted the saloon a couple of blocks up. It was a two-story adobe building that actually had two floors, not one and a false front. A narrow balcony ran along the front of the second floor.

The entrance was at the near corner. The sign that read BUCKINGHAM PALACE SALOON—BEER—LIQUOR—GAMES OF CHANCE—ENTERTAINMENT was so long it took up the front of the building and ran down the side, too.

Before heading for the saloon, Sam looked around for a livery stable. He found one on a side street and turned his horse over to a friendly, middle-aged Mexican who introduced himself as Pablo Garralaga.

"This is a fine horse, señor," the stableman said. "I will take good care of him."

"I'm sure you will," Sam said. "How much?"

"Fifty cents per night, señor. This includes feed and the finest care. And I will repair that damage to your saddle for free. I am skilled at such things."

Sam handed him two silver dollars, grateful that Garralaga hadn't asked how his saddle had gotten shot up.

"I'm not sure how long I'll be in town, but that'll get us started."

"Gracias, señor."

On the off chance that he might find out something else, Sam said, "Do you happen to know a couple of cowboys who've been in town about a week? One of them is tall and has a mustache, the other is shorter and has red hair."

Garralaga rolled his eyes.

"Those two! The little one, he is not so bad, but the tall one, he never stops talking! Always with the questions, questions, questions! He makes me tired just to listen to him."

"Then they're keeping their horses here?"

"Sí, señor. Over there." Garralaga pointed to a pair of stalls near the front of the barn.

Sam strolled over and looked at the horses in apparently idle curiosity. One was a buckskin, the other a wiry paint.

Actually, he was looking at the hoofprints they had left in the dust of their stalls, checking to see if either track was similar to the ones he had found out at the ambush site.

Neither hoofprint looked familiar, so to excuse his

actions he just nodded and commented, "Nice-looking horses," as he came back over to Garralaga.

"These hombres are friends of yours, señor?" the stableman asked.

"Not really. New acquaintances, I guess you'd say."

Garralaga shrugged and nodded, looking as if he didn't really understand but didn't care, either. As long as his customers paid their bills, whatever else they did was none of his business, his expression seemed to say.

"Can you recommend a good place in town to stay?" Sam went on.

"The Territorial Hotel is the only one in Flat Rock, but . . ." Garralaga hesitated.

"They might not want anybody with Indian blood staying there, is that it?" Sam guessed.

"I am sad to say that is true, señor. Myself, I don't care. All men's money spends the same."

"I understand."

"But there is a boardinghouse where you would be welcome, if there is room. A woman named Señora McCormick runs it. If you go there, tell her that Pablo at the livery stable sent you. Her late husband and I were amigos, before he passed away last year."

Sam nodded.

"I'll do that. I'm obliged, Señor Garralaga."

The stableman smiled and waved a hand.

"De nada."

He told Sam how to find the boardinghouse, and once again Sam postponed his trip to the saloon. He slung his saddlebags over his shoulder and walked toward the boardinghouse, carrying his Winchester.

Along the way he came to a general store, so he went inside to buy a new hat to replace the one that had been shot up the night before.

Bespectacled Noah Reilly smiled at him from behind the counter.

"Mr. Two Wolves!" he said. "I didn't expect to see you again this soon. What can I do for you?"

"I'm in the market for a new hat," Sam explained.

"Right over here," Reilly said, gesturing toward a set of shelves where a number of hats sat, gathering dust.

Sam found one that he liked. The new hat didn't have silver conchos on the band like his old one, but other than that it was very similar. Sam figured he could switch the bands if he wanted to.

He paid Reilly for the hat and settled it on his head. It would be good to have something to shade his head from the sun again.

The boardinghouse was a frame building, one of the few in town. In this part of the country, nearly everything was built of adobe.

The gray-haired woman who answered Sam's knock on the boardinghouse door asked, "Yes? Can I help you?" Her face wore a rather severe expression, but Sam thought her brown eyes looked kind.

Politely, he removed his new hat and said, "Señor Garralaga down at the livery stable recommended your place to me and said you might have a room for rent. That is, if you're Mrs. McCormick."

"I am," the woman said. "Eloise McCormick."

"My name is Sam Two Wolves." He waited to see if that was going to make any difference.

Apparently it didn't. Mrs. McCormick said, "I have a couple of vacant rooms. Would you like to take a look at them?"

"Ma'am, Señor Garralaga spoke so highly of you and your house, I'm sure that's not necessary. I'll take one of them."

She smiled, and that made her look younger.

"Well, then, come on. I'll show you the rooms anyway, and you can take your pick."

Sam choose a front room that looked out at the street. He liked to be able to see what was going on. The room was simply furnished but looked clean and comfortable.

"What brings you to Flat Rock, if you don't mind my asking?" Mrs. McCormick said. "Are you a scout for the army?"

"No, ma'am. You get many army scouts passing through here?"

"The cavalry sends out patrols from Fort Defiance every now and then. The Navajo behave themselves for the most part, but it doesn't hurt to remind them of what happened back in '63. My late husband was already out here then and served under Kit Carson." Mrs. McCormick gave Sam a keen look. "You're not a Navajo, are you, Mr. Two Wolves?"

"No. Half Cheyenne." Sam wondered how many times he was going to have to answer that question.

"I see. Clean linens once a week," she went on

briskly, "breakfast is at six in the morning, supper at six in the evening. I serve Sunday dinner at one, but not the rest of the week."

"Sounds fine to me," Sam said with a nod.

"Your next-door neighbor is Mr. Reilly from the general store, and he likes peace and quiet, so I hope you'll cooperate in that respect."

Sam smiled.

"Noah Reilly?"

"Oh, you know him?"

"We've met," Sam said.

"Well, good. You won't feel as much like you're in a strange place, then. How long do you think you'll be staying?"

Until someone tries to kill me again and I can find out why, Sam thought.

"I don't really know," he said. "I'll pay you for a week. Is that all right?"

"That'll be fine."

They concluded the arrangement, and Mrs. McCormick left the room. Sam put his saddlebags on the bed and leaned his rifle in the corner. He went to the window and pushed back the gauzy yellow curtain that hung over it.

The boardinghouse was on Flat Rock's only street, and from here Sam could see part of the front of the Buckingham Palace Saloon.

A couple of benches were on the boardwalk in front of the saloon, and on one of them sat the two cowboys he had met earlier, evidently just watching the world go by.

The tall, skinny one had his knife out again and was using it to whittle something. The shorter one's head drooped forward every now and then, as if he were having a hard time staying awake.

There was something about those two, Sam thought, something that bothered him.

Mrs. McCormick must have been elsewhere in the house, because he didn't see her in the parlor or foyer as he left the house. The saloon was only a short distance away, and it was finally time he paid that visit to the place.

Sam had to walk right past the two cowboys to reach the batwinged door, and just as he expected, they grinned at him in recognition.

The tall one continued whittling without missing a beat as he asked, "How was the food at the café? Best you ever et, right?"

"I wouldn't go quite that far," Sam said, "but it was good."

"Wait'll you taste ol' Harve's Irish stew. It's even better."

"Pie ain't bad, either," the shorter cowboy put in.

"Goin' to have a drink?" the tall one asked.

"More like a look around," Sam said. "I'm not much for drinking."

"Oh, yeah, because of the Injun blood, I reckon. The firewater don't agree with you." The man folded his knife and put it away. He held up what he'd been working on. It was a little whistle. "What do you think?"

"Looks good," Sam said. "Can you play it?"

"Not worth a lick," the tall cowboy said with a grin. He tossed it to a boy passing by in the street and added, "Here you go, son. Enjoy yourself."

The boy caught the whistle and said, "Gee, thanks, mister!"

He went on his way, tooting tunelessly on it.

The cowboy put his hands on his knees and pushed himself to his feet in a loose-jointed fashion.

"Come on, Wilbur," he said to his shorter companion. "We'll join this here fella."

Sam didn't recall inviting them along, but that didn't seem to matter. As the three of them walked toward the saloon's entrance, the tall cowboy went on, "They call me Stovepipe Stewart."

"On account of he's so tall and skinny," his red-headed friend put in.

"And this is my pard Wilbur Coleman," Stovepipe completed the introductions.

There didn't seem to be anything Sam could do but give them his name. "I'm Sam Two Wolves."

"Pleased to meet you, Sam. I figure it's sorta our duty to take you under our wing and show you around, you bein' new in town and all and us bein' old-timers."

Sam almost said something about how he thought they had only been in Flat Rock for a week, but he caught himself in time. He didn't want them knowing that he'd been asking questions about them.

Anyway, it didn't matter, because redheaded Wilbur Coleman laughed and said, "Yeah, real old-timers, that's us. We been in this burg all of a week."

"That's seven times as long as Sam here," Stovepipe pointed out.

"I suppose if you want to look at it that way . . ."

Sam pushed the batwings aside and stepped into the Buckingham Palace. He saw right away that it was an impressive place, with a long, mahogany bar on the right side of the room, cut-glass chandeliers that must have been freighted all the way up here from Phoenix, plenty of tables for drinking, and a large area of poker tables, roulette wheels, and faro layouts in the back of the room. There was a piano, too, but no one was playing it at the moment.

Even though it was the middle of the afternoon, the saloon was busy. Men stood at the bar, where a couple of drink jugglers waited on them. Several of the tables were occupied, too. Young women in short, low-cut, spangled dresses circulated among them, delivering drinks and smiles to the customers and ignoring hands that got a little too familiar.

A couple of poker games were going on, and men were trying their luck at faro and roulette, too. The only thing that was missing was a parade of saloon girls up and down the stairs to the second floor with men who wanted to buy their favors.

The tall cowboy was watching Sam keenly. He said, "The gals don't do that sorta business durin' the day, only at night. Lady Augusta says it ain't proper to be beddin' down for pay when the sun's out."

Sam gave Stovepipe a sharp glance.

"How did you know what I was thinking?"

"Well, you seemed to be takin' it all in," Stovepipe

drawled. "I sorta figured you'd get to that point in your thinkin' and wonder about it."

"Stovepipe's a demon for figurin' things out," Wilbur put in.

Sam looked around again.

"I've heard about this so-called Lady Augusta. Is she here?"

Wilbur bristled.

"So-called?" he repeated. "Are you doubtin' the word of the finest lady ever to set foot in Arizona?"

"Not really," Sam said. "But you have to admit, it is a little odd to think that a member of British nobility would wind up running a saloon in a backwater town in Arizona Territory."

"There ain't a thing in the world odd about it," Wilbur insisted. "She just got tired of all that foofaraw over yonder in England, and who could blame her? Sittin' around in musty ol' castles on spindly-legged chairs and sippin' tea with your dadburn pinky finger stickin' out! Who in the Sam Hill would want to spend your days doin' that?"

"Not me," Stovepipe said with a wide grin.

"Not me, neither," Wilbur said. "So don't go sayin' nothin' bad about Lady Augusta, Sam. I won't take kindly to it."

Stovepipe leaned closer to Sam and said in a loud whisper, "He's a mite smitten."

Sam felt a little like he had wandered into a lunatic asylum. The thing to do in a situation like that, he told himself, was to play along. He said, "Sorry, Wilbur. I didn't mean anything by it."

"That's all right," Wilbur said, still sounding a little huffy. "Just so's you know."

Stovepipe gestured toward the bar on the right-hand side of the room.

"Come on, Sam," he said. "I'll buy you a phosphate. We'll steer clear of the hard stuff."

"All right," Sam said. He was accomplishing his purpose just by being here. If any of those bushwhackers were in the room, they were getting a good look at him.

And of course, there was still a chance the two men with him were part of the very bunch he was looking for.

When they got to the bar, Stovepipe ordered cherry phosphates for the three of them, even though Wilbur made a face at that. The tall, lanky cowboy leaned his left elbow on the hardwood and asked, "What brings you to this wide place in the trail, Sam?"

"Flat Rock seems like more than just a wide place in the trail. It seems like a real town."

"Right now it is. I've seen 'em come and go, though. One of these days it's liable to dry up and blow away like so many others have. And you didn't answer my question."

"A man's business is usually his own," Sam said.

"That's Stovepipe for you," Wilbur said. "Always pokin' his big nose in where it ain't wanted."

"That ain't it at all," Stovepipe insisted. "I'm just naturally curious." He looked at Sam again and raised his somewhat bushy eyebrows.

"I'm looking for some fellows," Sam said. Maybe it was time to put a few of his cards on the table and see what he could shake out. "About a dozen men on horseback. They rode this way a few days ago."

He didn't say anything about finding the wagon tracks.

Stovepipe sipped his phosphate and got some of the bubbles from the fizzy drink on his mustache. He wiped the back of his hand across his mouth and said, "These hombres you're lookin' for are friends of yours?"

"I didn't say that."

"Then they're enemies?"

"Didn't say that, either."

"Aw, leave the fella alone, Stovepipe," Wilbur said.

"I'm just tryin' to help," the tall cowboy said. "Maybe I know those fellas Sam's lookin' for. What're their names?"

Sam just smiled and didn't say anything. He didn't want to admit that he didn't know the names of his quarry or even what they looked like. If Stovepipe and Wilbur were members of the gang, he wanted them to worry about him enough to be prodded into taking action.

Stovepipe looked like he wanted to press the issue, but just then a commotion erupted outside in the street. Hoofbeats thundered and men yelled. Everybody in the saloon swung around to look out the big plate-glass windows.

"What in blazes is all that?" Sam asked.

Stovepipe's craggy face had taken on a grim cast.

"Sounds like that bunch from the Devil's Pitchfork has come to town," he said. "And I reckon they're just about ready to raise hell and shove a chunk under the corner."

Chapter 15

The uproar made nearly everybody in the saloon turn toward the windows. The only ones who ignored it were the men at the poker tables who were intent on their cards.

A moment later, a man slapped the batwings aside and stalked into the Buckingham, followed by half a dozen more men. They were all rugged-looking, hard-bitten hombres in range clothes, Sam noted. A holstered revolver hung at the hip of each man.

Stovepipe Stewart leaned closer to Sam and said, "Yep, that's the Devil's Pitchfork bunch, some of 'em, anyway. John Henry Boyd's gun crew. Fella in the lead is Pete Lowry. Tough hombre. All of 'em are."

Sam had gotten that impression. Pete Lowry was a broad-shouldered man with a jutting shelf of a jaw that gave him a pugnacious appearance.

Lowry strode to the bar and thumped a fist on the hardwood to get the attention of one of the bartenders. It was really a wasted gesture, because nearly every eye in the place was on the newcomers already, and both bartenders were there to fill their orders.

"Whiskey for me and the boys!" Lowry snapped. "The good stuff, too, not that homemade swill."

"All we have is good stuff, Mr. Lowry," the nearest bartender said. "Lady Augusta don't go in for that panther piss."

Lowry's hand shot across the bar and grabbed the bartender's shirtfront. He jerked the man forward and roared, "Are you arguin' with me?"

Sam stiffened. He didn't like to see anyone being manhandled like that.

Stovepipe must have noticed the reaction, because he put a hand lightly on Sam's arm and said, "Hold your horses, son. You don't want to get on Lowry's bad side. He's not somebody you need for an enemy."

Sam forced himself to relax. Stovepipe was right. Anyway, it was none of his business what Lowry did, Sam told himself.

The bartender said, "No, sir, I'm not arguin' at all. I'll get you that whiskey, the finest we got, right away."

Lowry let go of him and nodded curtly.

"That's more like it. Pour it up, apron. After what happened last night, we need those drinks."

Sam wondered what had happened the night before. He didn't have to think about it for long, because as soon as Pete Lowry had knocked back the slug of whiskey the bartender put in front of him, he turned around and addressed the room in a loud voice.

"A bunch of damned savages raided the ranch last night," he said. "Killed two punchers and took off with fifty head of cattle. By God, there's gonna be a whole new Navajo war here in the Four Corners!"

Lowry's words shook Sam, although he managed not to show it. He had a hard time believing that Caballo Rojo or any of his people would have attacked the Devil's Pitchfork ranch. Even the proddy Juan Pablo just wanted to be left alone. None of them would go out of their way to draw attention to themselves by raiding a ranch and killing white cowboys. Sam would have staked his life on it.

Lowry seemed convinced of what he was saying, though. Several of the other ranch hands joined in, loudly and profanely insisting that the Navajo had gone on the warpath.

As Sam listened to Lowry and the other cowboys rant, he thought about what Noah Reilly had said earlier about people in this area still being nervous about the Navajo. This was going to make them even more so.

"A new Injun war," Stovepipe Stewart mused. "What do you think about that, Sam?"

"I think it's loco," Sam answered honestly and without hesitation. "If there are any Navajo still out there looking for trouble, there aren't enough of them to fight a war. I don't think they'd be foolish enough to risk that by raiding a ranch and killing some punchers."

He spoke a little too loudly. A man who stood not too far away at the bar overheard him and called, "Hey, Pete! This fella says you're lyin'. And from the looks of him, he might be a redskin, too!"

"Uh-oh," Wilbur said. "This ain't good."

Lowry swung around with a belligerent glare on his face.

"Who called me a liar?" he demanded. His angry gaze landed on Sam. "I'll bet it was you!"

Sam didn't see any point in lying, and it went against his nature anyway. He said, "I never claimed you were lying. I just said I thought it was unlikely any Navajo would be foolish enough to attack your ranch."

Lowry stomped toward him.

"Then how do you explain those missin' cows and two of my friends bein' dead?"

"I'm sorry about your friends," Sam said. "But maybe the cattle were stolen by rustlers."

"On unshod ponies? And those two fellas had arrows stuck in 'em! Navajo arrows!"

"Anyone can ride unshod ponies," Sam said. "And white men can use bows and arrows, too. It wouldn't be the first time whites have tried to blame the trouble they caused on Indians."

Lowry stopped in front of Sam, looked him up and down, and sneered.

"You don't talk like a redskin, but you sure look like one," he said. "Half-breed, ain't you?"

"I'm half Cheyenne," Sam said for what seemed like the dozenth time since he'd ridden into Flat Rock.

"No wonder you're defendin' those filthy savages. You're just like 'em."

"The Cheyenne and the Navajo have never been allies," Sam pointed out. "They're from totally different parts of the country. Anyway, the Navajo fought more wars against other tribes, like the Pueblo, than they ever did against the whites."

"A redskin's a redskin, and I got no use for any of 'em," Lowry snapped. "And I sure as hell got no use for a smart-mouthed one like you, mister!"

He launched a fist at Sam's head.

Chapter 16

Sam was expecting that. He'd had a hunch that Lowry was working himself up to a fight.

As the man lurched forward and swung, Sam ducked his head and bent at the waist. The punch sailed wide past his ear.

Thrown off balance by the missed blow, Lowry stumbled against Sam, who hooked a hard right into his belly. The breath went out of Lowry's body with a *whoof!*

Lowry's companions from the Devil's Pitchfork yelled and surged toward Sam. As Lowry doubled over from the pain of the blow, Sam grabbed his shoulders and shoved him into the path of the charging cowboys. A couple of them ran into him and knocked him off his feet. Tripping over Lowry, the men went sprawling. More of the cowboys got tangled up and fell.

That gave Sam time to slip his Colt from its

holster and say, "Just hold on, blast it! There's no need for—"

"Watch it, Sam!" Stovepipe warned.

Men were crowded around Sam. Someone in the bunch lashed out and drove the side of his hand against Sam's wrist.

Paralyzing pain shot up his arm. His fingers opened involuntarily, and the revolver slipped out of his hand and thudded to the sawdust-littered floor.

Another man caught hold of Sam's shoulder and jerked him around. He heard a shout of "Let's teach the redskin a lesson!" and then a fist seemed to explode in his face before he could get out of its way. The impact sent Sam stumbling backward.

He knew if he went down, there was a good chance these men would stomp and kick him to death. Because of that he fought desperately to keep his balance, but he felt it deserting him and knew he was about to fall.

At that moment, strong hands caught him from behind and kept him on his feet. Sam glanced around and saw it was Stovepipe Stewart who had caught him.

"Much obliged!" Sam gasped.

"Don't be thankin' me yet," Stovepipe warned. "Here they come!"

It was true. Not only were the Devil's Pitchfork hands closing in around Sam, several of the men who'd been in the saloon to start with had joined the fight, too, and all of them wanted his blood.

Sam put his back against the bar, hoping that the bartenders would remain neutral as they usually did when a brawl broke out. Stovepipe was on his right, Wilbur on his left, and both of the cowboys had their fists clenched and ready.

Sam wiped the back of his left hand across his mouth. That left a streak of blood on it from a bleeding lip.

"Are you two sure you want to take cards in this game?" he asked.

"You bet," Wilbur said. "We don't cotton to such bad odds."

"So we'll make 'em a little better," Stovepipe added.

"All right," Sam said.

That was all he had time to get out of his mouth before angry shouts filled the saloon and fists started flying.

Sam stood there with his back against the hardwood, slamming punches back and forth and trying to block the blows aimed at him. Quite a few of them got through despite his best efforts and rocked him. He stayed upright, though, and continued battling.

On either side of him, Stovepipe and Wilbur were doing the same. Stovepipe's big, knobby fists on the ends of gangling arms snapped out with surprising speed and force and sent more than one man flying off his feet.

Wilbur's style was different. With his stocky frame, he was more of a grappler. He got hold of two men, knocked their heads together, and then used their limp forms to trip up several more men.

With a bellow like a wounded buffalo bull, Pete Lowry plowed through the melee, knocking men aside in his attempt to reach Sam. Sam saw him coming and was able to get his feet set. He met Lowry's charge with a straight, hard left and followed it instantly with a right cross.

Unfortunately, neither blow seemed to have much effect on Lowry. That prominent jaw of his might as well have been made of iron.

Sam had a hunch the big man's weak spot was his gut and tried to land a punch there, but Lowry was already too close. He rammed into Sam and bent him backward over the bar.

Sam gasped as pain shot through him. Lowry began to hammer punches into his ribs.

Sam brought his cupped hands up and slapped them over Lowry's ears. That made Lowry jerk back and gave Sam room to lift a knee into the man's groin. Lowry didn't shrug that off. With a keening cry of pain, he doubled over again.

At least nobody else had pulled a gun yet, Sam thought. That was the only good thing about this ruckus. As long as the men were just whaling away at each other, someone might get killed, but it was less likely than if guns were involved.

Even with Lowry incapacitated for the moment, there were plenty of other angry men to take his place. They crowded around Sam, Stovepipe, and Wilbur, and their numbers actually worked against them because they kept getting in each other's way as they tried to throw punches.

Eventually, though, they would overwhelm the three men who stood together at the bar. Sam knew that, and he didn't know if he could count on any more help. It was unexpected enough that Stovepipe and Wilbur had pitched in to aid him.

Either they weren't members of the gang that had bushwhacked him and Matt, Sam thought as he blocked a punch and landed a haymaker on a man's jaw . . . or else they were playing a very deep game.

There was no time right now to ponder that, no time to do anything except keep on fighting and postpone their ultimate defeat as long as possible . . .

The roar of a shotgun blast seemed to shake the entire room.

It was loud enough to assault the ears and make every man in the place stop what he was doing. A shocked silence fell as the echoes of the blast faded.

Into that silence came the sharp, angry voice of a woman.

"What in blazes is going on here?"

Sam lifted his eyes to the stairs and saw her standing there, her auburn hair pulled back away from her lovely face, the dark blue gown she wore hugging the splendid curves of her body. Smoke curled from one barrel of the double-barreled Greener in her hands, telling Sam that she still had a load of buckshot in the weapon, ready to cut loose again.

Even without the faint British accent to her words, Sam would have known from her regal bearing that he was looking at Lady Augusta Winslow, the owner of the Buckingham Palace Saloon.

Chapter 17

Lady Augusta eased back the shotgun's other hammer. The sound was loud in the now eerily quiet saloon.

"I asked what's going on here," she said.

One of the bartenders spoke up.

"It was this Indian, ma'am," he said as he pointed to Sam. "He started it!"

"That ain't true," Stovepipe said. "Pete Lowry threw the first punch."

That accusation brought howls of protest from a dozen throats as the Devil's Pitchfork hands who were still conscious and on their feet loudly denied that Lowry had started the fight. Some of the other men in the saloon backed up their claim.

A jerk of the shotgun's barrels made the men shut up. Lady Augusta looked at Sam, Stovepipe, and Wilbur and said, "You there. You three seem to be at the center of this maelstrom. Come up here, now."

"Hear that, Wilbur?" Stovepipe asked with a quick grin. "You get to go upstairs and meet Lady Augusta."

"Pipe down," Wilbur snapped. A deep red flush spread over his freckled face. When Sam saw it, he realized that Wilbur had been worshipping Lady Augusta from afar. Evidently he had never actually met her.

"Make a path for them," Lady Augusta ordered. No one in his right mind wanted to argue with a shotgun. There was plenty of angry muttering going on, but the men moved back to make way for Sam, Stovepipe, and Wilbur.

Sam spotted his Colt lying on the floor underneath the brass rail at the bottom of the bar, where someone had kicked it during the fracas. He reached down, picked it up, and slid it back into his holster, then joined Stovepipe and Wilbur as they crossed the room toward the stairs.

When they reached the bottom of the staircase, Sam was uncomfortably aware that the shotgun was pointing more at him and his companions than it was at the rest of the men in the saloon. He didn't like climbing toward the menacing double maw of the barrels, but that seemed to be the most likely way he and his companions could get out of here with their hides relatively intact.

Lady Augusta drew back a couple of steps as they reached the second-floor landing. She still covered them with the Greener.

As she glanced toward the men down below in the saloon's main room, she said in a clear, commanding voice, "I want everything cleaned up and put back in its place down there. Every man who pitches in to help gets a free drink."

That sent men scrambling to pick up knocked-over chairs and right overturned tables. Even some of the men who had been in the middle of the fight were more interested now in earning that free drink.

Not Pete Lowry, though. He jabbed a finger at Sam and said, "Don't you believe a word that filthy redskin tells you, ma'am. He says he's half Cheyenne, but he could be lyin'. He could be one of those murderin' Navajo himself, come into town to spy on us!"

"That's insane," Sam said.

"Just hush," Lady Augusta said coldly. "Move down there to that open door. That's my suite."

Stovepipe looked at Wilbur again, who gave his lanky friend a warning glare. Stovepipe didn't say anything.

With the shotgun trained on the backs of the three men, Lady Augusta followed them along the corridor to her suite.

Downstairs, Zack Jardine slumped in a chair at one of the tables that had been set back on its legs and glared at Angus Braverman and Doyle Hilliard.

"Was that him?" Jardine asked.

Braverman nodded.

"Yeah. I got a good look at him that day, Zack. There ain't no doubt."

"He didn't look like he was hurt a bit, the way he

was brawling. What about those two men who sided him? Was one of them with him that day?"

Braverman shook his head in answer to this question.

"No, both of those hombres are older than the fella who was with the half-breed. I don't know what happened to him. He was hit, so likely he died, and now the 'breed's lookin' to settle the score for him."

"One of us should have shot him," Jardine said, keeping his voice low. "That idiot Lowry and his friends would've gotten the blame if that happened."

"I never got a clear shot at him, Zack, or I might've," Hilliard said. "Those boys from the Devil's Pitchfork were crowdin' around him too much."

Jardine grunted. Boyd, Lowry, and the other two-bit desperadoes from the Devil's Pitchfork thought they were tough hombres. The people of Flat Rock believed that, too.

They had no idea who the really dangerous men among them were.

"At least we know the rest of the boys did their job and ran off those cattle," Jardine commented quietly. He had split his forces the previous day, keeping half of his men here in Flat Rock and sending the other half to rustle some cows off the spread south of the settlement.

Jardine had told those men before they left that if they got a chance to ventilate some of the Devil's Pitchfork hands, not to hesitate. Dead cowboys and rustled cattle would go a long way toward stirring up the whites in the area against the Navajo.

Once those rifles he had hidden here in town were in the hands of the Indians, a shooting war would be inevitable. The hotheads among the Navajo would see to that, and they would find the settlers more than willing to fight.

Then the army would come in to clean out the hostiles, the government would take back the reservation land it had granted to the savages, and Jardine and his partner would be ready to take full advantage of that.

Deeds had already been drawn up, just waiting for the proper developments in Washington. Once they were signed, millions of acres would belong to Zack Jardine . . . the King of the Four Corners.

It had a nice ring to it.

Of course, most of those acres were flat, empty, and useless . . . but they surrounded areas where cattle could be run, and precious waterholes, and mines producing small but still lucrative quantities of gold, silver, and copper.

Besides, there was talk of running a rail line through here, and if that happened, the so-called worthless land would be worth even more. No land where the railroad wanted to go was truly worthless.

"At least we know the half-breed's here now," Braverman said, breaking into Jardine's grandiose thoughts. "We don't have to watch the trail for him anymore."

"It would be better if Joe and Three-Finger had done like they were supposed to," Jardine snapped. "We could have set a trap that would've made sure the meddling bastard was dead by now."

"We can still kill him," Hilliard suggested. "He's upstairs right now."

"With that Englishwoman," Jardine pointed out. "Lady Augusta's the belle of this whole region. We don't want anything to happen to her."

That brought another idea to Jardine's brain, one that had crossed his mind on previous occasions. In an area where most of the women were either washed-out whores or Navajo squaws, Lady Augusta Winslow was a shining light of femininity.

If he was going to be the King of the Four Corners, Jardine mused, maybe he could interest Lady Augusta in being his queen . . .

With a little shake of his head, he put aside that appealing thought and told Braverman and Hilliard, "Keep an eye on the 'breed, but don't let him know you're watching him. If you get a chance . . . get rid of him."

"What about those two cowboys?" Braverman asked.

Jardine shrugged.

"I don't have anything against them. But if they're in the way . . . well, the buzzards would be even happier with three bodies than they would with one, wouldn't they?"

Chapter 18

When Sam stepped through the door of the suite, he wasn't surprised to see that the sitting room was elegantly and sumptuously furnished, from the rug on the floor to the paintings on the walls to the ornate lamp on a gleaming table.

He had seen enough downstairs to know that the lady liked fine things.

"Sit down," she ordered as she came into the room behind them. "That divan will do."

Stovepipe took off his hat and said, "Ma'am, not to be argumentative, but that's a mighty nice piece of furniture to have three galoots like us sittin' on it. We're liable to get it a mite dirty."

"Never mind that," Lady Augusta snapped. "Sit."

The three men sat.

She lowered the shotgun as she faced them, but the weapon was still pointed in their general direction. She wouldn't have to raise it much in order to spray them with buckshot if she pulled the trigger on the loaded barrel. Shotguns were heavy enough that some women had trouble handling them, Sam thought, but not this supposedly genteel Englishwoman.

"Now tell me what happened down there," Lady Augusta ordered. She nodded at Sam. "You."

"Pete Lowry and some riders from the Devil's Pitchfork came in and started talking about how the Navajo raided their ranch last night, ran off some cattle, and killed a couple of hands." Sam inclined his head toward Stovepipe and continued, "I commented to my friend here how that seemed unlikely to me. Someone overheard me and told Lowry that I called him a liar."

Lady Augusta nodded.

"I can see how that would spark a confrontation. I've seen these other two around, sir, but not you. Who are you?"

"My name is Sam Two Wolves, ma'am. And before you ask, I really am half Cheyenne. No Navajo blood, despite what Lowry said down there."

"Yes, I didn't think you looked much like any of the Navajo I've ever seen, and there are plenty of them around here. This is supposedly their land, after all." She turned her attention to Stovepipe and Wilbur. "What about you two? Who are you, and what's your connection with all this?"

Stovepipe still had his black Stetson in his hand, and when he nudged Wilbur in the ribs with an elbow, Wilbur snatched his battered old hat off his head, too.

"They call me Stovepipe Stewart, ma'am," the tall,

skinny cowboy said. "This here's my pard, Wilbur Coleman."

Wilbur opened his mouth to say something, but all that came out was a nervous squeak.

"You got to pardon ol' Wilbur," Stovepipe went on. "He ain't much for talkin', especially around beautisome ladies."

Lady Augusta didn't smile, but Sam thought he saw a twinkle of amusement in her eyes for a second.

"Go on," she said solemnly. "Why were you involved in that fight?"

"Because we were sidin' Sam here," Stovepipe explained. "Didn't seem fair to us that so many fellas would jump one lone hombre and give him a thrashin' . . . especially when he was just tellin' the truth."

"Then you were sticking up for the underdog."

Stovepipe nodded.

"Yes'm, you could say that."

For a moment, Lady Augusta regarded them gravely, then nodded and turned to place the shotgun on a side table.

The sight of the Greener lying there on what was obviously an expensive piece of furniture was a little odd, Sam thought, a good example of the stark contrasts to be found in many frontier towns on the edge of civilization.

"I can respect such behavior," Lady Augusta said, "although my tolerance is strained when it results in damage to my saloon. You gentlemen are forgiven for your part in the hostilities." She crossed her arms over her bosom. "Now . . . what about the Indians? You don't believe there's any truth to what Pete Lowry said, Mr. Two Wolves?"

"I don't know for sure because I wasn't there," Sam admitted, "but it seems pretty unlikely to me that people who have been mostly at peace with the white men for more than fifteen years would risk starting a war again."

"But what if they're starving? What if they had to have those cattle in order to feed their families?"

She had a point there, Sam thought. Fifty cattle would feed Caballo Rojo's people for quite a while.

But that isolated canyon where the Navajo lived was two days' ride from here, and Sam hadn't heard Caballo Rojo, Juan Pablo, or any of the other warriors talking about raiding a ranch in the near future, or any other time, for that matter.

It hadn't appeared to Sam that the band was running short on food, either. Everyone seemed reasonably well-fed. Between the sheep they raised, the crops they grew, and the deer that roamed the area, none of the Navajo should have gone hungry.

They wouldn't have risked everything by attacking the Devil's Pitchfork. Sam was sure of it.

"I just don't see it happening that way," he told Lady Augusta. "Maybe I'm wrong."

"What other explanation is there?" she asked. "Or do you believe the incident never occurred?"

Stovepipe said, "You mean maybe Lowry and his boss made the whole thing up? Why would they do that?"

She smiled at him.

"You tell me, Mr. Stewart."

Stovepipe shook his head and said, "Sorry, ma'am, I can't. This whole business don't make heads nor tails to me."

"Well, it's really none of my affair. I was just curious what nearly got my saloon busted all to pieces, as you ruffians might say." She went to the door and opened it. "There's a door at the end of the hall that leads to the rear stairs. I suggest the three of you depart that way, rather than going through the main room downstairs. In fact, I insist upon it. Mr. Lowry and his friends may still be down there, and I don't want a repeat of what happened earlier."

"Neither do we, ma'am," Sam assured her as he got to his feet. Stovepipe and Wilbur followed suit.

"It was an honor and a privilege to make your acquaintance, ma'am," Stovepipe said. Beside him, Wilbur gulped, opened his mouth to say something, gulped again, and made a few incoherent noises. Stovepipe nodded toward his friend and added, "Wilbur says likewise, Your Ladyship."

"You're all welcome in the Buckingham Palace Saloon," she told them, "but not until the boys from the Devil's Pitchfork are gone. Agreed?"

Sam nodded and said, "That's fine with me. One run-in with Pete Lowry is plenty."

They stepped out into the corridor. As they did, Wilbur seemed to gather his courage. He turned around and said, "It sure was a pleasure to—"

Unfortunately, Lady Augusta had already closed

the door behind them, so she couldn't hear him. Wilbur stopped and looked crestfallen.

Stovepipe clapped a hand on his shoulder and said, "Come along, old hoss. Maybe you'll have another chance to talk to the lady some other time."

"Yeah, well, I could've talked to her now if you two blabbermouths would ever let a man get a word in edgewise," Wilbur muttered.

Sam chuckled. He hadn't ruled out the possibility that these two had some sinister motive in befriending him, but it was becoming more and more difficult to remain suspicious of them.

They took the rear stairs and went out a door that led into the alley behind the saloon.

"Where are you headed now, Sam?" Stovepipe asked.

Sam looked at the sky. The afternoon was getting to be well advanced.

"I thought I'd go check on my horse at the livery stable, then head for the boardinghouse where I'm staying. The lady who runs the place told me that supper was at six o'clock, and I've got a hunch she wouldn't look kindly on any of her boarders who were late."

"You gonna be in town for a while?"

"I don't know yet," Sam answered honestly. "Probably."

"Then I reckon we'll be runnin' into you again. And if you get into any more trouble, let out a holler. Wilbur and me are liable to be around somewhere close by. Flat Rock ain't all that big of a place, after all."

"I'll remember that," Sam promised. He lifted a hand in farewell as the two cowboys ambled off along the alley.

He wondered if Stovepipe's comments meant that the two of them planned to keep an eye on him . . . and if they did, why?

Pablo Garralaga at the livery stable wanted to know if Sam had found Mrs. McCormick's boardinghouse. Sam said that he had and thanked the liveryman for directing him there.

"Looks like a comfortable place," he said. "And as it turns out, the fella who has the room next to me is a man I met at the café earlier."

"And who would that be?" Garralaga asked.

"Noah Reilly."

Garralaga smiled.

"The little hombre from the general store?"

"You know him?"

"I buy goods there. And he comes by here every so often to rent a saddle horse from me."

Sam said, "He didn't strike me as the sort of fella to go riding around the countryside."

Garralaga shook his head.

"No, no, he tries to ride, but the poor little muchacho always comes back in such pain. He told me once that he used to live somewhere back East, and he came out here to Arizona for his health. He thinks that he should learn to ride so he will fit in better. I try to show him how to sit so he won't be so sore from the saddle, but it's no use. Some people should never get on a horse."

Sam supposed that was true, even though he had spent so much of his life on horseback it was hard to imagine that there were people who just couldn't ride.

He looked in on his own horse, said so long to Garralaga, and then strolled toward the boardinghouse. Along the way he mulled over everything that had happened since he rode into Flat Rock. He had met some people, gotten into a brawl, and had a beautiful Englishwoman who just might be nobility point a shotgun at him. It had been an eventful afternoon, but not a particularly productive one. He didn't feel like he was any closer to finding the bushwhackers than he had been before he arrived in town.

But they were still here somewhere, his instincts told him. It was just a matter of drawing them into the open and figuring out why they had tried to kill him and Matt. Once he had done that, he could decide on his next move.

At least he didn't have to worry too much about Matt right now, he told himself. That was one thing to be thankful for, anyway.

Chapter 19

Juan Pablo hadn't returned to the canyon by the next morning, and Matt wasn't sure what that meant. He hoped Sam and the Navajo hadn't run into trouble, such as another ambush attempt.

Elizabeth Fleming wasn't in the hogan when Matt woke up. He didn't see any point in asking the older woman about her, so he just kept quiet, ate the bowl of stew she gave him for breakfast, and sat motionless while she changed the poultices on his wounds.

He felt stronger now, and as a result he was even more restless than before. That afternoon it grew so warm and stuffy inside the hogan that Matt felt like he couldn't get a breath of air.

Finally he got to his feet, went to the door of the hogan, and stepped out into the sunlight.

This was the first time he had felt the sun in a long time. A week, maybe? Matt wasn't sure. Because of his injury, he had lost track of time. All he knew was that although the light was blinding to his eyes, the warmth of the sun on his skin felt wonderful and was very welcome.

He drew in a deep breath. As in any Indian encampment, the air was filled with the smells of smoke, grease, and human waste. Even that didn't bother Matt right now. He had been in plenty of so-called "civilized" places that smelled worse.

"Matt," a voice said behind him.

He turned and saw Elizabeth standing there. From the looks of it, she had been on her way around the hogan when she saw him and stopped short in surprise.

After a moment she took a step toward him and lifted a hand as if she intended to reach out and touch his bare chest. Other than the bandages wrapped around his midsection to hold the poultices in place, he was naked from the waist up.

Plenty of people were around, including Juan Pablo's wife, who had followed Matt out of the hogan. Feeling their eyes on him, he backed away from Elizabeth, then turned and pushed past the older women to go back inside.

His jaw was clenched in anger, most of it directed at himself. He had never in his life been one to run from trouble, and here he was retreating.

Not only that, as he turned away he had caught a glimpse of the hurt that flared in Elizabeth's eyes. That ate at him as well, and he seethed inside with resentment for the unaccustomed awkwardness that had put the both of them in this position.

That was a long day and an even longer night. Matt

was restless and had trouble sleeping. The bullet holes still ached at times and itched at others, and he couldn't help but wonder how Elizabeth was doing tonight.

Juan Pablo was bound to be back tomorrow with news of Sam, Matt told himself.

But Juan Pablo didn't return the next day, which increased Matt's worries about his blood brother. More and more he wondered if Sam and Juan Pablo had been ambushed. The thought that Sam might be lying out there somewhere on the plains, wounded or even dead, gnawed at Matt's guts.

His boredom at doing nothing but sitting around increased, too. His wounds had closed up and were healing. Some of his strength had come back, and while he knew he wasn't in shape yet to do a lot of hard riding or fighting, he felt too good to waste his days in inactivity.

Through sign language, he managed to tell Juan Pablo's wife that he wanted a shirt to replace his blood-soaked, bullet-torn one. She gave him a shirt made of soft, red-dyed wool that he slipped over his head.

"I'm going to take a walk," he told her. When she stared at him uncomprehendingly, he pointed to himself and then made walking motions with his fingers. The woman shook her head, but Matt ignored her and stepped out of the hogan.

He hoped he wouldn't run into Elizabeth this time. He needed to get a little exercise. That would just make him stronger, he thought.

As he strolled along the creek and passed some of the other hogans, he was aware that he was being given a lot of curious looks. Several children ignored the sheep they were supposed to be watching and started following him. They tagged along with him until their mothers angrily called them back. Some of the men watched him warily.

Even though Caballo Rojo had guaranteed his safety, having a white man around had to go against the grain for these people who had been rounded up, forced to walk hundreds of miles to Bosque Redondo, and kept there in captivity for years before they were allowed to return to their homeland.

Matt made sure he didn't do anything that could be mistaken for belligerence. He gave everyone friendly nods and smiles.

As he approached Caballo Rojo's hogan, he spotted the clan leader striding toward him. Caballo Rojo seemed to be bound on a specific errand, and Matt wondered if someone had gone to him and told him that the white man was wandering around the canyon.

Caballo Rojo stopped in front of him and rumbled, "Rest. Get stronger."

"I'm already getting stronger, Chief," Matt said. "I need to move around now. I need to do something."

Caballo Rojo shook his head.

"Rest."

"I will. I give you my word. I'm just taking a stroll."

Caballo Rojo looked like he didn't approve of the idea, but he didn't try to force Matt back to Juan

Pablo's hogan. He stood there scowling as Matt walked over to the creek and continued following it.

He would walk a little farther and then come back, he figured. After being shut up in that hogan for so long, the warmth of the sun and the interplay of light and shadow through the branches of the cottonwoods along the stream were very welcome.

Matt hadn't gone very far when a bend of the creek and the thickening of the trees partially obscured the hogans. He was about to turn around and go back when he heard voices up ahead.

The voices belonged to women, and instantly the possibility that they might be bathing occurred to him. Matt was too much of a gentleman to spy on any female in a situation like that, so he swung around to head away from the spot.

Then he heard a laugh that he recognized as Elizabeth Fleming's, and that stopped him in his tracks.

"Don't be a damn fool, Matt Bodine," he told himself out loud. "You better just get away from here right now."

He would have, too, but just then the voices got louder. With a crackling of brush, the women pushed into view behind him. His head was turned just enough for him to catch the motion from the corner of his eye. He heard a surprised gasp, and Elizabeth said, "Matt?"

He couldn't stop himself from looking around. When he did, he saw the redheaded woman standing there with three young Navajo women.

Their hair was wet, and their colorful blouses and

skirts clung to their damp bodies. They had been
bathing, all right, and Matt was glad he hadn't stumbled onto that scene. At least they were clothed now.

"Sorry," he said. "Don't worry, I'll be movin' on
now."

He turned to leave, but Elizabeth hurried to catch
up with him.

"You're feeling better?" she asked.

Matt nodded.

"Yeah, I'm stronger now. Those bullet holes are
healing. I felt like I needed to get out and move
around some. But I'm going back to Juan Pablo's
hogan now."

"I'll walk with you."

Matt didn't think that was a very good idea, but he
wasn't really strong enough to run away from her, so
there was nothing he could do.

Besides, that would have been rude. He didn't
want to cause trouble, but he didn't want to hurt her
feelings any more than he already had, either.

The other young women followed behind them,
talking in quiet but animated voices. Matt figured
they were gossiping about him and the white teacher
from back East.

That was all he needed, he thought. In some ways
these Navajo were like anybody else. They liked a
good juicy scandal.

Matt tried to walk a little faster as they approached
the hogans. When he did, the pounding heartbeat and
slight shortness of breath he felt told him he had

pushed his recuperating body just about as far as it wanted to be pushed right now. He slowed.

"When Juan Pablo comes back, I may have to go." Elizabeth looked saddened by that prospect.

"You're going to leave?"

"I need to find Sam." Matt had thought it might take a week for him to be strong enough to ride out on Sam's trail, but now he believed he might be able to do that sooner. Another two or three days ought to see him in good enough shape to leave.

And that would sure simplify matters with Elizabeth, too. Best he put some distance between him and her, Matt told himself, so she could go back to her teaching and not be distracted by him.

If he was honest with himself, he had to admit that he didn't want to be distracted by her, either. Not as long as Sam was gone and the mystery of who had bushwhacked them and why still went unanswered.

Those thoughts wheeled through Matt's mind, and he wished they would go away. Getting caught in a gunfight was easier, in a way, than trying to navigate human emotions and figure out what was the best thing to do.

Elizabeth didn't make it any easier by saying, "I wish you'd stay longer." She sounded determined to make that happen, one way or the other.

Matt didn't waste his breath arguing with her. They had gotten back to Juan Pablo's hogan, so he told Elizabeth, "I'll see you later." She looked like she was going to argue, so he went on, "I'm tired. I need to rest."

She nodded, although he could tell she was reluctant to do so. He ducked through the entrance before she could say anything else.

The older woman gave him a stern look when he came in, as if she were scolding him. He ignored her and sat down on the blankets, and as he did, he realized just how weary he really was. He stretched out on the soft, thick pile of blankets. It felt good, and before he knew it he had closed his eyes and dozed off.

Matt didn't know how long he had slept before he woke up to the sound of angry voices outside the hogan. Some sort of squabble was going on.

He probably would have ignored it, but then he recognized one of the voices as Elizabeth's. He rolled over and pushed himself to his feet. Ignoring the exclamations from Juan Pablo's wife, he stepped out into the late afternoon.

Elizabeth was there, all right. She looked angry and more than a little frightened as she tried to pull away from a man who had his hand clamped around her arm. He was holding her so tightly it had to hurt, Matt thought. Without pausing to ponder what he should do, he said, "Hey! Let go of her, mister!"

The Navajo released Elizabeth's arm, but as he did, he turned toward Matt. His hand dipped instead to the knife tucked behind the red sash at his waist. With a whisper of steel, the blade came out. The warrior lunged at Matt and lifted the knife to strike.

Chapter 20

Instinct took over. Matt's left arm came up to block the thrust of the blade.

At the same time his right fist shot out and smashed into the warrior's face. He twisted at the waist as he launched the punch so he could put as much power into it as possible, and pain jabbed through him as the move pulled at the healing bullet holes.

That was a lot better than standing there and letting the man sink the knife in his chest, though. As the man reeled back a step, Matt grabbed the wrist of his knife hand with both hands and wrenched on it. The Navajo grunted in pain as bones ground together in his wrist and the knife slipped from his fingers.

The warrior swung a left at Matt's head. Matt moved aside just enough to cause the blow to glance off his ear. It hurt anyway.

Matt hooked a left of his own to the Navajo's jaw. He knew that the longer this fight lasted, the less chance he had. The wound he had suffered and the long days of lying around had depleted his reserves of strength. He was already breathing hard, and his pulse hammered inside his skull in a wild, discordant drumbeat.

A loud, angry voice bellowed words Matt didn't understand, but the tone of command was unmistakable. The man he'd been battling abruptly stepped back. The man's chest heaved, and his face was flushed and twisted with fury. But with a visible effort, he restained himself from attacking Matt again.

Caballo Rojo stalked up and planted himself between Matt and his opponent. For a moment the chief shouted at the warrior who'd been manhandling Elizabeth.

Then he turned to Matt and said, "White man go back in hogan!"

"I didn't do anything," Matt protested. He pointed at Elizabeth. "I was just protecting Miss Fleming!" He looked at her. "What in blazes is this all about, anyway?"

Elizabeth was pale and obviously upset.

"The young women have been gossiping about us, Matt. Pino here thinks that I'm corrupting them by being here. Many of the Navajo harbor such resentment toward white people that they don't like me being here in the first place."

"So he was trying to get you to leave?"

"Yes, and some of them think we should both go." Elizabeth shook her head. "But I won't leave, not as long as I can help these people."

Whatever she was teaching them, Matt had his

doubts about how much it really helped the Navajo. He wasn't sure a young woman from Vermont could know anything that would help these people survive in this rugged wilderness.

Even so, he wasn't going to stand by and let her be mistreated. That went too much against the grain.

On a practical level, however, there wasn't much he could do. A number of men had gathered, and from the way they were glaring at Matt it was obvious whose side they were on. Outnumbered, weak, and wounded as he was, he couldn't stop Pino from doing whatever he wanted.

Caballo Rojo leveled an arm.

"Go back in hogan," he ordered Matt again.

"You're gonna just let him get away with it?" Matt demanded. He didn't expect Caballo Rojo to do otherwise, but it wouldn't hurt anything to try . . . he hoped.

Caballo Rojo didn't budge. His face was hard as a rock as he pointed at the hogan. Matt reined in the anger he felt boiling up inside him.

He wouldn't be doing Elizabeth any good by getting himself killed, and Caballo Rojo looked just about riled up enough to go back on his word.

Matt jerked his head in a curt nod.

"All right," he said. "But this is wrong."

"Wrong for white man not wrong for Navajo," Caballo Rojo insisted.

Matt looked at Elizabeth and said, "Sorry."

"I appreciate you trying to stand up for me, Mr. Bodine."

He took a deep breath.

"Maybe when I leave here, you ought to go with me."

"No, I don't think so. Like I told you, I intend to stay. But when you're gone . . ."

She didn't have to finish what she was saying. When he was gone, then the young women of the clan wouldn't have anything to gossip about where he and Elizabeth were concerned. The trouble would probably blow over.

Fine, he thought. If that was the way she wanted it, he could oblige her.

"As soon as I'm strong enough to ride, I'll head out. I need to catch up to Sam, anyway."

Elizabeth nodded and said, "Of course."

With a last glare directed at Pino, Matt turned toward the hogan. Juan Pablo's wife had come out to watch the confrontation. He brushed past her and went inside. He heard a lot of low-voiced talking outside, but he didn't understand it and didn't care.

He told himself he didn't care, anyway. It was easier like that.

But not by much.

The canyon settled down as night fell. The brief ruckus between Matt and Pino seemed forgotten. Juan Pablo's wife gave Matt his supper, as usual, and this time when she removed the poultices from his wounds, she didn't pack more in there.

Instead, she simply covered the bullet holes with a thin layer of moss and bound it into place as a makeshift bandage. Matt took that to mean they thought he no longer needed the medicinal powers of the roots and herbs the woman had been using on him.

His sleep was restless again that night. He couldn't stop thinking about Elizabeth and wondering how she was doing. He admired her determination but questioned her good judgment.

The next morning he slipped on the wool shirt again and left the hogan. The woman didn't even try to discourage him this time. He supposed she had given up on getting him to do what she wanted him to do.

He didn't know where Pino's hogan was, or he would have avoided it. He definitely didn't want to encounter Caballo Rojo this morning, either, so he steered clear of the chief's hogan and walked along the creek toward the mouth of the canyon instead.

He wouldn't get too close to it, he decided, because he didn't want to alarm the guards posted there, but walking part of the way and then coming back would be good exercise for him.

None of the Navajo tried to stop him as he left the hogan, although he saw several of them watching him. He supposed they knew he wasn't a prisoner here, so he couldn't be trying to escape. When he came closer to the mouth of the canyon, he was able to see out over the vast sweep of the plains, and it looked mighty appealing to him. He had always been fiddle-footed by nature and never liked to stay in one place for too long.

Luckily, Sam was the same way, so they had always been good trail partners as well as blood brothers.

Matt stopped suddenly and frowned as he spotted something unusual out on the prairie. Several miles east of the canyon, a large cloud of dust rose into the morning sky.

His first thought was that it might be coming from a cavalry patrol, but after watching the cloud for a few minutes, Matt decided it was unlikely so much dust would be kicked up by horseback riders.

That looked more like the sort of dust cloud that would come from a herd of buffalo on the move, or a bunch of cattle being driven to market.

Out here in this big, mostly empty country, only one of those things was a possibility. The closest buffalo herds were hundreds of miles away, in western Texas.

There were some ranches in these parts, though, and the punchers who worked on them might be moving some cattle.

Matt wished he was out there on a good horse, getting a close look at whatever was going on. He didn't have any particular reason for feeling that way, just curiosity and restlessness. He watched the dust cloud until it finally moved out of sight to the northwest. The wall of the canyon itself cut the cloud off from his vision.

He turned to walk back toward the hogans. As he did, his instincts told him he was being watched. He looked along the creek and thought he saw a flash of movement from the brush that lined the stream. Matt headed in that direction, but when he got there he didn't see anyone.

Maybe it was his imagination, he told himself, although he didn't really believe that. He had never been the sort to see things that weren't there.

No, it was more likely that someone had been spying on him, he decided. Elizabeth, maybe? She could have noticed him leaving the hogans and followed him out here, even though she had to know by now that wouldn't be a wise thing to do.

Or maybe somebody who *wasn't* his friend, like Pino, was lurking around and keeping an eye on him.

Matt didn't like the feeling that crawled along his spine when he thought about somebody watching him. Most of the time, when somebody spied on an hombre like that, they were up to no good, he thought.

He would just have to keep his own eyes open for trouble.

No one bothered him during the rest of his walk. When he got back to the hogan, he told Juan Pablo's wife, "See, I'm doing better. Getting stronger. I walked halfway out of the canyon and back, and I'm fine."

Some of that was bravado on his part. He was pretty tired. But he was convinced that he was getting stronger with each passing day. Another couple of days, he told himself. Then maybe he could start thinking about riding out on Sam's trail . . . assuming that his blood brother hadn't returned by then.

"Still no sign of Juan Pablo?" he asked the woman. She ignored him, which came as no real surprise. He was starting to think that she understood more of what he said than she let on, but she didn't want him to know that.

During the afternoon, the woman left the hogan on some errand. That was all right with Matt, because he'd gotten drowsy. He stretched out on the blankets to take a nap, and he was asleep almost as soon as he closed his eyes.

He slept lightly. That habit had kept him alive on more than one occasion. And like a wild animal, he had the ability to go from sleeping to being fully awake in an instant, which also came in handy.

In this case, it allowed him to realize something was wrong as soon as a faint noise came to his ears and his eyes popped open. Even in the middle of the day, the interior of the hogan was dim and shadowy. Matt caught a glimpse of an indistinct figure looming over him. That was all it took for his muscles to burst into action and send him rolling to the side.

At the same time, the intruder's arm swept down, driving a knife through the buffalo robes where Matt had been a split second earlier.

Chapter 21

Matt snapped a kick at the man and caught him in the side. The impact knocked the man across the hogan.

He was able to hang on to his knife. As Matt started to scramble up, the intruder bounced off the far wall of the hogan and came at him again, slashing back and forth with the blade.

Since Matt was still kneeling, he stayed low and threw himself forward in a diving tackle. The knife sliced through the air above his head, missing him as he caught the attacker around the knees. The man yelled as Matt knocked him off his feet.

Matt levered himself up and made a grab for the man's wrist. Before he could catch hold of it, though, the intruder struck again. The knife had a brass ball at the end of the handle to keep a man's grip from slipping off it. The intruder smashed this ball against the side of Matt's head.

Stunned, Matt fell to the side. His muscles refused to respond to his commands.

Which meant he was as good as dead, he thought, because the intruder would need only a second to slash his throat from ear to ear.

Amazingly, that didn't happen. As the world spun crazily around Matt, blurring his vision, he realized that somehow he was still alive. The man hadn't killed him after all.

Footsteps thudded on the hard ground somewhere nearby. Matt rolled onto his uninjured side, got an elbow under him, and lifted himself so he could raise his head and look around.

He was alone in the hogan.

The knife-wielding intruder was gone.

Matt was baffled why the man had fled instead of completing his mission of murder. The only explanation he could think of involved the involuntary yell the man had let out when Matt tackled him.

The would-be assassin must have worried that his outcry would draw attention to the hogan, and he didn't want to be seen emerging from the dwelling where Matt's murdered body would be found later. So he had abandoned his plan and gotten out quickly.

That didn't mean he wouldn't try again to kill Matt later on.

Matt sat up and took stock of himself. The bullet holes in his side hurt from all the activity, but as far as he could tell, they hadn't opened up and started bleeding again.

He was still sitting there when a figure loomed in the doorway, blocking the light. Matt looked up and saw Elizabeth Fleming standing there.

She hurried into the hogan and dropped to her knees beside him. Juan Pablo's wife followed her. The older woman's usually stolid face actually wore a worried expression for a change.

"Matt, are you all right?" Elizabeth asked. "Someone said they heard a shout from this hogan, and then a man ran out."

"That's right," Matt said. "Somebody snuck in here and tried to knife me."

Elizabeth's beautiful green eyes widened.

"Who in the world would try to do that?"

"I can only think of one fella I've had a run-in with lately."

"You mean Pino?" Elizabeth asked.

"He was ready to stick a knife in me earlier," Matt said.

Elizabeth shook her head.

"That was just a spur of the moment thing, because he was angry. I don't think Pino would deliberately murder anyone. He's one of the clan's spiritual leaders."

"Who else would come after me like that?"

"I don't know," Elizabeth had to admit.

A harsh voice spoke outside the hogan. She turned her head toward the doorway.

"That's Caballo Rojo," she said. "He wants to know if everything is all right."

"Not hardly," Matt said. He started to get to his feet.

Elizabeth took hold of his arm to help him. Out of the habit of being fiercely independent, he started to shake her off.

But he had to admit, having her there to lean on felt pretty good. When he was standing, she kept her hand on his arm.

They went outside and found Caballo Rojo standing there with his arms crossed, waiting to hear what had happened. Juan Pablo's wife followed Matt and Elizabeth out of the hogan and started talking before they could. A steady stream of Navajo words came from her mouth.

When she finally finished, Matt said to Caballo Rojo, "I don't know what she told you, but someone snuck into the hogan while I was dozing and tried to kill me."

The clan leader nodded solemnly.

"Who would do this?" he asked.

"Well, I think it was Pino."

Caballo Rojo shook his head.

"Not Pino. Pino is good man."

"I haven't had trouble with anybody else from your clan," Matt pointed out.

Stubbornly, Caballo Rojo said, "Not Pino." He jerked his head in an indication that Matt and Elizabeth should follow him. If that wasn't clear enough, he added, "Come."

They exchanged a glance. Since they were both here because Caballo Rojo had extended his hospitality to them, they couldn't very well refuse.

They followed the clan leader along the creek, past several of the other hogans and the grazing herd of sheep. When they came to another hogan, Caballo Rojo called out to someone inside.

Matt wasn't surprised when Pino emerged from the dwelling. The man gave him and Elizabeth unfriendly looks, then spoke to Caballo Rojo in Navajo.

When Pino was finished, Caballo Rojo turned to Matt and said, "Pino here." He made a flat, slashing motion with his hand. "All day."

Matt wanted to point out that Pino could be lying about that. Even if the members of the man's family backed him up on that, they could be lying as well.

But while Caballo Rojo might be a judge of sorts, this wasn't a court of law, Matt realized. No rules of evidence applied here. What Caballo Rojo believed was the only thing that mattered, and clearly the clan leader was on Pino's side in this dispute.

Anyway, to be absolutely honest about it, he *hadn't* gotten a good look at the intruder, Matt reminded himself. All he could be sure of was that the man had been dressed like a Navajo . . . and Pino was hardly the only one in this canyon who fit that description.

"All right," he told Caballo Rojo. "Maybe Pino didn't try to kill me. But somebody did."

Caballo Rojo shrugged as if to say that wasn't his worry.

"Fine," Matt said. "But I'll be sleeping with one eye open from now on, you can count on that."

Caballo Rojo grunted and turned away. Matt had the distinct impression that the clan leader was washing his hands of the whole matter.

Pino glared at Matt and Elizabeth again and went back in his hogan, leaving the two of them alone.

"I don't understand, Matt," Elizabeth said. "Why would any of these people want to kill you? No one here even knew you until you were brought in wounded."

"I don't have an answer," Matt admitted. "Maybe it would be best if I just got on my horse and left."

"You're in no shape to do that," Elizabeth said.

He winced as the wounds in his side twinged a little.

"I'm in no shape to fight off whoever wants me dead, either. But if I could make it to Flat Rock and find Sam, he could watch my back."

"You don't know if he's even there. He could have found the trail of those men who attacked you, and it could have led somewhere else."

She was right about that, Matt realized. His instincts told him there was some connection between the bushwhackers and the settlement, though.

For one thing, the men who'd taken those potshots at him and Sam had been using repeaters. Judging by what he had seen so far, the Navajo didn't have any rifles except a few old single-shot weapons. Matt was convinced the bushwhackers had been white men.

And where else in these parts would white men be found except in Flat Rock, or on one of the ranches in the area of the settlement?

As he pondered that, he sighed and said, "I won't leave today. I reckon I'm still not strong enough to do that. But I don't make any promises about tomorrow."

"You should come back to my hogan," she suggested. "I can watch over you and make sure nothing happens."

Matt wasn't sure a schoolteacher from Vermont would be able to stop somebody from trying to kill him, and besides . . .

"That would just scandalize these folks even more. They'd run us both out of the canyon, and you didn't want to leave yet."

"Maybe I've changed my mind," Elizabeth said. "Things are getting too tense here. Normally the Navajo are very peaceful people, but I'm starting to get a feeling that . . . well, that there might be trouble."

Matt looked up and down the canyon. He felt the same way. The hair on the back of his neck stood up and the skin prickled, as if someone was watching them.

Somebody who didn't have their best interests in mind.

"Tomorrow," he said. "Tomorrow, if you still feel the same way, we'll get out of here."

Elizabeth nodded in agreement.

Now all they had to do was live through the night, Matt thought.

Chapter 22

Mrs. McCormick had told Sam that she served breakfast at six o'clock. What he found waiting for him when he came into the dining room the next morning was worth getting up that early for.

The rich aroma of fresh-brewed coffee filled the room and mingled with other enticing smells, like that of fresh-baked bread and sizzling bacon.

Six men sat at the long table, including Noah Reilly. The little bespectacled clerk lifted a hand in greeting and smiled at Sam.

"Mr. Two Wolves!" he said. "Mrs. McCormick told me that you'd taken a room here. I'm glad to see you."

"You, too, Noah," Sam said.

Reilly pulled back the empty chair next to him.

"Here, have a seat."

The table was already set and had food on it. Sam saw platters full of bacon, biscuits, hotcakes, eggs, and hash brown potatoes. A couple of pots of coffee sat within easy reach, and so did a pitcher of buttermilk. There was gravy and honey for the biscuits, molasses for the hotcakes.

It was classic boardinghouse fare and Sam's stomach rumbled a little as he sat down next to Reilly, letting him know that he was ready for it.

Mrs. Reilly came in from the kitchen, carrying a tray with several jars of different jams and preserves on it.

"Good morning, Mr. Two Wolves," she said. "Have you met everyone?"

Sam shook his head.

"No, not really, just Noah here."

"Let me introduce you to the other fellows," Reilly said.

He went around the table giving Sam the names and occupations of the other boarders, adding jocular asides about their professions such as "You don't want to get too well acquainted with Cyrus here. He's the undertaker!"

Sam filed away the information in his head, knowing that he wouldn't remember most of it. The townsmen were all pleasant enough, although a couple of them were a little reticent in their greetings. Sam had a hunch that was because of his Cheyenne blood.

Overall, though, it was a pleasant meal, and Sam was stuffed by the time he was finished.

"What are your plans for the day, Sam?" Reilly asked as they walked out of the house after breakfast.

"I don't really have any," Sam replied with a shake of his head.

"Are you looking for work?"

"I might be." He wasn't, really, but he might have to use that as an excuse to hang around Flat Rock while he continued to search for the bushwhackers.

"Unfortunately, I can't offer you a job. Mr. Wilmott, who lives in Prescott, owns the store but entrusts the running of it completely to me. Right now the profits don't justify hiring another employee."

"That's all right, Noah," Sam said. "I don't think I was cut out to work in a store, anyway."

"That's true. It takes a certain, ah, type such as me, doesn't it?"

Thinking that he had offended the man, Sam started to apologize, but Reilly smiled and waved it away.

"No, no, I'm perfectly aware that I'm not the adventurous, swashbuckling sort," he said. "I think most of the time people are foolish to try to be something they aren't, so I'm perfectly content to clerk in a store. It's what I'm cut out for."

"Well, that's one way to look at it," Sam said. He shook his head. "I don't see how you stay as skinny as you do, eating at Mrs. McCormick's."

Reilly grinned.

"The dear lady *does* set a good table, doesn't she?" He patted his stomach. "I guess I'm lucky that I burn it all off."

Now that the sun was up, Flat Rock was coming to life.

Or at least as much life as this sleepy little settlement usually exhibited. A few pedestrians moved along the boardwalks, a couple of men on horseback made their way slowly along the street, and a wagon was parked in front of the general store.

The doors of the livery stable were open, and that gave Sam an idea. He said, "I'll see you later, Noah," and walked over to Pedro Garralaga's place.

The stableman was inside, tending to the animals in his charge. At this hour the heat of the day hadn't started to build up yet, so inside the barn it was cool and shadowy.

Garralaga said, "Buenos dias, Señor Two Wolves. You are out and about early this morning."

"I thought I'd go for a ride before the day gets too hot," Sam said.

"A ride? Where?" Garralaga made a gesture that took in their surroundings. "What's there to see around here?"

"You never know. A man never stumbles over anything interesting if he doesn't look around."

Garralaga grunted.

"There's not much anywhere in the Four Corners that's interesting. But suit yourself. You want me to saddle your horse?"

"No, I'll take care of it."

Sam's horse tossed its head and nuzzled his shoulder. He put his saddle on the animal, noting what a good job Garralaga had done on the repairs, and led the horse out into the aisle in the center of the barn.

As he did, he passed the stalls where the mounts belonging to Stovepipe Stewart and Wilbur Coleman were kept. He'd halfway expected to run into the mysterious cowboys by now, since they seemed to turn up wherever he was, but so far he hadn't seen any sign of them.

Obviously they were still in town, though, since their horses were here.

Sam said so long to Garralaga and rode out of Flat Rock, heading south. He had only the vaguest idea of where the Devil's Pitchfork Ranch was, but he knew it lay south of the settlement.

If he had told anyone he was heading for John Henry Boyd's spread, they probably would have advised him that he was loco. Boyd, Lowry, and the rest of the Devil's Pitchfork bunch had shady reputations to begin with, and now they were all stirred up because they believed the Navajo had killed two of their men and rustled fifty head of cattle.

Sam didn't believe that, but he knew he was running a risk by riding on Boyd's range. If any of Boyd's men caught a glimpse of his coppery skin, they would probably shoot first and then figure out who he was.

This trip served two purposes, though. Sam didn't want Caballo Rojo's people being blamed for something they didn't do. If the army was drawn into this, it would only make the trouble worse. The best way to avoid that was to find out what had really happened to the rustled cattle.

Also, Sam was still trying to draw out the men who had attacked him and Matt. He couldn't give them a much more tempting target than this.

Of course, that meant he was risking his life, but

he thought it was worth the gamble. He hoped so, anyway.

If nothing else, the landscape was spectacular in its stark beauty. Dark, rugged mesas thrust up imposingly from the flat land around them, as did towering spires of red sandstone. Ranges of rocky hills bordered vast sweeps of empty ground. Cliffs jutted up and ran for miles. Colors faded from brown to tan to red to black. It was almost like being in an alien world devoid of life, Sam thought.

But here and there, pockets of life did exist. Canyons cut into the hills and cliffs, and in their shaded reaches, springs bubbled up, allowing hardy grass and stunted trees to grow. Higher up in the mountains, the slopes were dark with pine and juniper. This was a hard land, but it would support people who knew how to use it.

The Navajo possessed that knowledge. It was part of their heritage, going back centuries.

Most white men didn't know how to use the land the way it was, Sam reflected. What they knew was how to *change* it. They would find a way to bring water into dry country and make it bloom. They would lay down steel rails to span vast distances. They would gouge holes in the earth and rip minerals from its heart.

In truth, Sam didn't know which way was better. But there had to be a land somewhere that would finally defeat the ingenuity of the white men.

If such a place existed, it just might be the Four Corners. Maybe someday they would realize that and leave it to the Navajo, the Pueblo, the Hopi . . . the people who were born to this forbidding landscape.

Despite those musings, Sam was still alert. His gaze roamed constantly over the country around him. Because of that, he was able to spot a thin line of smoke rising into the air a couple of miles ahead of him.

That was probably smoke from a chimney, he thought, and a chimney meant the headquarters of the Devil's Pitchfork Ranch. So he was on Boyd's range now.

Or rather, the range that Boyd claimed the use of. All this land was supposed to belong to the Navajo. Obviously that didn't matter to some people.

If the trouble between the white settlers and the Indians escalated to the point that the army was sent in, that would give the politicians back in Washington the excuse they needed to invalidate the treaty establishing the reservation.

Sam had no doubt that they would do it, and that thought made him frown. In other places, evil men had attempted schemes such as that. Although he and Matt had never encountered any themselves, Sam had heard about them. In Denver, he had overheard men discussing just such a plot that had been broken up by the famous gunfighter Smoke Jensen and other members of his family.

Sam didn't know if that was what was going on here, but it was possible.

And he found himself wondering if that bushwhack attempt on him and Matt could be connected to it in some way. That seemed far-fetched, but reality was often stranger than any fiction could ever hope to be.

He came to a pair of shallow hogback ridges about a mile apart. They ran roughly parallel for at least two miles, and the smoke rose at the far end of the valley they formed.

Also at the far end of the valley, looming over it, was an odd, three-pronged rock spire. As Sam looked at it, he realized that it resembled, at least roughly, a pitchfork.

That was where the ranch had gotten its name, he thought.

There wasn't much grass in the valley, but there was some and cattle grazed there.

Sam reined in and sat there looking toward the far end of the valley. That was where Boyd's ranch house was located, he thought. And it was from this valley that the cattle had been stolen.

He lifted his horse's reins, ready to start riding back and forth until he found the tracks that fifty head of stock must have left.

Sam had just heeled his mount into a turn when he heard a bullet whip past his ear, followed instantly by the sharp crack of a shot.

Chapter 23

Sam didn't know where the shot came from, but he could tell from the sound of the report that it had been fired from a rifle, probably a Winchester.

He also knew that the rifleman would have a harder time hitting him if he was moving, so he continued pulling his horse into a turn and jammed his heels into the animal's flanks to make it leap ahead in a gallop.

Sam leaned forward over the horse's neck to make himself a smaller target. As he did so, he saw a puff of gunsmoke spurt out from a spot about halfway up the ridge to his right.

That was the direction he was headed.

He was charging right toward the hidden bushwhacker.

Bushwhackers, he corrected himself as he spotted another jet of powder smoke from a different place on the ridge. There were at least two of them—again.

These would-be killers seemed to like working in pairs.

Sam gritted his teeth. This was what he had wanted, to draw the bushwhackers into attacking him again.

This time he intended to take one of them prisoner so he could get some answers. Chances were, the man wouldn't want to talk, but threatening him with some Cheyenne torture would probably loosen his tongue . . . whether Sam intended to follow through on those threats or not.

He was getting ahead of himself, Sam thought as he sent his horse plunging back and forth at zigzag angles to keep the riflemen from drawing a bead on him.

First he had to actually capture one of them.

And to do that he had to keep from being killed.

His horse suddenly gave a wild leap underneath him. Sam knew the animal must have been hit. As he felt himself come out of the saddle, he kicked his feet free of the stirrups. That was all he had time to do.

Sam sailed free through the air for a breathless second before the ground came up and slammed into him. He landed on his shoulder and rolled.

Pain shot through him, but he ignored it as his momentum made him roll over a couple of times. He let it carry him up onto one knee and looked around for some cover.

He knew he was going to need it.

Sure enough, more slugs plowed into the ground around him, spraying him with grit and gravel. Sam got his other foot underneath him and shoved himself upright.

Several good-sized rocks lay a few yards to his right. He flung himself toward them as another slug burned past his ear. A desperate dive landed him among the rocks. He hugged the dirt as a couple of bullets whined off the big chunks of stone.

A slug hit the ground right beside one of his outstretched feet, close enough that the impact made him wince. He drew his legs up as much as he could.

From up on that ridge, the bushwhackers could see down into this cluster of rocks. The area that was protected from their bullets was a tiny one. Sam tried to fit himself into it, but as big and rangy as he was, that wasn't easy.

He made himself as small as possible and then tried to catch his breath. His left shoulder ached from falling on it, but he moved his arm around enough to know that nothing was broken, only bruised and battered.

He moved his right hand to his hip. The Colt was still in its holster. Sam drew the weapon, and even though he knew the range to the ridge was too great for a handgun, he felt better holding the revolver.

If he stayed where he was, maybe sooner or later the bushwhackers would get tired of the standoff and come after him.

That was when he would have his chance to use the Colt.

On the other hand, if they were smart they might just try to wait him out. The sun was climbing in the sky, and he didn't have any shade here. It wouldn't be too many hours before his position would become unbearably hot.

Then his choice would be to leave his cover and probably get shot down, or stay there and bake.

The rifle fire stopped. Sam figured the two bushwhackers were up there on the ridge talking about the situation and trying to figure out what to do next.

He wondered if the shots would draw any attention from the Devil's Pitchfork. The sound of them might have reached the ranch headquarters.

But if the bushwhackers were two of John Henry Boyd's men, which Sam supposed was possible, then it wouldn't really matter.

Sam lifted his head just enough to glance at the ridge. As he did, a bullet slammed into the rock about a foot away. A stone splinter stung his cheek. More shots blasted and sent slugs ricocheting off the rock as he ducked down again.

Well, they were still up there watching and still wanted him dead, he reflected. He had established that beyond a shadow of a doubt.

Staying as low as possible, Sam turned his head to look for his horse. He didn't know how badly the animal had been wounded.

To his relief, he saw the horse grazing on the hardy bunchgrass about a hundred yards away. A bloody streak on its hip showed where a bullet had creased it for the second time, causing the violent reaction that had cost Sam his place in the saddle.

Sam's gaze lingered on the butt of the Winchester that rode in a sheath strapped under the left stirrup.

He wished he had the rifle. Pinned down like he was, the Winchester wouldn't do him much good, but with it the odds might not have seemed quite so overwhelming.

He blinked as beads of sweat popped out on his forehead and trickled down into his eyes. The heat was getting worse.

Already his mouth felt like cotton.

The shooting had stopped again. The bushwhackers were going to wait and let the sun do their work for them, Sam thought. How long could he stand it before he was forced into the open?

With no warning, more shots abruptly blasted out. Instinctively, Sam lowered his head even more, but after a second he realized that he didn't hear any bullets ricocheting off the rocks around him.

Not only that, but the sound of the shots was different as well. They were coming from somewhere else on the ridge.

And they weren't directed at him.

The duller boom of six-guns being fired came to his ears. It sounded like quite a battle was going on up there.

Sam risked a look and caught a glimpse of two figures on horseback vanishing over the top of the ridge. They were moving fast, and the shots that still rang out hurried them on their way.

Were those the bushwhackers, Sam wondered, or had whoever was trying to come to his aid been forced to flee?

Either way, he knew this might be the only chance

he had to get out of this trap. He leaped to his feet and broke into a long-legged sprint toward his horse.

No bullets came searching for him. When he reached the horse, he yanked the Winchester from the saddleboot, worked the lever to throw a round into the chamber, and whipped around toward the ridge, ready to return fire if any came his way.

Silence had fallen over the valley again. Sam turned his head to look all around him, searching for any other sign of a threat. He didn't see any, but he didn't relax his vigilance.

Movement on the ridge caught his eye. He picked out two riders working their way down the slope. They were too far away for him to make out any details, but something about them was familiar.

When they reached the floor of the valley and rode toward him, he realized what it was. He recognized the two horses: a buckskin and a paint.

That was Stovepipe Stewart and Wilbur Coleman riding toward him.

Sam's forehead creased in a frown as he thought about the two cowboys. From the looks of it, they had rescued him from the bushwhackers.

But there had been two bushwhackers, too, Sam reminded himself. It was possible Stovepipe and Wilbur could have been the men he had seen retreating over the ridge. They could have pretended to flee, circled around, and be riding toward him now intending to claim that they had saved his bacon.

But why would they do that? Maybe to gain his trust, Sam thought.

However, there was no doubt in his mind that the hidden riflemen wanted him dead. Those shots had come too close to be any sort of warning or ruse.

Which meant that if Stovepipe and Wilbur had been the ones shooting at him, they might be riding up to Sam now in apparent innocence so they could blast the life out of him as soon as they got close enough.

Those thoughts went through his head in a flash. He looked at the approaching cowboys again.

Their rifles were booted, and their Colts were holstered. They were in rifle range now, so Sam brought the Winchester to his shoulder, leveled it at them, and called out, "Hold it right there, you two!"

Stovepipe and Wilbur reined in. Stovepipe leaned forward in the saddle with a puzzled frown on his craggy face.

"Why in Hades are you pointin' that rifle at us, Sam?" he asked. "It appears to me we just done you a mighty big favor, the sort that usually prompts a fella to say gracias instead of threatenin' to ventilate somebody."

"I'm just trying to make sure I have everything sorted out the right way," Sam said. "What are you doing out here? Following me?"

Stovepipe surprised him by answering, "Yep. That's exactly what we were doin'."

Sam's frown deepened as he asked, "Why would you do that?"

Stovepipe rested both hands on his saddle horn and grinned. He said, "Because Wilbur and me, we got a hunch that you might be lookin' for the same fellas we are."

Sam was curious enough now that he lowered the rifle slightly.

"Come on over here so we can talk easier," he said. "But don't try anything funny, because I'll be watching you."

"We wouldn't dream of it," Wilbur said.

They hitched their horses into motion again and rode slowly toward Sam. He kept the rifle pointed in their general direction and his finger was ready on the trigger.

When they were close enough, he called, "All right, stop there. Now dismount one at a time."

Stovepipe looked at Wilbur, who shrugged.

"All right, I'll go first," Stovepipe said. "Don't get trigger-happy now, Sam."

The lanky cowboy swung down from the saddle. Holding on to his horse's reins with one hand, he raised the other hand to shoulder height.

"See? Not tryin' anything funny."

"Now you, Wilbur," Sam said.

Wilbur dismounted and didn't make any threatening moves, either.

Once they were both on the ground, Sam lowered the rifle to his waist. He could still fire from the hip with blinding speed if he needed to.

"What's this about us looking for the same men?" he asked.

"Well, in order to tell you about it, I'm gonna have

to ask you to believe a couple of things we can't prove right now," Stovepipe drawled. "The first bein' that we ain't who we seem to be."

"You mean you're not a couple of drifting grub-line riders?" Sam asked. "Yeah, I had started to figure that out."

"Truth of it is," Stovepipe went on, "we're lawmen . . . sort of."

That took Sam by surprise, but he tried not to show it.

"How can you sort of be lawmen?"

"We ain't federal marshals or Rangers or even local badge-toters. We're private operators, I reckon you could say. Range detectives. We work most of the time for the Cattlemen's Protective Association."

Sam knew about the CPA. It was a loose-knit organization with members stretching from Montana to the Rio Grande. In fact, he and Matt both belonged to it, that is, assuming their ranch managers had remembered to send in their dues. The blood brothers didn't keep track of such things.

"If you work for the CPA, you ought to have papers showing that," Sam said.

Stovepipe shook his head.

"Well, see, that's why I said we couldn't prove it right now. We ain't exactly workin' for the CPA on this case. They've loaned us out, I reckon you could say?"

"Loaned you out?" Sam repeated. "To who? And what case are you talking about?"

"We're workin' for the War Department in Washington," Stovepipe said. "Undercover-like, which is why we got no bona fides on us sayin' who we are."

Beside him, Wilbur spoke up.

"Are you sure we ought to be tellin' him all this, Stovepipe? For all we know, he could be part of the gang."

"Then who was that shootin' at him a while ago?" Stovepipe wanted to know.

Sam wasn't sure whether to believe anything they had told him, but he said, "For what it's worth, that wasn't the first time somebody tried to bushwhack me. It's the third attempt in the past week, and I'm convinced they were all by the same bunch."

Stovepipe let out a low whistle.

"Sounds like you've made yourself some powerful enemies, Sam."

"Yeah, and I still don't have any idea why."

"Oh, shoot, we can tell you that." Stovepipe looked over at Wilbur again.

The smaller man shrugged and nodded, telling him to go ahead.

"It's about two things, Sam," Stovepipe said. "Money . . . and guns."

Chapter 24

Sam looked at the two of them intently for a moment, then said, "You're going to have to explain that."

Stovepipe nodded.

"Figured I'd have to. You see, about a month ago a shipment of rifles—brand-new Trapdoor Springfields—were on their way to the garrison at Fort Defiance when the wagon they were in was waylaid." Stovepipe's face grew grim. "The troopers ridin' escort with the guns were wiped out."

"Do the authorities believe that the Navajo did that?" Sam asked.

"Nope," Stovepipe replied with a shake of his head. "One of the troopers was shot to pieces but lived long enough to talk to some freighters who came across the massacre. Before he died he said it was white men who jumped 'em, and the shod hoofprints around the place indicated that, too."

"But just because it wasn't Indians who stole the rifles," Wilbur put in, "that don't mean those guns won't wind up in Navajo hands before it's all said and done."

"The Navajo are peaceful people," Sam protested. "They've been mistreated, but despite that all they want is to be left alone."

"I ain't gonna argue with you about how they been treated," Stovepipe said. "But you're a mite too young to remember a Navajo headman name of Manuelito. He wasn't a very peaceful fella. From what I've heard, even the other Navajo were a mite nervous around him. He gave Kit Carson a pretty good fight over in New Mexico Territory a while back."

"I've heard of Manuelito," Sam said. "That was nearly twenty years ago."

Stovepipe nodded.

"Yeah, but there are still some firebrands among the Navajo who think the ol' boy had it right. They think tryin' to get along with the white men ain't worked out too well for their people, and it's 'way past time to start killin' again."

Sam thought about Juan Pablo and the fierce resentment he felt toward the whites. It wouldn't take much to get him to be in favor of a new Navajo war, and there were bound to be others like him among the clans.

"So you think whoever stole those rifles intends to sell them to the Navajo," he said. "That doesn't make any sense. What would they use to pay for them? Sheep? Blankets?"

"Didn't say nothin' about anybody payin' for those

Springfields. But they could still wind up in Navajo hands, like Wilbur said."

"Only if the thieves *want* to start a war."

Stovepipe shrugged.

Those same thoughts had gone through Sam's mind earlier. Judging by what these two self-proclaimed range detectives were telling him, he had been on the right track.

But he wanted to see if their thinking matched up with his, so he said, "Where does the money come in?"

"The money's to be made when somebody comes in and grabs all this reservation land once the government rounds up the Navajo again and marches 'em back to Bosque Redondo or some other hellhole. This is the largest reservation in the whole blamed country. It ain't just in Arizona. It stretches over into New Mexico and up into Colorado and Utah as well. Millions and millions of acres. If they throw the whole thing open for settlement, instead of just the isolated patches here and there, it'd be worth a fortune." Stovepipe shrugged. "Leastways, it could be, if there was a way to get water in here from the Colorado to the west and the Rio Grande to the east. Wouldn't be easy, but with a big enough payoff waitin' for 'em, you can bet folks'd figure out a way to do it."

It was a long speech, but everything Stovepipe said lined up with the theory that had formed in Sam's mind.

He thought about the marks he and Juan Pablo had found on the ground at the base of that bluff where the first bushwhack attempt had been made.

"The stolen rifles were in one wagon?" he asked.

"That's right. Twelve crates with forty guns in each one. Nearly five hundred Springfields."

"A crate with forty rifles in it would be pretty heavy, wouldn't it?"

"I reckon so," Stovepipe said. His deep-set eyes narrowed. "I'm startin' to get the feelin' you know more than you're tellin' us, Sam. We've laid our cards on the table. Now it's your turn."

Sam drew in a deep breath and let it out. He had to make the decision whether to trust these two men. His instincts told him that they had been truthful with him, and the facts they had provided went a long way toward explaining everything that had happened over the past week or so.

"All right," he said as he made up his mind. "I think a friend of mine and I nearly stumbled right into those rifles being delivered to whoever they're intended for."

"You're talkin' about Matt Bodine?" Stovepipe asked.

Sam's eyebrows rose in surprise.

"How do you know about Matt?"

Wilbur said, "We've been workin' out here on the frontier for quite a while, mister. You reckon we never heard of Matt Bodine and Sam Two Wolves?"

"You were mixed up in that Joshua Shade business a while back," Stovepipe added. "Reckon that varmint might not have ended up at the end of a hangrope where he belonged if not for you two fellas."

"Where is Bodine?" Wilbur asked. "He's not dead, is he?"

"Not that I know of," Sam said. "But he was wounded, and I had to leave him with somebody while I went looking for the men who bushwhacked us. I think that's tied in with those rifles you told me about."

"So where's Bodine now?"

"With some Navajo about a day's ride northwest of here."

Stovepipe and Wilbur looked at each other again.

"You better tell us the rest of it," Stovepipe said.

For the next five minutes, Sam did so, explaining how someone had opened fire on him and Matt, wounding Matt and leading to them being discovered by Caballo Rojo, Juan Pablo, and the rest of the Navajo.

"I think the bushwhackers must have tried to kill us because we came along just as they were about to deliver those rifles to someone," he said. He told Stovepipe and Wilbur about the marks he had found on the ground at the base of the bluff. "Those were definitely wagon tracks I saw, and they looked like it was heavily loaded. And a crate full of Springfields would have left an impression on the ground like that, too."

Sam grunted and shook his head.

"And I thought at first that it was a coffin."

"Not a coffin," Stovepipe said, "but in the wrong hands, what was in it sure might fill a bunch of 'em."

"I backtracked the bunch to Flat Rock," Sam

went on. "I think they must've gotten spooked and postponed the deal. They probably have the rifles hidden somewhere close to the settlement. The boss, whoever he is, put guards on the trail outside town to see if anybody followed them. When I did, they tried to kill me again."

"And they trailed you out here today and tried again, more'n likely," Stovepipe said.

"And why did *you* follow me?"

"Just keepin' an eye on you," Stovepipe said. "To tell you the truth, we sorta thought you might attract trouble like a magnet, given your reputation for gettin' mixed up in things."

"And we weren't completely convinced you weren't mixed up somehow with the gang we're lookin' for," Wilbur added.

Stovepipe winced.

"Now, you didn't have to go and tell him that."

"Just like you didn't have to tell Lady Augusta that I like her," Wilbur shot back.

Sam said, "So when somebody tried to kill me, that convinced you that I wasn't one of the gang?"

"Didn't figure they'd be shootin' at you if you was one of 'em," Stovepipe said.

Wilbur nodded at his companion.

"That's what he said. If I had as many thoughts crammed into my head as Stovepipe does, I swear I'd go plumb crazy. That's why I mostly let him do the figurin'."

"And what I'm studyin' on now," Stovepipe said, "is what brought you out here today, Sam. The hombres out at the Devil's Pitchfork don't cotton much to strangers."

"Especially ones with Indian blood," Sam said. "I know. But I got curious about those cattle that were stolen from out here. Boyd and Lowry blamed the rustling on the Navajo, but that just doesn't seem right to me. Caballo Rojo and his people are the closest ones to the settlement, and I spent enough time with them to know they wouldn't do such a thing."

"Most of 'em probably wouldn't," Stovepipe agreed. "But all it takes is a handful who take after Manuelito."

Sam shrugged.

"Maybe. But the whole idea is to increase the tension between the white settlers and the Navajo until a shooting war is inevitable. The men behind it are even going to give the Navajo those rifles to make it unavoidable. Right?"

"That's the way it looks to me," Stovepipe replied with a nod.

"So rustling cattle and making it look like the Navajo are responsible would just up the stakes."

"He's right, Stovepipe," Wilbur said. "I reckon he's about as good a detective as you are."

"I never claimed to be no genius. What you say makes sense, Sam. The same bunch is playin' the settlers and the Indians against each other to set up a land grab." Stovepipe rubbed his beard-stubbled chin. "Question is, what are we gonna do about it?"

"The first step is to find out who they are," Sam

said. "Maybe if we track those stolen cows that will tell us something."

"It sure might." Stovepipe inclined his head toward his horse. "All right if we mount up again? We've all decided to trust each other?"

Sam slid his Winchester back in the saddleboot.

"I think so. And we'll come closer getting to the bottom of this if we work together."

Stovepipe nodded and said, "Sounds good to me."

All three of them swung up into their saddles. As they started looking for the tracks left by the stolen herd, Wilbur said, "You know, there's somethin' that's botherin' me. You said you left your partner Bodine with the Navajo, Sam?"

"That's right."

"There's got to be at least a few members of that clan who are workin' with the gang that stole the rifles."

That same worry had started gnawing at the back of Sam's thoughts.

"You're probably right," he said. "And if that's true, they might want to get rid of Matt just to make sure he doesn't stumble over what's really going on."

Stovepipe said, "Yeah, and that means we'd better find the varmints we're lookin' for and bust up their plans as quick as we can . . . because the longer your pard spends with those Injuns, the more danger he's in."

That thought made Sam's jaw clench tightly. Matt was stuck there in the canyon, trying to recover from his wounds, probably with no idea that lurking among the Navajo was at least one man who wanted him dead.

"Speakin' of danger . . ." Wilbur said.

The other two men looked at him and saw him pointing toward the southern end of the valley.

"Riders comin' fast," Wilbur went on. "I'll bet it's John Henry Boyd and his bunch of gun-throwers, and they ain't gonna be happy to find us here."

Chapter 25

All three men reined in and turned their horses to face toward the oncoming riders. Wilbur moved his hand toward the butt of the gun on his hip, which drew a sharp comment from Stovepipe.

"Don't do it," the lanky cowboy warned. "There's too dang many of 'em."

Sam was already keeping his hands in plain sight, well away from his weapons, so Stovepipe didn't have to say anything to him.

As the crew from the Devil's Pitchfork approached, they spread out so that they formed a half-circle around Sam, Stovepipe, and Wilbur. That was menacing enough, and the expressions on the hard-bitten faces of the men were even more so.

To a man, they looked like they wanted to whip out their six-guns and start blazing away at these interlopers on Devil's Pitchfork range.

Sam recognized the ugly, jut-jawed face of Pete Lowry. Lowry rode near the center of the group, and beside him was a man who carried himself in the saddle with such an air of command that he had to be John Henry Boyd.

The two of them kept coming after their companions halted, not stopping until they were within twenty feet of Sam and the two range detectives. Then they reined to a stop as well.

"Look at that, boss," Lowry said, confirming Sam's hunch that the other man was John Henry Boyd. "We don't have go lookin' for those damned rustlers after all. They've come to us."

"You've got that wrong, mister," Stovepipe said. "We ain't rustlers."

"Then who are you?" Boyd demanded. He was an old man, with white hair under his black Stetson and a face like worn, cracked saddle leather. "And what in blazes are you doing on my land?"

Sam felt a flush of anger. This wasn't Boyd's land, and in the technical sense it wasn't even open range, the sort of graze that hundreds of cattlemen across the frontier claimed.

No, this was Navajo land, and the only reason Boyd was able to stake such a claim on it was that the authorities looked the other way . . . and probably had been paid off to do so.

However, Sam wasn't here today to right that particular wrong. Instead he said, "We're looking for the rustlers, too, Mr. Boyd. We want to find out what happened to your cattle and where they were taken."

"Don't believe him, boss," Lowry snapped. "These are the fellas we had that run-in with in town yesterday. The redskin claims to be a Cheyenne 'breed, but I think he's a Navajo spy."

Boyd turned to his segundo and said, "You blasted fool. You can tell by looking at him that he's not Navajo. Not all Indians look alike, you know."

That surprised Sam. Before he could start feeling too kindly toward Boyd, though, the rancher went on, "But that doesn't mean he's not a damned rustler anyway. A couple of white men and a Cheyenne 'breed can be owlhoots just like anybody else."

"I never stole a cow in my life," Wilbur said angrily, "and neither did Stovepipe."

"And if we *were* the rustlers, what would we be doin' back out here?" Stovepipe added. "Comin' back to the scene of the crime would be kind of a durned fool thing to do, wouldn't it?"

"Not if you were lookin' for more stock to steal," Lowry said.

"In broad daylight?" Sam asked.

Boyd leaned forward in his saddle.

"Then what are you doing here? I asked you before, and I don't intend to ask you again."

"And I reckon we told you," Stovepipe said. "We're lookin' for them rustled beeves."

"What business is it of yours?"

Sam glanced at Stovepipe and wondered what the man would say. He thought it would be a mistake to reveal their real identities to Boyd and the rest of the Devil's Pitchfork crew. For all he and his two companions knew, Boyd was behind the scheme to smuggle guns to the Navajo and start a new Indian war here in the Four Corners.

Boyd already had a foothold here with his ranch. He would be in a good position to try to take over the rest of the region. Certainly he and his men could have lied about the rustling just to stir up the settlers in Flat Rock that much more.

He shouldn't have worried about Stovepipe, Sam realized a second later. A lazy grin spread over the range detective's face as he said, "Shoot, we figured there might be a reward, and we're gettin' a little short on funds. Thought you might be more inclined to give us some ridin' jobs, at the very least, if we found them cows for you."

Boyd glared at them.

"That's what you thought, is it? What I'm inclined to do is run the three of you off my land. Either that, or string you up."

"That's what I'd do, boss," Lowry said as he gave Sam a baleful look.

"I don't want to waste the time on either of those things, though," Boyd went on. "In fact, we've lolly-gagged around here enough."

Without warning, he shucked his Colt from its holster and pointed it at Sam, Stovepipe, and Wilbur.

"Drop your guns," he ordered. "You're coming with us."

Lowry looked as surprised as anybody.

"John Henry, what're you doin'? You can't trust these varmints!"

"I never said I trusted 'em. Why do you think I told

them to drop their guns?" Boyd's voice hardened. "I won't tell you *that* again, either."

"Reckon we'd better do what the man says," Stovepipe drawled. He gave Sam and Wilbur a look that meant *Play along*. Sam understood that well enough. He didn't see what else they could do right now.

He had seen the muscles in Boyd's arm and shoulder tense before the rancher went for his gun. Sam was confident he could have beaten Boyd to the draw if he had tried to. He might have been able to get the drop on the rancher and use him as a hostage to get past the other fifteen men in the Devil's Pitchfork crew.

But that wouldn't have gotten him any closer to the answers he was looking for, Sam thought as he carefully used his left hand to slide his Colt from its holster. He pitched the revolver to the ground, where it was joined by those belonging to Stovepipe and Wilbur as well.

"Now the rifles," Boyd commanded. "And I want that knife of yours, too, redskin."

Again Sam swallowed the anger he felt. He leaned toward the opinion that Boyd and his men weren't the ones who had bushwhacked him and Matt. Since that bunch obviously wanted him dead, they would have gone ahead and opened fire as soon as they rode up. Sam, Stovepipe, and Wilbur would have put up a fight, but they couldn't have stopped the bunch from the Devil's Pitchfork from wiping them out.

That didn't mean Boyd wasn't an arrogant, unpleasant son of a bitch anyway.

But maybe cooperating with the rancher would make it easier for Sam and his companions to find out what they wanted to know.

For that reason, Sam drew his bowie knife and tossed it to the ground as well.

"Now back off some," Boyd ordered. When Sam, Stovepipe, and Wilbur had done that, Boyd jerked his head at a couple of his men, who dismounted and hurried forward to collect all the discarded hardware.

"Come on," Boyd said. "You want to find out what happened to those rustled cows, you said. Well, so do I. We'll follow the trail together."

Lowry said, "I still think this is a bad idea, boss. They're part of that bunch, I tell you."

"Well, if they are," Boyd said, "we've got us some hostages, don't we?"

He led the pack toward the northwestern corner of the valley. Following the commanding gestures Pete Lowry made with his gun, Sam, Stovepipe, and Wilbur fell in just behind Boyd. The other hard-bitten gunmen of the Devil's Pitchfork crew kept them mostly surrounded as they followed the rancher.

"This is what we want," Stovepipe said to Sam from the corner of his mouth. "We get to find out where those stolen cows went, and Boyd sees that we ain't rustlers."

Sam nodded and said, "That's what I thought."

Lowry snapped, "Shut up, you two. I don't want you back here plottin' behind the boss's back."

"You know, you're a mighty touchy sort, mister," Wilbur said. "What happened, your ma take your favorite play-pretty away from you when you were little?"

"Why, you . . ." Lowry growled as he moved his horse closer to Wilbur's paint. He lifted the revolver he still held. "I oughta bust your skull open!"

"Pete!" Boyd's sharp tone rang out. "That's enough." The white-haired rancher looked back over his shoulder. "But I warn you, mister, don't try my patience any more than it already is. If you do, I'm liable to turn Pete loose on you."

"Sure, Wilbur here understands," Stovepipe said quickly. "Don't you, Wilbur?"

"I reckon," Wilbur said with obvious reluctance.

Sam hoped that Wilbur would behave himself and not get them killed by potential allies.

They already had more than enough enemies who would be happy to take care of that.

Chapter 26

Zack Jardine was on his way back to the Buckingham Palace Saloon when he saw Angus Braverman and Doyle Hilliard gallop into town.

For the past half-hour, Jardine had been talking to his partner in this enterprise and the discussion hadn't gone very well, so he was in a bad mood to start with.

His anger flared up even more at the sight of Braverman and Hilliard. He had told the two men to keep an eye on that blasted half-breed and to finish him off if they got the chance.

Now, from the way they were hurrying, Jardine figured that they had fouled up again some way.

He lifted a hand to catch their attention as they started to ride past in the street. Both men reined in sharply, sawing the bits in cruel fashion.

"What the hell's going on now?" Jardine demanded.

"It's that redskin," Braverman replied, not surprisingly. "He's gone out to the Devil's Pitchfork."

Jardine wasn't expecting to hear that. As his eyes

widened, he said, "Why in blazes would he do that, after the run-in he had with Lowry and that bunch the other day?"

Hilliard said, "It looked to us like he was tryin' to find the trail of those cows that got run off a couple nights ago."

At that news, Jardine felt like spewing a string of vile curses. Realizing that wouldn't do any good, he said, "I hope you took care of him."

Braverman grimaced and looked uncomfortable as he shifted in the saddle.

"We tried, Zack, we really did."

"But?" Jardine said ominously.

"But those two drifters who sided him in that saloon brawl showed up and came mighty close to partin' our hair with lead. We had to get out of there while we still could."

Jardine glanced around to make sure no one else was within earshot, then said, "You stupid sons of bitches. Now not only Two Wolves is out there poking around where he doesn't belong, but so are those two cowboys. I've got a bad feeling about them."

"It gets worse, boss," Hilliard added with a shake of his head. "We were watchin' from a distance, and we saw Boyd and his crew come up and grab the red-skin and the other two."

"They didn't kill Two Wolves and his friends?"

That was probably too much good luck to hope for, Jardine thought.

Hilliard confirmed that hunch by saying, "No, they disarmed the three of 'em but didn't hurt them as far as we could tell. Then the whole bunch rode off to the northwest, the same direction those boys took the cows."

Jardine took a deep breath and tried to reassure himself that everything would be all right.

"We figured all along that Boyd and his men would try to trail the herd," he said. "They won't be able to find it."

"That's what that Injun claimed," Braverman said. "But we don't know that for sure."

"Who knows those godforsaken canyons better than a Navajo?" Jardine asked.

"But Boyd's got Two Wolves with him now. He's Cheyenne, but maybe he can track as well as a Navajo can."

Jardine took off his hat and ran his fingers through his thick black hair. The whole deal had seemed so simple at first . . .

All they had to do was steal those rifles before the guns made it to Fort Defiance, deliver them to the hotheads among the Navajo who wanted war with the whites, stir up the settlers by rustling a few cattle and killing a couple of punchers, and then sit back and let nature take its course.

When the fighting was all over, the redskins would be herded out of the Four Corners, and Jardine would be ready to swoop in and take over.

He scowled at Braverman and Hilliard as he recalled that if they hadn't been so trigger-happy a week earlier, maybe none of the problems that currently plagued him would have cropped up. That incident had fouled up the delivery of the rifles, and the plan hadn't recovered yet from having that kink thrown into it.

Now this unlikely alliance between Two Wolves, those two mysterious cowboys, and the crew from the Devil's Pitchfork threatened to make things even worse.

Jardine sighed and settled his hat back on his head.

"There's only one thing we can do about it now," he said. "Angus, get a fresh horse and ride for the place where the cattle are being held as fast as you can. Warn the boys watching them that trouble may be on the way."

"You really think I can get there before Boyd and the others do, boss?"

"I don't know, but you can damned well try," Jardine snapped. "There's a good chance, because you know where you're going and they don't. Now get a move on."

"You want me to go with Angus, Zack?" Hilliard asked.

Jardine shook his head.

"He's a lot lighter than you. On a fresh horse he can move pretty fast." He scowled at Braverman. "Didn't you hear me? Go!"

Braverman nodded and pulled his horse around.

"You bet!"

He headed for the livery stable to change mounts.

"I'm sorry things didn't work out, boss," Hilliard said. "It's like that damned Injun's got some sort of redskin spirits lookin' out for him! Every time we think we're about to ventilate him, he gets out of it somehow."

"Two Wolves' luck can't last forever," Jardine said as hate filled his heart. "And when it runs out, I hope I'm looking at him over the barrel of a gun."

Fifty cows and the half-dozen men pushing them along couldn't help but leave a lot of tracks.

Unfortunately, even though there hadn't been any rain in this arid country in a long time, the wind blew and sometimes wiped out marks left in the dust.

Not only that, but there were stretches of rocky ground as well where the hooves of cattle and unshod horses didn't leave any impressions.

Because of those things, following the rustlers' trail was more difficult than one might think it would be. However, Sam had anticipated that, so he wasn't surprised when the tracks disappeared about five miles northwest of the ranch and the riders from the Devil's Pitchfork had to search for them again.

As prisoners, Sam, Stovepipe, and Wilbur rode along with Boyd and the other men. They didn't have any choice.

After an interval of futile searching, Sam suggested, "Why don't you let me have a look, Mr. Boyd?"

The three prisoners were sitting their horses with Boyd, Lowry, and another man to guard them while the rest of the Devil's Pitchfork hands rode back and forth across the range, looking for the trail.

"Don't listen to him, boss," Lowry said in response

to Sam's suggestion. "It's bound to be a trick of some sort."

John Henry Boyd frowned.

"What if he was to find the tracks of those rustlers?"

"Well, of course he might find 'em," Lowry blustered. "I still say he's probably one of 'em. He already knows where they went."

Boyd looked at Sam, who shook his head.

"I don't have any idea," he said. "But I'm pretty good at finding a trail, if I do say so myself."

"So's Stovepipe," Wilbur put in. "He's got eyes like a hawk."

Stovepipe grinned.

"Better than a nose like a buzzard, I reckon."

Boyd frowned in thought as he rasped his fingers over the silvery stubble on his chin. After a moment, he nodded.

"All right, if you think you can find the trail, have at it," he told Sam and the two cowboys. "But we'll be right behind you, and if you try anything funny, you'll wind up blasted out of the saddle quicker than you can blink."

"No tricks," Sam promised. "We want to find those cows as much as you do."

"You know, I almost believe you," Boyd said. "Which makes me wonder why you feel that way."

"Because maybe then you'll realize that we're not your enemy, and neither are the Navajo."

Lowry's beefy face flushed even more.

"What about those unshod hoofprints we found? What kind of white man would ride an unshod horse?"

"The kind who's trying to make everyone think he's an Indian," Sam said. He lifted his reins and heeled his mount into motion. "Come on."

After all that, he was going to feel like an utter fool if he couldn't find the trail, he thought wryly.

Less than fifteen minutes had gone by, however, when he spotted a rock that was a little darker than the same sort of rocks scattered all around it. The stone had been turned over recently and the burning sun hadn't had the chance to bleach as much color out of it.

Sam reined in and swung down from his horse. As he hunkered on his heels to study the ground, John Henry Boyd called a question from behind him.

"You find something, Two Wolves?"

"Maybe," Sam said. He spotted another darker rock a few feet away, and another after that. He straightened and walked forward slowly, leading his horse.

The signs were small, in some cases so tiny as to be almost invisible, but they were there. Sam followed them for a good fifty yards before he found an actual hoofprint. It had been left by a cow, and he came across more and more of them as the ground became softer again.

"Here," he said, pointing. "They came through here."

He lifted his arm and leveled it in a generally northwest direction, toward the area of buttes, ridges, and canyons where Caballo Rojo and his people lived.

"And they went that way," Sam said, hoping he wasn't wrong about the Navajo.

Boyd grunted.

"Then so will we," he said as he slipped his revolver from its holster.

He pointed the gun into the air and fired three shots, signaling his widespread riders to converge on him again.

"You're leading the way now, Two Wolves," the rancher said.

"The redskin might be leadin' us into a trap, boss," Pete Lowry warned.

"I don't care if he is," Boyd snapped. "We'll fight our way out of it. I want my cows back, and I want a shot at the mangy coyotes who killed my men."

At that moment, Sam almost felt some admiration for the crusty old cattleman. He could appreciate the loyalty Boyd felt toward the men who rode for the Devil's Pitchfork brand.

The riders gathered and the whole group struck out, again following the trail left by the stolen herd. Stovepipe brought his horse up alongside Sam's and said quietly, "That was good trackin', son. Couldn't have done better myself, I reckon."

"You don't fool me, Stovepipe," Sam said. "I'll bet you picked up some of the same sign I did."

The range detective grinned.

"Well, you was doin' such a good job of leadin' the way, I didn't see no need to get in *your* way."

"So you let me take the credit with Boyd, so maybe he'll trust me a little more."

"Credit's somethin' I never cared overmuch about," Stovepipe admitted.

After another hour or so of following the trail, the riders began to get into an area that seemed a little familiar to Sam. Of course, most of the rugged landscape in the Four Corners region looked similar.

The rock formations jutting up from the arid plains were infinite in their variety, however, and Sam began to see some he was sure he had seen before.

That meant they were getting into the area where he and Matt had been bushwhacked.

And *that* meant they weren't that far from the canyon where he had left Matt with Caballo Rojo's people.

Elizabeth Fleming was there, too, Sam recalled. He had spent a considerable amount of time wondering how his blood brother was doing, and that included wondering what was going on between Matt and Elizabeth.

Sam didn't have any real romantic interest in the redheaded Eastern teacher himself, but he knew how Matt was any time he was around a pretty girl.

Flirting came as naturally as gun-handling to Matt Bodine, and Sam hoped that hadn't led to any trouble while Matt was supposed to be recuperating from those bullet holes in his hide.

Chapter 27

Matt made good on his promise to sleep with one eye open after the attempt on his life.

Not literally, of course, but with the skills developed during a dangerous life on the frontier, he slept lightly that night.

His instincts remained on alert to warn him of anything that wasn't the way it was supposed to be. He wished he had his guns, but Caballo Rojo had ordered something done with them.

The only weapon he had was a fist-sized rock he had managed to sneak into the hogan. If anybody attacked him, he planned to brain the varmint with the rock.

The result of all that was that Matt was still tired when he rolled out of his blankets the next morning, but nothing else had happened.

Well, one other thing, he amended as he sat up and looked across the hogan.

Juan Pablo was back.

The Navajo was as stone-faced and unfriendly-looking as ever, Matt saw. He hadn't heard Juan Pablo come in, and he felt a slight prickling of his nerves. He should have been aware of the man's arrival.

Juan Pablo was standing up, though, so it was possible he had just stepped into the hogan. His wife knelt by the fire, preparing breakfast. If there was going to be any sort of reunion between them, obviously they intended to wait until they were alone for it, which was just fine with Matt.

"Good morning," he said as he got to his feet. As soon as he'd seen Juan Pablo, he had wondered about Sam. "Is Sam back, too?"

Juan Pablo shook his head.

"The half-breed followed the trail of the men he sought toward the settlement of Flat Rock two days ago," he answered. "I have not seen him since."

Matt was disappointed that Sam hadn't returned to the canyon. He asked, "Where have you been all that time since?"

Juan Pablo frowned, as if tempted to tell Matt that was none of his business, but then he said, "It took a day to return from the spot where I left your friend. The other day I spent cleansing myself of his presence."

"And now you're dirtied yourself up again by comin' back here where I am."

Juan Pablo grunted.

"You said that, white man, not I."

"Well, I'm not gonna be here much longer. I'm leaving today."

And so was Elizabeth, he thought, but he didn't mention that just yet.

"Fine," Juan Pablo said with a curt nod.

"Aren't you gonna ask if I'm in good enough shape to travel?"

Juan Pablo's silence was an eloquent indication of how little he cared about the answer to that question.

The man's wife had a pot of stew ready. When she held out a bowl to him, Matt shook his head.

"Thank you," he told her. He had exchanged very few words with her, and neither of them had understood what the other was saying.

But despite her sometimes disapproving demeanor, she had taken good care of him, and he appreciated that. He smiled at her and nodded, hoping that she understood he was grateful to her, and then stepped out of the hogan.

The air had that welcome coolness desert air always did, early in the morning. Matt breathed deeply of it and didn't feel quite as tired.

He heard his name called, turned around, and felt even better.

Elizabeth was coming toward him, beautiful in her dark green long-sleeved blouse and long skirt.

"You're all right," she said as she came up to him. Matt smiled.

"Did you expect something different?"

"After what happened yesterday, I didn't know what to expect," she said. "Do you still want to leave today?"

Matt's answer came without hesitation.

"That's right. There's still something bad brewing here. I don't know what it is and I wish I did, but my guts tell me we'll be better off getting out while we can." He paused. "You're still coming with me, aren't you?"

"I don't know . . . I hate to leave these people. I'd like to think I've done them some good. They're going to be able to make their way better in the white man's world because of me."

She didn't understand, Matt thought. The Navajo didn't want to make their way in the white man's world. They wanted to be left alone to live in their own world, in their own way.

You couldn't convince the "Lo, the poor Indian!" people of that, though. Folks who believed they were going to make somebody change for their own good were doomed to failure.

He wasn't going to say that to Elizabeth. For one thing, it wouldn't do any good. He couldn't change her beliefs any more than she could change those of the Navajo.

But he could get her out of what might well turn out to be a dangerous situation, and he was going to try his best to do so.

"I really think you ought to come with me. I mean, since I've been wounded and all . . ."

He ought to be ashamed of himself for playing that card, he thought as he saw sympathy light up her eyes. Somebody like Elizabeth couldn't resist the urge to help somebody. But if it got her clear of this canyon, he was willing to do it.

Anyway, he was wounded. That was just the truth. And while he felt stronger today than he had since winding up here, he still thought it would be a good idea to have somebody around to look after him, if need be.

"All right," she said. "I'll come with you." She smiled. "Anyway, there's nothing stopping me from coming back here later on, is there?"

"Not a thing," he agreed. They could deal with what would happen later once they were out of here.

"Of course, we don't know if Caballo Rojo will allow us to leave," Elizabeth pointed out.

She was right. That could be a problem.

So the thing to do was tend to it right now, Matt decided.

He took her arm and said, "Let's go talk to him."

They walked along the creek toward Caballo Rojo's hogan. With the air still holding that hint of coolness and the sun not blazing down in the canyon like it would later in the day, this would have been a pleasant moment if not for the fact that Matt was worried about what the Navajo headman would say.

Caballo Rojo was sitting outside his hogan, working with a bit of silver, fashioning it into some small piece of jewelry. He looked up for a second as Matt and Elizabeth approached, but otherwise he didn't acknowledge that they were there.

"Caballo Rojo, I'd like to talk to you," Matt said. "I know you understand me, even without Juan Pablo here to translate for me. I want to thank you for your hospitality, for seeing that I was taken care of while I was recovering from my injuries."

Caballo Rojo grunted but still didn't look up again.

"Now that my wounds are healing, I think it's time for me to leave," Matt went on. "I'd like to have my horse, my guns, and the rest of my gear returned to me."

No response from the headman. Matt and Elizabeth traded worried glances. This wasn't going the way they had hoped.

But there was nothing they could do except go ahead with their plan. Matt said, "Miss Fleming is going to go with me, to help me in case my injuries trouble me."

Caballo Rojo finally lifted his head. He shook it slowly from side to side in stubborn refusal.

Elizabeth said, "Do you mean you don't want me to go with Mr. Bodine, Caballo Rojo?"

From behind them, a harsh voice said, "Caballo Rojo means that neither of you will leave this canyon."

Matt turned sharply and saw Juan Pablo standing there. The Navajo had one of the single-shot rifles in his hands, and the weapon was trained on Matt's belly.

Behind Juan Pablo stood three more men, one of them armed with another rifle, the other two with bows and arrows. They glared menacingly at Matt and Elizabeth.

Juan Pablo smiled, though, the first smile Matt had seen on the Navajo's face.

It wasn't a pretty expression.

"What's going on here?" Matt demanded. He looked over his shoulder at the headman. "Caballo Rojo—"

"I have already spoken to Caballo Rojo," Juan Pablo broke in. "I have told him how you plan to go to the settlement and lead the white men back here so they can attack us and wipe out all of our people."

"That's not true!" Elizabeth cried. "Caballo Rojo, you must believe me. I've never done anything except try to help your people, and Mr. Bodine would never betray you after you helped him the way you did."

"Lies, all lies," Juan Pablo said with the calm self-assurance of a man who knows that he has already won. "Like all the other whites, you seek only the destruction of the Diné. But your treachery will bring about only your own destruction."

He lifted the rifle.

"No, you will never leave this canyon . . . alive."

Chapter 28

The trail of the rustled cattle continued to angle toward the canyon where the members of Caballo Rojo's clan made their home. Sam grew more worried as he saw that.

Was it possible that the Navajo really *were* to blame for stealing that stock and killing Boyd's punchers?

Sam didn't want to believe that was true, but he couldn't deny the evidence of his own eyes . . . especially when the line of cliffs where the canyon was located came into view.

As he and the other riders came closer, however, the tracks began to turn more to the north. Relief went through Sam as he realized that the trail was going to lead past the entrance to the Navajo canyon.

This was the closest he had been to the place since leaving several days earlier, and he couldn't help but wonder how Matt was doing. It would be easy enough to ride over there and see. It wouldn't take long.

That is, it would have been easy if he and Stove-pipe and Wilbur weren't prisoners of the Devil's Pitchfork crew.

As it was, Sam knew that Pete Lowry would be only too happy to gun them down if it looked like they were trying to escape, and so would some of the other men.

He wasn't sure he wanted Boyd and his men to know those Navajo hogans were hidden in the canyon, anyway. That might cause trouble for Caballo Rojo and his people in the future.

So as the cliffs fell behind them, Sam felt mingled relief and worry. Relief that the trail of the stolen cattle hadn't led straight to the Navajo, and worry about Matt.

He wasn't sure why that had started nagging at him, but the bond that existed between the blood brothers sometimes enabled them to sense when the other one was in trouble.

Sam hoped that wasn't the case now.

"That looks like hellacious country ahead of us," John Henry Boyd commented. "I don't reckon I've ever been up this far before. Can't be far to the Sweet-water Hills." He pointed to a range of low but rugged peaks with sides deeply seamed by canyons and crevices. "That must be them."

Pete Lowry said nervously, "Boss, I've heard that those hills are haunted."

It struck Sam as odd that such a sentiment would be expressed by the hard-nosed segundo. Even the tough-est hombre could be touched by superstition, though.

A harsh laugh came from Boyd.

"Ghosts didn't steal those cattle or ventilate those two boys, Pete. If they're in those hills, the varmints who took 'em there are flesh and blood, and bullets will put holes in 'em. We're not turning back now."

"Never said anything about turnin' back," Lowry responded in surly tones. "Just tellin' you what I've heard, that's all."

The trail grew dim, and once again Sam and Stovepipe had to search for it. This time it was the tall, lanky cowboy who found the tracks they were looking for.

There was no doubt now that they were headed straight for the Sweetwater Hills.

"Looks like there's a heap of places to hide in those badlands," Stovepipe said.

"Then it's a good thing we've got you with us," Lowry said. "Since you're one of the gang, you can tell us how to find the rest of your bunch."

Wilbur said, "I thought it was the Navajo who were responsible for what happened. Now you're sayin' it's a gang of white outlaws? Sort of changin' your tune, ain't you, Lowry?"

Lowry snarled at him.

"Give me five minutes with a Bowie knife and I'd get the truth outta you, you short-growed little runt."

Wilbur's face flushed with anger as he said, "Blast it, I'm not that short! It just looks like it because I hang around with this beanpole here."

He jerked a thumb at the grinning Stovepipe.

"Beanpole, eh? I ain't sure I like that name. I'm just gettin' used to Stovepipe."

"Pipe down, all three of you," Boyd warned. "Two Wolves, what do you think?"

"Your cattle are probably stashed in some canyon up there in the hills, all right," Sam said. "And it won't be easy to find."

"You don't know anything about it?"

Sam shook his head.

"I'm just following a trail, like you."

"I've got a hunch you're telling the truth." Boyd silenced Lowry's protest with a look before the segundo could even say anything. "Pete, give 'em back their guns."

"Boss, that's a mistake—" Lowry began.

"If it is, it's my mistake to make!" Boyd said. "I still give the orders in this bunch."

Lowry nodded.

"I never said you didn't, John Henry." With obvious reluctance, he turned in the saddle and motioned to the men who had taken charge of the weapons belonging to Sam, Stovepipe, and Wilbur. "Give 'em back their guns."

Sam felt a little better once the familiar weight of the Colt was back in its holster, the Winchester was in the saddleboot under his left thigh, and his bowie knife was nestled in its sheath on his left hip. He knew the situation was still full of risk, but at least now he could fight if he had to.

"Let's go," Boyd said once the three men were armed again. The rancher added, "But just in case you're trying to double-cross us, we'll still be keeping a close eye on you and your friends, Two Wolves."

"No double cross," Sam said. "We're on the same side."

Lowry snorted.

"If that's true, it's the first time I've ever been on the same side as a damn redskin."

"There's a first time for everything," Sam told him with a smile. He didn't have to like Lowry—that seemed pretty unlikely—but they might soon be fighting side by side, so it was a good idea if they could trust each other.

Several rugged mesas loomed between the riders and the hills. They would have to weave among those mesas to reach their destination, unless they went around and risked losing the trail . . . because it appeared that the stolen herd had been driven through those big, flat-topped formations.

Sam cast occasional glances toward the tops of the mesas as the group started into the forest of rock. This would be a good spot for an ambush, he thought. Riflemen hidden atop one of those mesas would have a good vantage point.

But the sides of most of the formations appeared to be sheer. Men might be able to climb some of them, but it would be difficult.

Knowing that didn't stop Sam from worrying. He had survived more than one bushwhack attempt already in the past eight or nine days. It might be pushing his luck to live through another.

"Where in blazes did the tracks go?" Lowry suddenly asked.

Sam studied the ground, then looked over at Stovepipe, who nodded.

"They're gone, all right," the range detective said. "Maybe we can pick 'em up on the other side of these mesas."

"Let's have a look," Boyd said. "Those cows had to go somewhere."

But when they emerged from the cluster of rock formations, half an hour of searching turned up no sign that the cattle had come this way, even to the keen eyes of Sam and Stovepipe.

"That's just loco!" Wilbur said. "They went in there. They had to come out somewhere!"

"Maybe they doubled back and come out on the same side they went on," Stovepipe suggested. "Might be a good idea if we was to split up, Mr. Boyd, and make a circle around the whole place."

"Don't let them talk you into that, John Henry," Lowry warned. "If they split us up, it'll be easier for somebody to jump us."

Stovepipe frowned.

"All that mistrust is gettin' a mite annoyin'," he said.

"I'm not splitting my men," Boyd decided. "But we'll circle around these mesas like you said, Stewart. That sounds like a good idea to me. Your friend's right about one thing . . . Those cows have to be somewhere."

With Sam and Stovepipe leading the way, watched hawkishly by Lowry, the group started around the area dotted with mesas. It was pretty extensive, so circling it took more than an hour.

They found the place where they had followed the tracks among the mesas, but that was all. By the time they got back to where they had started on the far side, Sam had to admit that something odd had happened.

The rustled cattle had gone in there, but they hadn't come out.

"There's only one answer," he said.

"Yeah, I agree," Stovepipe said.

"What are you talking about?" Boyd asked.

Stovepipe pointed at the sky with a thumb. Sam nodded in agreement with him.

"What the hell!" Lowry exploded. "You're sayin' those cows sprouted wings and *flew* away? Because that makes as much sense as thinkin' they climbed one of these mesas."

"We just need to look harder," Sam said. "We missed something."

Lowry snorted to show how much stock he put in that.

The tops of some of the mesas were probably a square mile in area, Sam thought, maybe even a little more than that. There might be enough grass growing on one of those to support a small herd of fifty head, plus the horses of the rustlers who had stolen them.

If he was right about the motive behind the rustling—that it was intended solely to stir up Boyd and the other ranchers in the area to the point where they would support a war against the Navajo—then the thieves wouldn't care about the money they could make from selling the cows. They could let the stock starve on top of a mesa and still come out ahead.

That still left the question of how the rustlers could have gotten the cattle up there, but Sam figured if they found the right mesa, they would also find the answer. For now, all they could do was look.

And that depended on John Henry Boyd.

The rancher rubbed his jaw again as he frowned in thought. Finally, he nodded.

"Let's take a closer look at all these mesas," he said. He added, "And get your rifles out. I've got a bad feeling crawling around in my guts."

Sam understood that. He had the same feeling.

The men rode around the base of each mesa as they came to it, looking for some sort of hidden trail. In some places, it was hard to get close because over the centuries huge slabs of rock had broken loose from the sides of the mesas and fallen around them.

It was possible some of those slabs might conceal the start of a trail, Sam thought. It wouldn't have to be very wide. With only fifty cows to hide, the animals could be driven up single file if need be.

The sun blasted down, making the air so hot and dry it seemed to sear the lungs if a man took a deep breath. Sam was grateful for the shade provided by the hat he had bought back in Flat Rock. As the search continued, the sweating men became more impatient and frustrated.

Finally, Pete Lowry said, "This is crazy. There

aren't any cows on top of these mesas, John Henry. It just ain't possible."

"Then we got to admit them critters vanished into thin air," Stovepipe said. "And I'm havin' a hard time believin' that."

"So am I," Boyd said. "We'll keep looking."

"It's already so late we won't be able to make it back to the ranch today," Lowry pointed out.

"The boys we left there will be able to look after things. I want those cattle. More than that, I want whoever shot two of my punchers. They're not gonna get away with that, by God."

Lowry grumbled to himself but didn't argue anymore.

Sam gazed toward one of the largest mesas, which sat about three hundred yards away. It rose some eighty feet to its table-like top. Slabs of red stone littered the ground around its base, and lightning-like cracks in the rock zigzagged their way up the walls in places.

Sam frowned. There was something about the mesa . . .

"That's it," he said under his breath as understanding dawned inside him.

"What did you find, son?" Stovepipe asked as he brought his horse alongside Sam's mount. The range detective kept his voice pitched low.

Equally quietly, Sam said, "Look at those cracks, Stovepipe. On some of them, the slope is gentle enough a cow could make it up them."

"Yeah, but most places, they ain't. I'm lookin', but

I don't see one anybody could climb that goes all the way to the top."

"But look at the line connecting one crack to the next one."

"What line? I don't see any—" Stovepipe stopped as his eyes narrowed. "Son of a gun. Is that a ledge?"

"I think so. It's narrow enough that it's hard to see, but it runs almost level over to another crack."

"And there's another one a mite higher up leadin' to the next crack after that," Stovepipe said. "They're like steppin'-stones, with little ramps in between. You don't notice the ledges because your eyes are fol-lowin' the cracks."

Sam nodded.

"That's the way it looks to me. The cracks are more pronounced, so you can see them better."

"That ain't no natural formation. The cracks may be, but the ledges connectin' 'em ain't. They must go all the way around the mesa."

"The Navajo probably carved them, no telling how long ago," Sam said. "They could put lookouts up there to watch for their enemies, and they could fire arrows down or throw rocks off to ambush those enemies."

"You reckon those ledges are wide enough for cows, or a man on horseback?"

"Only one way to find out," Sam said as he lifted his reins.

Before he could heel his horse into motion, Pete

Lowry said, "Hold on there, breed. Where do you think you're goin'?"

Sam hesitated.

"I have an idea where the men we're looking for might be," he said. "But they're probably watching us right now, and I don't want them to realize that I've figured out their secret."

"I don't believe you," Lowry said. "I still think this is some sort of trick."

Boyd rode over and asked, "What's going on here?"

Lowry nodded toward Sam.

"The 'breed says he's figured it out. I think he's just tryin' to get away from us, though, so his friends can open fire on us."

"That's not true," Sam said. "Look at that big mesa in front of me, Mr. Boyd. I think I see a trail leading up to the top."

Boyd frowned.

"Where? I don't see any trail, just a bunch of cracks like the whole thing's about to come tumbling down in an avalanche."

"I'll bet it's a lot more stable than it looks. I want to amble over there and take a closer look, but if the rustlers are up there, I don't want them to realize that I know they're there."

Boyd nodded slowly.

"That makes sense, I reckon. Go ahead, Two Wolves . . . but Stewart and Coleman stay here, and if any lead starts to fly, they'll die before we do. You've got my word on that."

When Sam hesitated again, Stovepipe said, "Go ahead, son. We'll take that chance, won't we, Wilbur?"

"Do we have any choice?" the redhead asked gloomily.

"Not a dang one," Stovepipe said with a grin.

"Keep an eye on the top of the mesa," Sam told Boyd. "If I was trying to set up an ambush, I wouldn't tell you where it was coming from, now would I?"

"Likely not," the rancher agreed, although Lowry still looked skeptical.

Sam started his horse toward the mesa, moving at a deliberate pace. Several of the Devil's Pitchfork hands were still searching around the other mesas, so what he was doing didn't look too suspicious . . . he hoped.

Because he could feel eyes on him. The same instincts that had warned him of danger many times in his adventurous life were setting off alarm bells inside him now.

That warning was justified, too, because he was still a hundred yards from the base of the mesa when a rifle cracked and a bullet whistled past his ear.

Chapter 29

The hot breath of the slug was much too close for comfort. Sam leaned forward in the saddle and kicked his horse into a gallop as more shots blasted. Dirt and rocks spouted from the ground as bullets struck around him.

The closest cover was at the base of the mesa itself. The riflemen on top of the formation would have trouble firing straight down at him. The big slabs of fallen rock would give him some protection as well.

As he raced toward the mesa, Sam glanced over his shoulder at his companions. Stovepipe, Wilbur, Boyd, Lowry, and the other men from the Devil's Pitchfork were scattering as bullets whined among them, too. The riders hunted cover as fast as they could.

One man wasn't fast enough, though. He went backward out of the saddle as a slug smashed into him. One of his feet caught in the stirrup, and the panicky horse dragged him across the rough ground, causing his body to bounce grotesquely.

As Sam reached the rocks at the base of the mesa, he yanked his rifle from its sheath and swung down from the saddle. He dropped the reins and hoped the horse wouldn't run off too far.

Bringing the Winchester to his shoulder, Sam cranked off several rounds as fast as he could toward the top of the mesa. He had seen spurts of gunsmoke from up there and had a general idea where the ambushers were.

He didn't expect to hit any of them, but with luck he could force them back for a second, which would give Stovepipe and the others more time to find shelter.

As slugs began to search for him, Sam ducked behind a chunk of sandstone that was taller than he was. Bullets smacked into the top of the slab, some drilling into the sandstone and others whining off as ricochets.

But none of them reached Sam, and that was all that mattered right now.

Sam slid along the rock, reached the corner of it, and snapped a couple more shots at the mesa's rim, working the rifle's lever swiftly between rounds.

Then he sprinted toward another rock that brought him closer to one of the cracks in the mesa wall.

When he reached cover again, he looked out over the flats in front of the mesa. The rest of the men who had come here with him were out of sight now, hidden behind boulders and some of the smaller rock formations that gave this landscape something of an alien look. Sam heard shots booming out from them as they returned the fire of the rustlers on top of the mesa.

While his companions were keeping the rustlers busy, Sam worked his way closer. When he reached one of the cracks, he saw that it ran deep enough into the rock to form a ledge angling upward. That ledge was wide enough for a couple of cows to ascend it.

Driving cattle up to the top of the mesa by this route would be difficult, and once the beasts were up there, getting them down would be even harder. But maybe the rustlers didn't intend to bring them down, Sam thought. As he had reasoned out earlier, selling the stolen stock had never been the goal.

Once the Navajo had been moved out, the rustlers could leave those cattle up there to starve if they wanted to. Such cruelty wouldn't be beyond men who had set out to start an Indian war.

Sam started up the crack in the rock. For several yards, the climb was an easy one. When it grew steeper, he came to one of the connecting, man-made ledges that were hard to see from a distance.

Up close like this, it was obvious that the path had been hewn out of the stone by hand. All the sharp edges had been rounded away by erosion, though, which indicated that long years, maybe even centuries, had passed since the work had been done.

Sam had heard legends about Old Ones, people who had been in this part of the world even before the Navajo, and he wondered if this path was some of their handiwork. Those Old Ones had disappeared mysteriously, sometime in the dim past, so if they had turned this mesa into a watchtower, obviously that hadn't been enough to save them in the end.

The continuing racket of gunfire from above and below brought Sam out of his momentary reverie. The past might be fascinating, but the present was dangerous and needed his full attention.

He walked out onto the ledge, keeping an eye on the rim some seventy feet above him. After about fifty feet, he came to another of the zigzagging cracks and was able to climb it to the next man-made ledge.

As he moved higher and higher, his route carried him around the curve of the mesa, so he couldn't see his companions anymore. He heard the shots, though, as the battle between the rustlers and the Devil's Pitchfork crew continued.

Sam didn't know how many men he would find on top of the mesa. It would have taken at least five or six to steal that herd and drive them out here, but once the cattle were hidden atop the mesa, fewer men would be needed to keep an eye on them. Some of the rustlers could have headed to town, leaving only a couple up there.

It had sounded like more than two rifles firing at him, however, and Sam figured there were at least four men he would have to deal with when he reached the top.

Those weren't good odds. He would have felt a lot better if Matt had been here with him. Being outnumbered two-to-one didn't mean much to the blood brothers. They had faced odds like that many times in their adventurous lives and were still alive and kicking.

But now that he had started up, there wasn't much he could do except keep going. If he was able to come in behind the rustlers and get the drop on them, he could force them to surrender.

A sudden grating of rock somewhere above him made him jerk his head up.

Sam's eyes widened as he saw a boulder almost as big as he was plummeting toward him.

He was on one of the ledges at the moment, so he threw himself into a dive that carried him out of the boulder's path. It slammed into the ledge a few feet behind him as he landed. His momentum sent him sliding toward the brink of the curving ledge.

Sam had to drop his rifle to slap both hands against the sandstone and stop himself. Luckily the Winchester didn't bounce off. The boulder rebounded from the ledge and fell the rest of the way to the ground, where it landed with a crash that raised a little cloud of dust.

Sam grabbed the rifle and scrambled to his feet. Obviously, the rustlers knew he was trying to climb the mesa, so he wouldn't be taking them by surprise after all.

And if they could try to drop one boulder on him, probably they could make another attempt. He ran along the ledge toward the next crack in the rock. The mesa wall bulged out above it, so that would give him some protection.

His heart pounded as he climbed several feet up

the sloping crack. He was safe here, but whether he retreated or forged ahead, as soon as he stepped out onto another of those open ledges, he risked having a boulder dropped on his head.

But he couldn't stay here forever, Sam told himself. Boyd and his men might be able to lay siege to the mesa and starve out the rustlers, but they would be starving out Sam at the same time.

He looked up. The crack in which he had taken shelter became too steep after another ten feet for cattle and horses to use it as a trail . . .

But a man could climb it, Sam thought.

A grim smile tugged at his mouth. It wouldn't be easy—in some places the crack was almost vertical— but it could be done. And most importantly, the rustlers couldn't get at him with either boulders or bullets while he was making the ascent.

He would need both hands, though, so he took off his belt and used it to rig a sling for the Winchester. When he had the rifle hung over his shoulder, he hurried along the slope until it turned upward at a steeper angle. Ignoring the ledge that had been cut into the rock, he started up the natural crack, crawling now because of the angle.

Somewhere above him, a man yelled, "Can you see him?"

"Blast it, no!" another man answered. "He's found himself a hole somewhere!"

"Well, let him stay there," the first man said. "Let him stay there and rot!"

Sam smiled again.

He continued climbing. The crack narrowed, grew steeper still, turned into a chimney. Sam pulled the Winchester around so that it hung in front of him, pressed his back against one side of the opening and his feet against the other, and worked his way up inch by inch.

After a while the strain set his muscles to trembling slightly. He slipped a little but caught himself before he fell.

There was nowhere for him to go except up, so he kept struggling to lift himself, again and again. Sharp places in the wall gouged his back through the buckskin shirt. He ignored the pain and continued climbing.

The shots would taper off, then flare up again. From down below, it would be very difficult for any of the men on the ground to get a clear shot at the rustlers on the mesa.

From the sound of it, though, Stovepipe, Boyd, and the others had found good cover for themselves, though, and continued throwing lead at the cattle thieves.

At the very least, that kept the rustlers occupied and gave Sam the chance he needed to make his way to the top.

The crack angled again, rather than going almost straight up. Sam stretched out in it to rest for a moment.

But not for too long, because the men who had come here with him were still at risk as long as they were trading shots with the rustlers. He had come to regard Stovepipe and Wilbur as friends, and the men from the Devil's Pitchfork were allies, at least for the moment.

Sam moved the Winchester around to his back again and resumed the climb, once more proceeding on hands and knees. A few minutes later, he saw the end of the crack not far above him.

His first impulse was to climb out right away, but he stopped where he was instead and listened intently. He heard the shots coming from the other side of the mesa, but he heard something closer as well: a man clearing his throat.

He'd suspected that the rustlers might leave a man over here on guard, in the area where they had seen him last. If he just poked his head up without being careful about it, he would probably get a bullet through the brain.

Sam looked around and found a fist-sized chunk of sandstone. The guard was to his right, so he drew back his arm as much as he could in the narrow confines of the crack and threw the rock in that direction. It sailed up and out and came thudding down on the ground atop the mesa.

Sam followed the rock, moving fast.

As he emerged from the crack with the Winchester cradled in both hands, he threw himself forward on his belly. About twenty feet away, a man in range clothes was turning toward him. The rock had done its job and served as a distraction, causing the guard to take his attention off the crack for a second.

The rustler held a rifle, too, and it spat flame and

lead as he hurried a shot at Sam. The bullet hit the ground well to Sam's left.

Sam fired more deliberately, and his aim was true. The .44-40 round punched into the rustler's mid-section and doubled him over. The man dropped his gun and howled in pain as he clutched himself. He staggered to the side.

That took him too close to the edge. He let out a sudden scream as he toppled off into empty air. The scream continued for the couple of heartbeats it took him to fall all the way to the rocks next to the mesa.

As Sam scrambled to his feet, he heard the soggy thud of the rustler's landing. That grim sound ended the scream.

He ran toward the other side of the mesa. With all the other shooting going on, the rest of the rustlers might not have noticed the shots Sam had traded with the guard, but he couldn't count on that. He had to move fast while he still had the chance.

As he had suspected, the mesa had some grass growing on its top and even a few small bushes. Off to Sam's right was a basin where the top of the mesa had sunk, creating a rock-lined pool that held water from the occasional rains.

Gathered around that pool were the cattle that had been stolen from John Henry Boyd's ranch. They didn't need to be fenced in. They wouldn't get far from the water, and anyway, where would they go?

Beyond the pool was a rope corral made from a couple of lassos and some stakes pounded into the hard ground. Four horses were inside the corral.

Since Sam had already killed one man, that meant there were three more rustlers up here.

He got instant confirmation of that a second later when three men emerged from behind the horses and charged toward him, guns blazing.

Chapter 30

Sam was outnumbered and the scrubby vegetation atop the mesa offered no protection.

So he angled toward the only cover he could find, the cattle clustered around the pool.

Bullets sang around him. He returned the fire as he ran, working the Winchester's lever and snapping shots toward the rustlers.

One of the cows let out a bellow as a stray slug struck it. Sam ducked between two of the beasts. One of them swung its head and nearly hooked him with a horn. He bounced off the sturdy flank of the other cow.

Sam kept his head down as one of the rustlers shouted, "Where the hell did he go?"

"He's in amongst the cattle!" one of the other men answered. "Spread out! We'll circle them!"

Sam couldn't afford to let that happen. He yanked his hat off his head and slashed right and left with it, swatting the rumps of several cows. At the same time he fired his Winchester one-handed into the air and let out a howl like a panther.

The cattle reacted as he hoped they would. The normally stolid beasts around him spooked at the racket and at being swatted, and in a herd of cattle, when one cow panicked, they all panicked.

The herd surged away from the pool in a full-on stampede, straight at the rustlers.

Even over the pounding of hooves, Sam heard the frightened yells that came from the three men as they tried to get out of the way.

He had his own scrambling to do, since he was in the midst of the cattle when they began to run. He leaped from side to side to avoid the lumbering beasts, but he was still pummeled.

If he fell, he would never get up again. The cattle would trample him to death. Sam knew that. He dropped his rifle, willing to lose the Winchester if it would save his life, and used both hands to grab the horns of a steer charging past him. The steel-spring muscles in his legs vaulted him onto the animal's back.

Sam hung on for dear life.

With his legs clamped around the steer's neck, Sam used his grip on the horns to twist the beast's head. That forced it toward the edge of the stampeding herd.

He had lost track of the three rustlers, but he had more pressing worries at the moment. The steer began to buck.

Sam had heard that down in Texas, cowboys had started to have what they called rodeos, competitions

that centered around ranch work. One of them was
bull-riding, or so he had been told.

This was a steer, not a bull, but the ride was a
thrilling and dangerous one anyway. Sam thought a
couple of times that the steer was going to throw him
off, but he managed to stay on until the animal
reached the edge of the herd.

He let go of the horns and piled off, leaping desperately to put as much distance between himself and
the stampede as possible. When he hit the ground, he
rolled away fast and came up running.

Dust choked him, but at least none of the cattle
ran over him. When he looked back, he saw that he
was clear.

Now he could start looking for the rustlers again,
he thought as he blinked grit out of his eyes and drew
the Colt that had stayed thronged down in its holster.

The thing about a stampede on top of a mesa was
that the cattle didn't have very far they could go.
When the leaders reached the edge, they began to
turn, and the herd started to mill. Sam ran around the
confusion, searching for the three men.

The first one he found wouldn't ever steal any
more cows. The man hadn't been able to get out of
the way, and the thundering hooves had pounded him
into a gory mess that barely resembled anything
human.

The second man had been more fortunate, but not
much. Both of his legs were broken. His groans of
agony led Sam to him.

But just like a broken-backed rattlesnake can still

bite, this crippled rustler was dangerous. When he spotted Sam, he heaved himself up with one hand and lifted a revolver with the other. Flame geysered from the muzzle.

Sam flung himself aside and returned the fire. He didn't have time for anything fancy. The rustler's head snapped back as a red-rimmed hole appeared in his forehead and Sam's bullet drilled into his brain.

Sam grimaced. He wanted to take at least one of the men alive so they could question him. Now that might not be possible.

He swung around looking for the third man, and as he did, the scrape of boot leather on rock warned him.

But not in time for him to get out of the way. The last rustler slammed into him from behind, driving him off his feet.

Sam went down with the man on his back. The rustler must have lost his gun in the chaos of the stampede, otherwise he would have just shot Sam. Instead he looped an arm around Sam's throat from behind and started trying to choke the life out of him.

Sam tried to buck the rustler off, just as the steer had bucked under him. The rustler clung with the same tenacity Sam had, though.

Heaving himself up on hands and knees, Sam rolled, thinking that maybe he could break the man's grip that way.

Instead the arm across his throat just pressed harder, cutting off his air as effectively as if it had been an iron bar.

Sam still had his gun. He struck behind him with it in an attempt to knock his attacker unconscious.

The rustler ducked his head and pressed his face into the back of Sam's neck.

"I'm gonna kill you, redskin!"

Sam heard the harsh whisper, although it sounded muffled because of the roar of blood in his ears. His vision was beginning to blur as a red haze dropped over his eyes.

He had no choice.

He pushed the Colt's barrel against the man's leg and pulled the trigger.

The rustler screamed in his ear and let go of him. Sam arched his back, throwing the man to the side. He rolled away and came up in a crouch, holding the Colt ready to fire again if he needed to.

But all the fight had already gone out of the rustler, along with a great deal of blood. As the man screamed again, a crimson fountain shot into the air from the wound in his thigh. He pawed at it, but the blood just ran between his fingers like a river.

Sam knew his bullet had torn an artery. He had intended just to inflict a flesh wound, something to make the rustler let go, but now he saw that the man had only moments to live unless that bleeding could be stopped.

Sam leaped forward and slammed the Colt against the rustler's head, knocking the man out. There was no time to waste in struggling with him.

He dropped the gun and pulled the man's belt off, then wrapped it around the thigh as high as he could above the wound and pulled it tight. Slipping the Colt's barrel into a loop he fashioned in the belt, he began twisting it.

As the belt tightened and cut into the flesh of the rustler's leg, the gush of blood slowed. Sam used both hands to twist the Colt and draw the makeshift tourniquet even tighter. The blood stopped.

A grotesque rattle came from the man's throat.

"Blast it, no!" Sam burst out. He held the belt tight with one hand on the gun and used the other hand to feel for a heartbeat. The rustler's eyes were open and staring, and the muscles of his face were slack.

After a minute, Sam had to admit to himself that he wasn't going to find a heartbeat. The fourth and final rustler on top of this mesa was dead.

Sam had just heaved a sigh of disgust when he heard a man's voice call his name. He turned his head to look and saw Stovepipe Stewart running toward him, followed by Wilbur Coleman and John Henry Boyd.

"Sam, you all right?" Stovepipe asked as he pounded up. "Lord, that's a lot of blood!"

"It's all his," Sam said. He released the tourniquet and pulled his gun loose from the dead man's belt. "I was trying to wing him, but I nicked an artery instead."

"I'll say you did," Wilbur put in. "Looks like he bled practically a whole lake."

Weariness gripped Sam as he got to his feet.

"What about the rest of you?" he asked. "Was anybody hurt?"

"One of my riders, Ben Conroy, was killed," Boyd said grimly. "Couple men got creased, but that's all." He looked around the mesa. "Any more of the varmints up here?"

"None breathing," Sam told him. "There were four men with the cattle."

"This is just about the craziest thing I ever saw," Boyd went on. "Who'd be loco enough to drive cattle up a narrow little trail like that to the top of a mesa?"

"Somebody who knew the chances of you findin' 'em would be mighty small," Stovepipe said. "If it wasn't for Sam's eyes, likely we never would've spotted the way up here."

Boyd looked at Sam and nodded. He waved a hand to indicate the cattle and the dead rustlers.

"I reckon this proves you didn't have anything to do with that stock being stolen, Two Wolves. You wouldn't have done what you did if you were part of this bunch."

"If you check the bodies, you'll see that they're all white," Sam pointed out. "Not Navajo."

In his habitual gesture, Boyd rubbed his chin.

"Yeah, I reckon I was wrong about that, too," he said.

"You ever seen this fella before, Mr. Boyd?" Stovepipe asked as he nodded to the man who had bled to death.

Boyd frowned.

"I don't think I have."

"I have," Wilbur said. "I don't know who he is, but

I remember seein' him in Flat Rock durin' the past week or so."

Stovepipe nodded and said, "I was just thinkin' the same thing, pard. Let's have a look at the others."

"You won't be able to tell much about one of them," Sam warned. "He got caught in the stampede."

"Got to pick him up with a shovel, eh?" Stovepipe hunkered on his heels next to the man Sam had shot in the head. "Well, we'll let that one go. This one, though, I've seen him in town, too. Don't you think, Wilbur?"

"Yeah, he looks familiar," the freckle-faced puncher agreed.

"So the gang's holed up in Flat Rock," Boyd said. "We'll go in there and clean out the whole place if we have to."

"That won't do any good," Sam cautioned. "You don't know who else is part of the bunch. What we need to do is figure out a way to draw them into the open."

"Yeah, maybe," Boyd said with obvious reluctance. "I know my boys, though, and they're gonna want to go in shooting."

"You'll have to keep them from doing that." Sam turned toward the rope corral, which had survived the stampede intact as the cows went around it. "I want to take a look at their horses. Maybe that'll tell us something."

"I was just thinkin' the same thing," Stovepipe said. Together they examined the rustlers' mounts. The brands were ones that Sam didn't recognize, and neither did Boyd.

"That just means they didn't come from any of the spreads around here," the rancher said. "I figured as much."

All four horses were unsaddled, but as Sam ran his hands over the flanks of a leggy roan, he said, "This one is hotter than the others. He's been run hard fairly recently."

"You reckon one of those fellas made a fast trip out here?" Stovepipe asked.

"That would mean the rustlers left three men to keep an eye on the cattle," Sam said. "That sounds reasonable."

"Then why'd the fourth man come out here all hell-for-leather?" Wilbur asked.

"To warn the other hombres that we were tryin' to trail the stolen herd," Stovepipe answered. "That the way it lays out to you, Sam?"

"Yeah. The men who tried to bushwhack me this morning hurried back to Flat Rock to tell their boss that I wasn't dead. They must have seen the two of you join up with me, and then Mr. Boyd and his men came along and we all started trailing the cattle. The boss sent word to his men out here, hoping they'd get rid of us."

"They jumped the gun a mite," Stovepipe drawled.

"Yeah, one of them has a habit of doing that," Sam said. He thought it was very likely that the man who had taken that first shot at him and Matt was dead now, one of the four men who had been killed here on top of the mesa.

"Getting those cows down off this mesa is gonna be a chore," Boyd complained. "I'll be damned if I'll leave them up here, though. We'll wait until morning and see if we can drive them back down that trail."

"That's up to you and your men," Sam said. "Now that you've decided that Stovepipe and Wilbur and I are trustworthy after all, there's something else we need to do."

"What's that?" Stovepipe asked.

Sam thought about Matt. The canyon where Caballo Rojo's clan lived wasn't very far away. They might not be able to reach it by nightfall, but he thought he could find it even after darkness had fallen.

"Let's just say I want to go visit a sick friend."

Chapter 31

This had been one of the longest days of Matt Bodine's life.

He knew it had been hard on Elizabeth, too, but at least she had been in the shade part of the time. He had been baking in the blistering sun all day, tied to a stake. Standing there like that for hours had caused the wounds in his side to ache like a bad tooth.

But he could tell the bullet holes weren't bleeding again, just hurting, and that was something to be thankful for, anyway.

They hadn't really hurt Elizabeth, either, just forced her to sit beside Juan Pablo's hogan and watch Matt's torment. That was the only other good thing about this ordeal.

He looked over at her now and saw how her face was pale and drawn with the strain. He tried to summon up a smile to let her know that everything was all right, but he couldn't quite manage it.

Things weren't all right, though, and they both knew it. Juan Pablo and his followers intended to kill both of them. It was just a matter of time.

Juan Pablo had at least a dozen men backing his play. Matt didn't know if Caballo Rojo was one of them, or if the clan headman was just staying out of this for the time being because he didn't want Juan Pablo challenging him for leadership of everyone who lived in the canyon.

But the Navajo had been drifting in from their homes along the creek all day, gathering here to look at the captive white man, and some of them seemed very happy about it. The men had taken turns standing guard over Matt, although with his hands tied behind his back and his torso lashed to the stake, he wasn't about to go anywhere.

He supposed it made them feel like they were accomplishing something to stand there clutching their old rifles and glaring at him.

Matt didn't look directly at them. He didn't want to give them the satisfaction of letting them see what bad shape he was really in. The sun had baked his brain until his vision was fuzzy, his thoughts were clouded, and despair gripped his heart. He felt like the heat had leached every bit of moisture out of his body. His tongue was swollen and his mouth as dry as cotton.

His head drooped forward, but he wouldn't allow himself to pass out. Even though he was helpless, he wanted to know what was going on around him.

Because of that, he saw movement as someone approached him late that afternoon. The sun had started its slide toward the western horizon, which gave him a certain amount of blessed relief although the canyon still felt like an oven.

Through slitted eyes, Matt watched as Juan Pablo walked up to him, as haughty, cruel, and arrogant as if he were old Manuelito come back to life.

"Bodine," Juan Pablo said. "This day has taught you that the Navajo are still a proud people."

"I never . . . doubted that." Matt had to force the words out through his parched throat and mouth and past blistered lips. "But there is no pride . . . in cruelty. You have . . . nothing to be proud of . . . Juan Pablo."

The man's face darkened in anger. He stepped closer and backhanded Matt viciously across the face.

The blow brought a cry of alarm and outrage from Elizabeth. She started to get to her feet, but Juan Pablo's wife, who stood near her, clamped a hand on her shoulder and forced her back down on the ground.

"For too many years, my people have done what the white man told them to do," Juan Pablo said. "They have treated us like animals! They have told themselves they are being generous to us by allowing us to live on our own land, while at the same time they try to take more and more of that land away from the Diné. But soon they will all be gone. We will drive them out."

"A couple dozen of you?" Matt asked. "How are you going to do that? You won't stand a chance."

"More men will come, from all over this land you white men call the Four Corners." Juan Pablo sneered. "As if your states truly mean anything. They are false boundaries." He swept an arm around him. "Everything, as far as a man can ride on a good pony, belongs to the Diné. And when the other clans hear that we are driving the whites from our midst, they will come to help us. The uprising will spread and soon will be complete. Then all those who are not Diné will either leave . . . or die."

There was a slim chance Juan Pablo was right, at least partially, Matt thought. He had studied enough history to know that most revolutions started small. The ones that succeeded grew until they reached the point where they couldn't be stopped.

But that wouldn't happen here. It couldn't. There weren't enough Navajo to stand up to the army. Even if Juan Pablo was able to get all the clans to rise in rebellion, the cavalry would come in and crush them. Many of the men would be slaughtered, and the rest would be rounded up and probably forced back to Bosque Redondo with their families.

It would be a tragedy all the way around.

Juan Pablo was too worked up to see that. His eyes glowed with the fervent belief of a would-be messiah. He saw himself as the one who would lead his people to well-deserved glory.

Instead, he would just lead them to death, Matt knew.

It wouldn't do any good to say that. Juan Pablo was long past the point where he could hear it.

Still, Matt had to try. He said, "If you let us go, Miss Fleming and I will try to help your people. We'll tell everyone that the Navajo land should be left to the Navajo."

Juan Pablo shook his head.

"You think those who have built the town of Flat Rock will abandon it? You think the white ranchers who have driven their cattle onto our land will take them away?"

He was right about that, Matt thought bleakly. Once settlers had moved into an area, they hardly ever gave it up. The government would have to force them to do so, and Matt didn't figure there was much sentiment in Washington for something like that.

"There's no reason you can't all learn to live together," he said.

A bark of fierce laughter came from Juan Pablo.

"Foolishness," the Navajo declared. "The rattlesnake and the scorpion are more trustworthy than the white man."

Matt sighed. He was at the end of his rope. He just wished there was some way he could save Elizabeth.

Maybe Caballo Rojo wouldn't allow Juan Pablo to kill her. The headman had let her stay here in the canyon and try to teach the children. He must have thought she was doing some good for his people.

But as the sun dipped below the peaks to the west and a red glare filled the sky, Matt looked at Juan Pablo and saw the fanatical glare on the man's face.

Caballo Rojo was no longer the most powerful man in this canyon.

Juan Pablo was, and he would delight in exercising that power.

Suddenly, one of the Navajo men came running toward them, shouting in what sounded like alarm. Juan Pablo swung around sharply.

The words flowed swiftly as the newcomer reported to Juan Pablo. Matt couldn't follow any of what was being said.

But he didn't like the cruel smile on Juan Pablo's lips as the man turned back to him.

"Your friend has returned," Juan Pablo said. "He approaches the canyon now, with two more white men."

Matt's heart sank. Under any other circumstances, he would have been very happy to hear that Sam was back. Now, though, his blood brother was riding into a trap and didn't know it. If there was just some way to warn him . . .

Matt opened his mouth to shout. He didn't know if the sound would carry beyond the canyon walls, but he could try, anyway.

Before he could make a sound, Juan Pablo stepped forward and struck swiftly with the rifle he held. He rammed the butt into Matt's stomach, causing Matt to gasp and double over as much as the ropes would allow.

Juan Pablo brought the rifle up and crashed the stock against Matt's jaw. The brutal blow drove Matt's head back against the thick stake to which he was tied. The double impact sent red explosions cascading through Matt's brain.

When those explosions faded, nothing was left except an all-enveloping blackness.

Chapter 32

The sun was down by the time Sam, Stovepipe, and Wilbur reached the Navajo canyon, but the western sky was still filled with a reddish-gold glow.

During the ride down here from the mesa where the rustlers had been holed up, Sam and Stovepipe had discussed the situation and agreed that everything they had discovered so far supported the theory they had put together.

"Big question is, who's behind it," Stovepipe said. "Got to be somebody in Flat Rock."

Sam nodded.

"There's another big question," he said. "Where are those rifles?"

"Also in Flat Rock, or somewhere close by. That'd be my guess, anyway. I don't reckon the boss would want them too far away from him until he's ready to try deliverin' 'em to the Navajo again."

"I wonder how come he's waited this long," Wilbur put in.

Stovepipe pointed a thumb at Sam.

"I reckon that's because of our new pard here."

"Me?" Sam said.

"Yeah, you and your friend Bodine. You spooked the fella who's in charge of this bunch. He wanted to make sure you weren't gonna cause too much trouble before he tried deliverin' the guns again. That's why folks keep tryin' to shoot you." Stovepipe frowned. "You know you might as well've painted a big ol' target on your back, the way you rode into Flat Rock and started pokin' around."

Sam chuckled.

"Well, I was trying to stir up a hornet's nest," he said. "I guess I succeeded."

"I'll say you did," Wilbur agreed.

Sam pointed to the mouth of the canyon up ahead on their right.

"That's where we're headed," he told his two companions.

A worried frown appeared on Wilbur's face.

"Those Indians aren't gonna try to lift our hair, are they?" he asked.

"They were friendly enough when I left," Sam said.

That was only partially true, he thought. Caballo Rojo had tolerated the presence of the blood brothers, and Juan Pablo had barely contained his hostility toward them, only because his clan headman said so.

Sam had been gone for several days, and he knew that things could have changed during that time. But he hoped that he and his companions could ride into the canyon without putting their lives in too much danger.

Anyway, Matt was there, so Sam didn't have much choice in the matter. He had to find out how his blood brother was doing.

They rode into the mouth of the canyon. Sam glanced up at the spots on the walls where sentries were usually posted. He didn't see anybody, but that didn't concern him greatly. The light was growing dimmer, and anyway, the Navajo were seen only when they wanted to be seen.

Sam looked along the creek. The first of the hogans wouldn't be visible until they were deeper in the canyon. He listened and heard the bleating of sheep somewhere up ahead. That was a perfectly normal sound, and he probably would have thought something was wrong if he hadn't heard it.

But at the same time, his nerves had grown taut. Something *was* wrong, he realized, although he didn't know what it was.

Stovepipe must have shared some of the same instincts. The lanky range detective began, "I'm startin' to get a bad feelin' about—"

He didn't have a chance to finish. Men suddenly rushed out of the brush on both sides of the riders. Sam twisted in the saddle to see who was attacking them. He had time to recognize the Navajo clothing, then one of the men reached up in an attempt to grab him and haul him off his horse.

Sam kicked the man in the chest and knocked him

away. He started to yank his mount around, calling to Stovepipe and Wilbur as he did so.

"Get out of the canyon!" he told them. "Back the way we—"

Something crashed into the back of his left shoulder and made him slump forward over the neck of his horse. Sam thought at first he'd been hit by an arrow, but then he realized that would have been a sharper pain. From the way his arm had gone numb, he figured out that he'd been clouted by a club.

The Navajo warriors swarmed around the three riders. Wilbur drew his gun, but a club knocked it out of his hand before he could fire. Men grabbed Stovepipe and dragged him off his horse. Sam found himself hauled to the ground as well.

Heavily outnumbered as they were, Sam knew their chances of winning this fight were slim. He had no idea why Caballo Rojo's men were attacking them, but that answer could wait for later.

Right now he just wanted to break free and get out of here.

That wasn't fated to happen. Another club smashed into the back of his knees and made his legs collapse under him. Men pummeled and kicked him as he went to the ground.

Sam couldn't see Stovepipe and Wilbur any more, but he doubted if they were faring any better. He could hear the commotion as the struggle continued nearby.

Sam grabbed an attacker's leg and heaved, upending the man. That gave him a little breathing room.

He launched a kick of his own and landed it solidly in another man's groin. As the Navajo warriors fell back for a second, Sam rolled onto hands and knees and started to lever himself to his feet.

Before he could get up, a club struck him in the back of the head, sending him sprawling to the ground again. He landed with his face in the reddish dirt. The taste of it filled his mouth. He felt consciousness slipping away from him and tried desperately to hang on to it, but the effort was doomed.

The last thing he was aware of before oblivion claimed him was the brutal thud of moccasin-shod feet landing on his ribs.

Red light flickered and glared against Matt's eyelids, gradually rousing him from the stupor that gripped him. He groaned as he moved his head from side to side in an attempt to shake loose some of the cobwebs from his brain.

The movement was a mistake. It made Matt feel like he was spinning crazily through a hellish void. When he forced his eyes open and saw flames leaping up in front of him, that only reinforced the feeling.

But it was just a campfire, he realized after a moment. He sagged against the ropes binding him to the post. His captors had built a fire that lit up the area in front of Juan Pablo's hogan.

And he was no longer the only prisoner, Matt saw to his horror.

A few yards away, Sam Two Wolves sprawled

motionless on the ground. For a terrible few seconds, Matt thought his blood brother was dead.

Then he saw the slow rise and fall of Sam's chest and knew that he was still alive. Relief flooded through Matt.

It was tempered by concern, though, because Sam was unconscious and Matt couldn't tell what had happened to him. Sam might be badly wounded and dying even as Matt stood there staring at him.

Two men Matt had never seen before lay near Sam. Both were white and looked like cowboys. They appeared to be out cold, too. All three men had their hands tied behind their backs.

Matt looked around for Elizabeth and didn't see her. She might be in Juan Pablo's hogan, he thought. Juan Pablo wasn't visible, either, but two of his followers stood nearby, holding rifles and scowling at Matt and the other prisoners.

Sam groaned, causing Matt's attention to snap back to him. After a moment, Sam shook his head and blinked his eyes open. He winced as the garish light from the fire struck his face. Then he lifted his head a little and started to look around.

"Over here, Sam," Matt called softly.

Sam muttered something Matt couldn't make out. He blinked again as he stared toward the post where Matt was tied.

"Matt?" he said. "Is that you?"

"Yeah, it's me." A grim smile curved Matt's mouth. "I'd come over there and let you loose, but—"

"You're not going to say that you're a little tied up at the moment, are you?"

"I was thinkin' about it, yeah."

"I can see that. Is that Juan Pablo's hogan?"

"Yeah."

"I take it this is his doing?"

One of the Navajo guards spoke sharply in his native tongue. He gestured with the rifle, and Matt knew he was telling them to be quiet.

Matt ignored the guard and said, "That's right. He plans to lead the clan in an uprising and try to get the other clans to join in. But they won't stand a chance."

"They might with nearly five hundred new Springfields to lure the other clans into joining them," Sam said.

Matt's eyes widened.

"Five hundred Springfields?" he repeated. "What are you talkin' about, Sam?"

"If Juan Pablo is the leader of this would-be rebellion, then he has some white allies. The gang that bushwhacked us in the first place stole a shipment of rifles bound for Fort Defiance. They were about to deliver them to the Navajo when you and I came along and fouled up the works."

Matt struggled to wrap his mind around what Sam was telling him.

"You know this for a fact?" he asked.

"At the moment, I don't have any proof, but I'm reasonably sure the theory is correct."

"That's good enough for me," Matt said. "Who are those two rannihans with you?"

Before Sam could answer, the guard who had tried to get them to stop talking earlier stepped closer and aimed a kick at Sam's head. Sam rolled out of the way and pulled his legs around in a sudden move, sweeping the Navajo's legs out from under him. The man let out a startled yell and then hit the ground.

"Maybe not the smartest thing you've ever done," Matt said as the guard scrambled back to his feet with murder in his dark eyes.

At that moment, Juan Pablo stepped out of the hogan. He barked an order at the guard, who stopped in his tracks and then moved back with obvious reluctance.

Juan Pablo stood over Sam and said, "When the time comes for you to die, half-breed, I will kill you. You betray your blood by siding with the white men. You no longer deserve to live."

"What about you?" Sam demanded. "You're liable to get a bunch of your people killed if you go through with your plans."

"And those who are left will mourn their deaths. But the people who live will be free. The white men will be gone."

Matt said, "It'll never happen, Juan Pablo. The government won't let it. They'll send in the army to wipe you out."

"This is our land. We know how to fight here better than the white man's army."

Much as Matt hated to admit it, Juan Pablo had a point there. The Navajo knew this country, knew how to survive here, knew how to strike hard against the enemy and then hide. Normally a peaceful people, content to farm and hunt, to weave blankets and make jewelry, when aroused they could be fierce, implacable foes. Kit Carson had learned that, back in the old days.

Rooting them out of this wasteland and rounding them up wouldn't be easy . . . but the army had almost limitless resources to do so.

That wasn't the case with the Navajo. They could fight a war and deal out plenty of damage . . . but in the end they would lose.

Juan Pablo didn't want to hear that. So Matt asked him, "What are you going to do with us?"

"You will all die, of course. When the sun comes up tomorrow morning, you will be killed." Juan Pablo's lips curved in a cruel smile. "You will be the first to die from the weapons that will save our people."

"What do you—" Matt began, but before he could finish the question, Juan Pablo turned and strode away, taking the guards with him and ignoring the prisoners now as if they were no longer worthy of his notice.

It didn't really matter. Matt had a hunch he knew what Juan Pablo meant by that threat.

Sam did, too. He said, "The Springfields. Juan Pablo's going to get those army rifles tonight."

Matt nodded.

"Yeah, that's the way it sounded to me, too. We've got to get loose and find a way to stop him. He's gonna get a lot of people killed for no good reason."

As if to punctuate Matt's statement, a swift rataplan of hoofbeats sounded in the night, fading as the riders moved away.

"That's Juan Pablo and some of his men going to take delivery on those rifles," Sam said.

"Yeah," Matt agreed. "And they'll bring 'em right back here so Juan Pablo can have his little firing squad in the morning."

One of the men who had been brought in with Sam began to stir. He lifted his shaggy head and shook it. After a moment his bleary-eyed gaze landed on Sam.

"Thought you said these Navajo were friends of yours, Sam."

"I said they didn't kill us and they let Matt stay here to recover from those bullet holes. That's a big difference from being our friends."

"Yeah, I reckon." The man looked at Matt with his deep-set eyes. "You'd be Matt Bodine?"

"That's right," Matt said. "Who are you?"

"A fella who wishes we'd gotten a mite more hospitable reception. Name's Stovepipe Stewart."

Sam said, "And this other fella is Wilbur Coleman." Sam lowered his voice. "They're range detectives, Matt. They've been helping me track down the men who bushwhacked us and figure out what it's all about."

"Stolen Springfield rifles, I'm bettin'," Matt said.

"You'd win that bet," said Stovepipe. "How's Wilbur?"

"He's breathing," Sam said, "but he's still out. I guess they dragged the two of you out of your saddles and walloped you with clubs, too."

"Yeah. From the way my ol' noggin feels, they got in some good licks, too." Stovepipe rolled his shoulders to get some of the kinks out. "Well, you boys tell me what's goin' on, why don't you?"

"Juan Pablo intends to murder us at dawn," Matt said.

"By shooting us with those Springfields," Sam added. "Which means he's going to get them tonight."

"Dang it. I guess the big boss in Flat Rock decided he didn't need to wait no longer. Or maybe this here Juan Pablo fella sent word to him that he's got all four of us hogtied, so he's anxious to get rid of us while he's got the chance." Stovepipe sighed. "I wish we had ol' John Henry and the boys from the Devil's Pitchfork with us again right about now."

"All right," Matt said. "One of you is going to have to explain all that."

For the next five minutes, both Sam and Stovepipe filled him in on everything that had happened since the blood brothers split up, along with explaining the theory they had worked out about some gang trying to start an Indian war so they could take over after the army forced the Navajo out of the Four Corners.

"That makes sense," Matt said when they were finished. "Do you know who's behind it?"

"No clue," Stovepipe said.

Sam added, "We figure they're operating out of the settlement, but we don't even know that for sure."

Wilbur groaned and started to come around. Stovepipe scooted over closer to him and said quietly, "Take it easy, pard. You're all right. We're sorta between a rock and a hard place at the moment, but we'll get out of it."

"Speakin' of rocks, I feel like an avalanche landed on top of me," Wilbur said. "And I'm tied up, blast it!"

"We all are," Stovepipe told him dryly.

"Well, when we get loose, we're gonna have a heap of score-settlin' to do, that's all I can say!"

"You're right about that, pard—"

Stovepipe broke off with a sharp intake of breath as he glanced toward Matt.

A second later, Matt knew why the range detective had reacted that way. He heard the shuffle of soft footsteps behind him, and then he felt the touch of cold steel against his skin.

Chapter 33

Matt's breath froze in his throat for a second as he felt the knife press against his wrist.

Then the blade moved, and the tug that came on one of the ropes binding him told him that the keen edge was sawing through it.

The rope parted and fell away. Whoever was wielding the knife moved on to one of the others and started cutting through it.

Matt's hands had gone numb from being tied so tightly. As the blood began to rush back into his fingers, he felt like they were being stabbed with thousands of tiny pins.

Painful though it might be, it was a good feeling.

"I don't know who's back there," he said in a half-whisper, "but I'm sure obliged to you for turning me loose."

"I think it's Juan Pablo's wife," Sam said. "I couldn't see very well in the shadows, but it certainly looked like a woman."

The last of the ropes came loose. After the ordeal of that long, blistering day he had gone through, he almost fell without their support.

He caught himself and half-turned, reaching out to grasp the stake to which he had been tied. Bracing himself with that grip, he looked into the stolid face of the Navajo woman who had fed him and tended to his wounds.

"Gracias," he told her. Maybe she would understand his gratitude if he expressed it in Spanish. He waved his free hand toward the other prisoners. "Can you cut my friends loose, too?"

Before Juan Pablo's wife could even take a step in their direction, Sam said, "Matt, somebody's coming!"

Matt bit back a curse. He straightened and grabbed the knife away from the woman. She let him take it, willingly.

"Better get back in the hogan," he said. "You don't want them knowing you helped us, whoever it is."

She might not have understood the words, but fear was universal. She turned and scurried into the earthen dwelling, the long skirt rustling around her legs as she moved.

Matt heard voices coming closer. There wasn't time to cut Sam, Stovepipe, and Wilbur loose from their bonds before the men got there.

So, clutching the knife, Matt broke into a shambling run that carried him around the hogan and out of the circle of light cast by the fire.

He leaned against the hogan to catch his breath. Even that momentary burst of action had winded him.

As he stood there, he heard startled yells from the returning guards when they realized he was gone. The men shouted what sounded like questions at Sam and the other two prisoners, who didn't respond.

At any moment now, they would come searching for him, Matt thought. He drew himself deeper into the shadows behind the hogan and waited.

The angry voices split up, which was a lucky break for Matt. As weak as he was, he couldn't have fought two men at once. He knew he'd be doing good to deal with one of the guards.

His fingers tightened on the handle of the knife as one of the men came around the hogan toward him. They probably thought he had fled, abandoning the others, and wouldn't expect to find him lurking so close by.

The man's footsteps thudded on the ground. Matt saw him loom up out of the darkness.

He struck without warning as the guard stepped past him, bringing down the butt end of the knife's handle against the back of the Navajo's head. The blow drove the man to his knees. Matt kicked him in the back and sent him sprawling. His rifle clattered on the ground.

Matt sprang forward and grabbed the weapon. A shot might rouse others along the creek, so he used the stock to knock the guard out cold.

Panting from the exertion, Matt turned from the unconscious man just in time to see the other guard charging at him from the shadows.

He still had hold of the rifle, so he thrust it out in

front of him like a spear. The second Navajo's momentum carried him into the barrel, which dug deep into his belly and doubled him over. Matt stepped forward and brought his knee up, catching the man under the chin.

The guard went down, just as unconscious as his companion.

Matt fell against the hogan. Battling the two men had taken every bit of his strength.

But he had to summon up more from somewhere, he told himself, because Sam and the two range detectives were still prisoners. With a groan, Matt pushed himself away from the hogan and started around it at a shambling run.

He emerged into the firelight and was almost at the entrance when Elizabeth Fleming ran out of the hogan and almost collided with him. She grabbed his arm to steady herself and exclaimed, "Oh!"

"Are you . . . all right?" Matt asked, still breathless and dizzy.

"Yes, Josefina just untied me."

Matt had to think for a second to remember that Josefina was the name of Juan Pablo's wife. He had heard it used only occasionally.

From the ground nearby, Sam asked, "Matt, what happened to those two guards?"

"They're both . . . knocked out . . . for now."

"Better cut us loose while you got the chance," Stovepipe said.

"Give me the knife," Elizabeth suggested. "You look like you're about to fall down, Matt."

"Feel like it . . . too." He pressed the knife into her hands. "Be careful, but . . . don't waste any time."

As Elizabeth took the knife and knelt beside Sam, Matt saw movement from the corner of his eye and turned to look toward the hogan's entrance. He saw the woman emerging from the dwelling with her arms full of gunbelts and holstered revolvers.

"Son of a gun!" Matt said as he recognized his own twin Colts. "They were . . . hidden in there . . . the whole time!"

The woman practically dumped the weapons into his hands. He staggered a little under their weight.

When Matt turned toward the prisoners again, he saw that Elizabeth had succeeded in freeing Sam. His blood brother leaped to his feet and flexed his hands a few times to get the blood flowing in them again.

"Give me my gun," he said as he came over to Matt.

Sam took his gunbelt and strapped it around his hips. Stovepipe was free by then, and he hurried over to retrieve his revolver as well, followed by Wilbur.

Matt felt strength flow back into him as he buckled on the pair of Colts. It might not be real—the return of his guns had buoyed his spirits, and that could account for the fresh energy—but for now he would take it.

"I'm not sure what's goin' on here," he said, "but it sure does feel good to be free again."

"You can thank Josefina for that," Elizabeth said. She still clutched the knife, which Matt now recognized as Sam's bowie. "It was her idea to cut you loose and to untie me."

"Why would she betray her husband like that?" Sam asked as he took the knife from Elizabeth and slid it into the sheath attached to his gunbelt.

With a grim little smile, Elizabeth said, "It was either that or cut my throat, and don't think she didn't consider doing that instead."

"But why?" Matt asked.

"She freed us so you can take me out of the canyon and get me far away from Juan Pablo."

"Oh," Matt said as understanding dawned on him.

"What're you talkin' about?" Wilbur said. "You mean—Oh, shoot!"

His face was already red in the firelight. It became more so as he flushed.

"Yes, he was going to take me as a second wife once his armed uprising succeeded. Josefina doesn't want that. So she thought that if she turned you loose, you'd escape and take me with you."

"She was right about that," Matt said. "Where are our horses?"

Elizabeth took hold of his arm.

"Come on, I'll show you."

The group hurried along the creek for a quarter of a mile, then Elizabeth led them to a brush corral where a number of horses milled around. It was dark away from the fire in front of Juan Pablo's hogan, but Elizabeth had been here in the canyon for months and knew her way around, even when she had to navigate by starlight.

"Our horses still have the saddles on them, Matt," Sam said, "but I don't see yours."

"That's all right," Matt told him. "I can ride bareback if it means getting out of here." He paused. "We have to stop Juan Pablo, Sam. If he gets his hands on those rifles, innocent folks will die."

"I know," Sam agreed. "But I'm not sure where we'll find the place the gang plans to deliver them."

Stovepipe said, "I reckon if it was me, I'd head for the spot where they planned to turn 'em over to the Navajo the first time . . . that bluff where you two boys got bushwhacked to start this fandango."

Matt and Sam exchanged a glance and nodded to each other.

"It's worth a try," Sam said. "Let's get mounted up. Elizabeth, you can take one of the saddled horses. I'll ride bareback, like Matt."

"You don't have to do that," she said.

"Don't worry," Sam told her with a grin. "Remember, I'm half-Cheyenne. I was riding without a saddle almost before I could walk."

"He's telling the truth," Matt said.

The horses inside the corral were nervous, but Sam, Stovepipe, and Wilbur were adept at handling them. They moved the brush gate aside and led out the animals they wanted, and a moment later all five riders were mounted.

"We'll have to get past the guards at the mouth of the canyon," Sam said. "They're not expecting trouble from in here—"

As if to give the lie to his words, shouts of alarm suddenly rang out, echoing back from the canyon walls.

The two guards Matt had knocked out must have regained consciousness.

"Blast it!" Matt exclaimed. "I should've cut their throats, or at least gagged them!"

"I'm glad you didn't kill them," Elizabeth said. "Juan Pablo is leading them into trouble, but they're not bad people at heart."

Stovepipe said, "No offense, ma'am, but I reckon they'll ventilate us if they get half a chance."

"We'll have to try not to give them a chance," Sam said. He urged his horse into a gallop. "Let's go!"

Chapter 34

Zack Jardine tossed back the glass of whiskey and thumped the empty onto the table.

"Angus should have been back by now," he said with a dark scowl. "Something happened out there."

Dave Snyder, Joe Hutto, and Doyle Hilliard were sitting at the table with Jardine. Hilliard, who was Braverman's best friend, leaned forward and with a worried frown on his face asked, "You want me to take a ride out to that mesa, Zack? I can find out what's goin' on."

Jardine considered the suggestion for a moment, then shook his head.

"No. The cattle don't matter that much. We're gonna get those rifles in the hands of the Navajo tonight, and by this time tomorrow, the war will be started and nothing can stop it."

Hilliard, Snyder, and Hutto looked surprised. This was the first they had heard about delivering the rifles to the Indians tonight. They had to be wondering how the arrangements had been made, since Jardine had been right here in Flat Rock all day.

Jardine smiled faintly at that thought. He liked to keep a few of his cards close to the vest, and one of them was the fact that he had a partner in this enterprise, a partner none of the other men knew about.

That partner was the one who had ridden out and met with Juan Pablo earlier today, after Two Wolves had formed that unlikely alliance with the Devil's Pitchfork crew.

When Jardine had heard about that, he had known that it was time to make their biggest move yet in this game. Being cautious was all well and good, but at some point decisive action was needed.

This was that point.

"Go down to the Mexican's place and get the wagon ready," Jardine went on. "Bring it to the alley behind the saloon, and we'll go get the guns."

His men didn't know where the rifles were hidden. Only Jardine and his partner knew that, because they had unloaded the crates after the first attempt to deliver the rifles to the Navajo.

The time for secrecy was over, though.

"All right, boss," Snyder said. "Do we get all the other fellas who are in town together?"

"That's right. We'll all ride out with the wagon."

That was only seven or eight men. The other members of the gang were either wounded or out at the mesa with the rustled cattle.

But that ought to be enough, Jardine told himself.

Nobody knew what was really going on here, so they couldn't prepare for it.

The three men hurried out of the Buckingham Palace. Jardine poured himself another drink and leaned back in his chair to enjoy it. His gaze roamed across the room and lingered on the beautiful Lady Augusta Winslow, who stood at the bar talking to one of the bartenders.

Jardine's eyes narrowed. Once he was the King of the Four Corners, that lovely but stuck-up British bitch would be his for the taking. She wouldn't dare turn him down. He had made a few advances already, only to be politely rebuffed.

She would learn, he thought. He would do the teaching, and it would be a lesson Lady Augusta would never forget.

He'd intended to sip the whiskey this time, but thinking about what he would do with the English-woman made him swallow the fiery stuff fast. He stood up and went out the side door, then along the alley to the back of the building.

His men showed up with the wagon about ten minutes later, with Hilliard at the reins. Jardine climbed to the seat and took over the team, forcing Hilliard aside. He was the only one who knew where he was going.

He drove along the back alley behind the buildings along Flat Rock's main street. When he came to one of the larger buildings, he brought the vehicle to a stop and got down. The building was made of boards freighted in from Phoenix. The floor sat on piers, so there was a crawl space underneath it.

Jardine went up some steps to a small rear porch and knocked on the door there. A moment later it opened and a man stepped out.

"It's time," Jardine said. "Let's get those rifles out."

"Of course," Noah Reilly said. "I'll be glad to get them out of here."

Reilly came down the steps, took a key from his pocket, and used it to unfasten a padlock on a short door that opened into the crawl space under the general store. He stepped aside so Jardine could reach inside and grasp the handle on the end of the nearest crate.

It hadn't been easy for the two of them to wrestle those crates into and out of the crawl space, but Reilly was stronger than his small stature would indicate. Still, Jardine was glad that after tonight they wouldn't have to do this anymore.

Jardine grunted with effort as he slid the first crate out.

"Load it up," he told his men. He reached into the crawl space for another.

He supposed his men were surprised to find out that he and Reilly were working together. That wouldn't be the case much longer, Jardine thought. Reilly had some idea that once they were successful, he would be the power behind the throne, so to speak, because the whole plan had been his idea to start with.

Jardine wasn't going to let that happen. Once the Navajo had launched their bloody uprising and the army came in, Reilly wouldn't be any more use. Jardine could get rid of him without jeopardizing anything, and that was exactly what he planned to do.

Of course, Jardine thought as he pulled another crate out into the alley, Reilly might have the same thing in mind for him. If that was the case, the little storekeeper was going to be mighty disappointed.

But not for long, since he'd be dead soon.

The other men didn't say anything. They just lifted the crates of rifles and slid them over the lowered tailgate into the wagon. Curious or not, they knew to keep their mouths shut.

"Can you find the rendezvous point in the dark?" Reilly asked Jardine when all the guns were loaded.

"Don't worry about that," Jardine said. "I know these parts better than you do. We'll be there a couple of hours before dawn."

"Juan Pablo should be waiting for you." Even in the gloom of the alley, starlight reflected off the lenses of Reilly's spectacles. "And in another month or so, we'll be well on our way to being rich men."

Jardine grunted.

"Can't be too soon to suit me," he said.

"That's true for me as well. I've spent my entire life working for other men. But not much longer."

Jardine tried not to grin. Taking orders was really all that little varmints like Reilly were good for. They didn't have any business being in charge of anything. Not like big, strong hombres like him.

"Let's go," he said curtly to his men. "We've got rifles to deliver. See you tomorrow, Noah."

"Good luck," Reilly called as Jardine stepped up onto the wagon box again.

"Thanks," Jardine said, but he knew he didn't really need luck.

He was going to be the King of the Four Corners. It was his destiny.

Matt, Sam, Elizabeth, Stovepipe, and Wilbur sent their horses racing along the creek toward the mouth of the canyon. Matt hoped Elizabeth was a good rider. In the dark like this, it would be easy for a horse to take a spill.

The guards who were shouting for help were between them and the canyon mouth. As the five riders came closer, men carrying rifles charged toward them.

"Hunker down!" Matt shouted as orange flame spurted from the muzzles of those rifles.

They leaned forward, over the necks of their mounts, to make themselves harder to hit. Matt sensed as much as heard a bullet humming past his head, but that was the closest any of the slugs came to him.

The Navajo who tried to stop them fell behind, as did the fire in front of Juan Pablo's hogan. Shots still blasted sporadically, but now the men were firing blindly and the chances of them hitting were very slim.

But even wild shots got lucky and found their targets every now and then, Matt knew, so he stayed low and kept his horse moving fast, and hoped that the others would, too.

He looked over his shoulder. The riders were strung out a little now. He was in the lead, followed by Stovepipe, Wilbur, and Elizabeth. Sam was bringing up the rear, and Matt knew his blood brother was doing that on purpose to protect Elizabeth.

They were almost at the mouth of the canyon now. Matt wasn't surprised when shots rang out from the sentries posted there.

Wilbur yelped in pain. Stovepipe turned to him and called, "How bad is it, pard?"

"Just nicked me, the varmint!" Wilbur replied. "Keep goin', Stovepipe. Don't slow down!"

"Wasn't intendin' to," Stovepipe said. "But you holler if you need any help, hear?"

Matt knew he was operating purely on the excitement of battle and the urgent need to escape from this canyon. He drew his right-hand Colt and triggered a few shots toward the places where he had seen the flare of the sentries' guns.

He wasn't really trying to hit anything. He just wanted to give them something to think about and make them duck.

From the back of the group, Sam's revolver roared, too. Matt knew he was trying to do the same thing.

The effort seemed to work. The running horses flashed past the sentries and through the entrance to the canyon. Now they were out in the open, with the cliffs rapidly falling behind them.

"Will . . . will they come after us?" Elizabeth gasped.

"I don't know," Sam said as he pulled his mount up

even with hers. "Juan Pablo left some of his followers behind to guard us and keep an eye on Caballo Rojo and the men who don't want a war. I don't know if they would risk leaving the canyon completely unguarded."

"Some of them might come after us, though," Matt said as the riders slowed slightly and grouped up again. "They won't want us to interfere with Juan Pablo gettin' his hands on those guns."

"But that's dang sure what we need to do," Stovepipe put in. "Think you can find the place where the gang was gonna turn 'em over before?"

"I believe I can," Sam said. "Matt was unconscious for a lot of that time, so he doesn't know exactly where it is."

"I trust you, though," Matt said. "I—Whoa!"

He swayed suddenly in his saddle as a wave of dizziness washed over him. Wilbur was close enough to reach out and grab his arm in a steadying grip.

"You're in no shape for this, Matt," Sam said. "We need to find a place where we can leave you and Elizabeth before we go after Juan Pablo and the rifles."

"Not hardly!" Matt shook his arm free from Wilbur's hand. "I'm obliged for your help," he told the redhead, "but I'm fine now. And I'm comin' along to help you stop Juan Pablo, Sam. You can get any other ideas out of your head right now."

"I see that being wounded hasn't kept you from being as stubborn as ever."

Elizabeth said, "Well, I'm stubborn, too, and you're not leaving me behind, either. You can't afford to take the time to find a safe place for Matt and me. The lives of too many innocent people are at stake."

"The lady's right about that," Stovepipe drawled. "But if you can't keep up, Matt, we may have to leave you behind."

"I'll keep up," Matt promised grimly. "Come on. We're burnin' starlight."

Stovepipe laughed.

"First time I've heard that one," he admitted.

With Sam in the lead now, they pushed on, stopping occasionally to rest the horses when it became obvious that none of the Navajo from the canyon were pursuing them. Without Juan Pablo there to tell them what to do, uncertainty probably reigned.

The stars wheeled through the dark heavens overhead. Matt figured it was well after midnight by now. The rush of blood that had kept him going earlier was wearing off now, and weariness gripped him.

As Sam had said, though, he was too blasted stubborn to give up. His iron will kept him in the saddle.

Then, finally, Sam held up a hand to signal a halt. As the others gathered around him, he said quietly, "That bluff where Matt and I were bushwhacked the first time is maybe half a mile away. We'd better dismount and go the rest of the way on foot. Elizabeth, can you hold the horses?"

"Of course," she said. "But what about Matt?"

He drew his Colt and replaced the shells he had fired earlier when they were escaping from the canyon.

"I'm going," he said as he snapped the revolver's

cylinder closed. He looked at Sam. "And don't try to stop me."

"Wouldn't think of it," his blood brother said. "Even with you in bad shape, there's nobody I'd rather have siding my play than you, Matt."

Stovepipe said, "All right, fellas, let's go see if we can catch us some gun-runners."

Chapter 35

Jardine hauled back on the lines and brought the wagon to a stop. Around him, his men reined in as well.

The dark, looming bulk of the bluff told Jardine that they were in the right place. He had been confident in his ability to find his way out here, even at night, but it was nice to know that he'd been right.

Now all they had to do was wait for Juan Pablo to show up.

The man was a damn fool, Jardine thought with a wry smile. Juan Pablo actually believed he could rouse the whole Navajo nation against the whites and lead his people to victory. He had no idea how doomed to failure they really were.

That failure would lead to Jardine's success, though. Once the Navajo were cleaned out of the territory like the vermin they were, the way would be clear for a man with guts and brains to seize power . . . a man like him, Jardine thought with a self-congratulatory smile as he took a cigar from his shirt pocket and clamped it between his teeth.

"How will we know when the Indians are here, boss?" Snyder asked from his horse as he brought the animal alongside the wagon.

"They should be here already," Jardine said. He turned halfway around on the seat and reached behind him into the wagon bed. Finding the lantern that was sitting there, he lifted it and set it on the seat beside him.

Then he snapped a lucifer to life with his thumbnail, lit the lantern, and held the flame to the tip of the cigar, puffing until it was burning, too. He stood up, held the lantern out at the end of his arm, and swung it back and forth three times.

"That's the signal, eh?" Snyder asked.

"Shut up and be ready for trouble," Jardine said as he set the lantern on the wagon seat again. "There shouldn't be any, but I don't trust those damned redskins."

Jardine left the lantern burning. He picked up his own rifle and sat with it across his lap. An air of tension gripped him, and he knew it extended to his men as well.

The Navajo weren't paying anything for the rifles, although Juan Pablo had promised payment later on, once they had run out all the whites.

Jardine fully expected Juan Pablo to try to doublecross him on that angle, although Juan Pablo had no idea that Jardine didn't really care.

But the Indians might try to get fancy and kill

the men who had delivered the rifles to them. It was unlikely, but it could happen.

If it did, the Navajo would learn quickly that half a dozen tough men armed with Winchester repeaters were more than a match for a motley bunch of savages armed with bows, arrows, and a few ancient single-shot rifles.

If it became necessary, Jardine would wipe out Juan Pablo and the men he brought with him, then start over and arrange a deal with some other power-hungry redskin. The delay in his plans that would cause would be mighty annoying, but unavoidable.

Don't borrow trouble, he told himself. Maybe everything would go off without a hitch tonight.

Jardine suddenly sat up straighter as he heard hoofbeats. Somebody was coming, and it had to be Juan Pablo. Who else would be out here in this isolated spot at such a wee hour of the morning?

Jardine heard a few muttered curses as his men gripped their rifles tighter and waited for the newcomers to arrive. As the hoofbeats thudded to a stop, Jardine stood up and lifted the lantern again so that its glow spread out on the arid, rocky landscape around the wagon.

He knew he was making a target out of himself, almost daring somebody to shoot at him, but at the moment he didn't care. He felt invulnerable, as if no one would ever dare to challenge him.

Soon enough, that would be the truth.

The lantern light revealed the glaring, hawk-like face of Juan Pablo, who was accompanied by five other Navajo warriors. Juan Pablo edged his pony ahead of the others and demanded, "You have the rifles?"

"Would we be here if he didn't?" Jardine shot back. He set the lantern on the wagon seat and waved his free hand toward the crates. "Here they are."

"Open the boxes. I would look at them."

Jardine smiled.

"You don't trust me, amigo?"

"I would look at them," Juan Pablo said again.

"All right, fine." Jardine turned to Snyder and Hilliard. "Pry the lid off one of those crates." He look at Juan Pablo again. "But only one. We're not going to sit out here the rest of the night prying lids off and nailing them back on."

Juan Pablo's scowl didn't lessen any, but he gave a curt nod of agreement.

When Snyder and Hilliard had one of the crates open, the Navajo moved his pony nearer the wagon and leaned over so he could look into the bed. The rifles were wrapped in oilcloth.

"Show me," Juan Pablo snapped.

"Oh, for God's sake," Jardine muttered. "Dave, get one of the guns out."

Snyder unwrapped one of the Springfields and used a rag to wipe the packing grease off it.

Juan Pablo held his hands out.

Snyder glanced at Jardine, who nodded. He handed the rifle to Juan Pablo, who snatched it and held it close to study it. The Navajo weighed the weapon in his hands, then opened the loading mechanism in the breech that gave the rifle its "Trapdoor" designation.

"Bullets?"

"Ten thousand rounds in those boxes," Jardine explained, pointing to the smaller boxes that contained the ammunition.

Juan Pablo shook his head.

"Not enough to fight a long war."

"But enough to get you started," Jardine said. "There's more ammunition in the settlements, and it'll be yours for the taking."

That was true, as far as it went. A lot of those rounds wouldn't fit these Springfields, but that wasn't his lookout, Jardine thought.

Anyway, all it would take was a couple of bloody raids and the army would be on its way from Fort Defiance to begin the forced removal—or extermination, if it came to that—of the Navajo.

Despite what Juan Pablo had just said, this wouldn't be a long war at all.

"All right," Juan Pablo finally said as he handed the rifle back to Snyder. "We will take the wagon, too."

"Of course," Jardine said. "That's part of the deal."

"When this is over, you and your men will be the only whites allowed on Navajo land."

"As we agreed," Jardine replied with a grave nod.

He stood up so that he could climb down from the wagon box again and turn the vehicle over to the Indians. His men had brought along an extra saddle horse for him to ride back to Flat Rock.

But before Jardine could get down, there was a

huge crash that shook the wagon, and the impact
flung him off and sent him tumbling to the ground.

Matt, Sam, Stovepipe, and Wilbur were all experi-
enced at moving quietly through the shadows when
they needed to, so they were able to approach the
bluff without alerting any of the men gathered at the
base of it.

Sam had spotted the lantern when it first flared to
life. The light gave them something to steer by and
confirmed their hope that the delivery of the rifles
would take place here where it had been supposed to
happen more than a week earlier.

They couldn't climb to the top of the bluff using
the trail Sam had found when he first explored this
place with Juan Pablo, so instead the four men had
circled around and found another place where the
bluff was shallower and could be climbed.

Juan Pablo had known all along what had happened here, Sam thought as they made their way
toward the rendezvous. Sam recalled how the Navajo
had tried to persuade him not to investigate.

He was lucky Juan Pablo hadn't just tried to kill
him outright. He probably would have if he hadn't
known that he would have to return to the canyon and
try to make Matt believe some lie about what had
happened. At that point, Juan Pablo might have still
been worried about crossing Caballo Rojo.

Now the renegade didn't care anymore. He wasn't
going to let anything or anyone stop him.

Or at least, that's what he thought.

The four men slipped along the edge of the bluff until they were above the spot where the white men were delivering the rifles to the Navajo. The big, cruelly handsome man on the wagon box seemed to be the leader of the gang. He gave the orders as Juan Pablo demanded to take a look at the merchandise he was getting.

Stovepipe tapped Sam on the shoulder and put his mouth almost against Sam's ear to whisper, "If we was to put our shoulders against the boulder there and roll it off, I reckon it'd fall right on top of that wagon."

The range detective was pointing at a good-sized boulder that perched at the very edge of the bluff. Sam studied the angles and realized that Stovepipe was right.

The boulder wouldn't be easy to budge, but if they could drop it on the wagon, it would probably bust the vehicle all the pieces, not to mention surprising the hell out of the gun-runners and the Navajo.

Sam nodded his agreement with the plan.

He motioned for Matt to stay back and let him, Stovepipe, and Wilbur shove the boulder off the bluff, but Matt shook his head and moved into position with them, planting his feet and resting his left shoulder against the rock.

They waited until the men below were talking again, then heaved against the boulder. The voices covered up any tiny scraping sounds the rock made as it shifted.

But it didn't shift enough to overbalance. Again the four men paused until the boss on the wagon gave more orders. When he did, they put their shoulders and legs into the effort.

Stone grated against earth, and suddenly the boulder was moving. With their feet dug in, Sam and the others continued to shove. The boulder tipped over . . .

And was gone, plummeting through the air to land with a huge, shattering crash in the back of the wagon below.

The abrupt lack of resistance made Sam, Matt, Stovepipe, and Wilbur sprawl at the edge of the bluff. Wilbur might have toppled over himself if Stovepipe's hand hadn't shot out to snag his collar and haul him back.

As they scrambled to their feet, Matt saw several of the white men recover quickly from their surprise and start to raise the rifles they held. Matt's hands dipped to his own twin Colts.

Wounded though he might be, Matt Bodine's draw was swift and a thing of beauty. The guns seemed to leap into his hands like magic. Less than a heartbeat later, Colt flame bloomed in the darkness as shots roared out from both revolvers.

A couple of the outlaws grunted and toppled out of their saddles as Matt's slugs ripped into their bodies.

Sam, Stovepipe, and Wilbur had their guns out and blasting by now, too. Sam snapped a shot at the boss of the gang, who had been knocked clear of the wagon when the boulder came crashing down on it.

The man scrambled to the side and avoided Sam's bullet. He had managed to hang on to his rifle. Working the lever with blinding speed, he sprayed lead toward the top of the bluff as he ran toward one of the suddenly riderless mounts.

That forced Matt, Sam, Stovepipe, and Wilbur to pull back and cease fire for a moment, and as they did, Juan Pablo kicked his horse forward and raced over to one of the shattered crates that had fallen out of the wagon. He reached into it and began pulling out rifles, which he tossed to his men as they followed him.

The men on the bluff continued to trade shots with the outlaws, and because they were occupied with that, they couldn't stop the handful of Navajo from looting the broken crate. Matt saw Juan Pablo grab a box of ammunition and leap back onto his pony. Matt snapped a shot at the warrior, but the bullet whined past Juan Pablo's head harmlessly.

"They're gettin' away with some of those rifles!" Matt called to Sam.

"I know!" his blood brother replied. "And the boss is getting away, too!"

Indeed, the leader of the gang had made it to one of the horses and swung up into the saddle. He kicked the animal into a run that carried him out of the circle of light cast by the lantern, which was still burning even though it had half-fallen against the rail at the side of the wagon seat.

With their boss deserting them, the rest of the gun smugglers lost their enthusiasm for the fight. Three of them were down. The others wheeled their horses and galloped off into the night, taking a different direction than the fleeing Navajo.

Matt lowered his guns and asked, "Now what do we do?"

The scream that cut through the night answered the question. The men's heads jerked toward the sound.

That scream came from Elizabeth Fleming, and as the cry was abruptly silenced, Matt knew that Juan Pablo must have stumbled over her.

Chapter 36

"That's Elizabeth!" Matt yelled. "Come on!"

Sam caught his arm. "She had our horses with her, and Juan Pablo's probably scattered them by now."

"But we've got to go after them!"

"There are a couple of horses down there," Sam said, nodding toward the mounts whose riders had been shot off of them. "Stovepipe and I will take them. You and Wilbur stay here and guard those rifles."

"Blast it, Sam—"

"The two of you are wounded," Sam cut in. "Stovepipe and I aren't. Anyway, somebody's got to guard those rifles, otherwise Juan Pablo is liable to circle back around and try to grab some more of them. So *he* may come to *you*."

"I hope so," Matt said as he reached for fresh cartridges in the loops on his shell belt. "I surely do."

Wilbur protested, "I ain't hurt that bad. I told you it was just a scratch, Stovepipe."

"I know that," the lanky range detective said as he

rested a hand on his partner's shoulder for a second, "but like Sam says, somebody's got to look after them guns, and I don't know anybody I'd trust more'n you to do it, pard."

"All right, all right," Wilbur grumbled. "Don't go butterin' me up. Just get after those varmints and help that girl."

"Plan to," Stovepipe said as he finished reloading his revolver and snapped it closed.

He and Sam made their way down the narrow trail to the base of the bluff, followed by Matt and Wilbur. The first thing Sam did when he reached the wrecked wagon was blow out the stubbornly burning lantern. The light just made them better targets.

During that brief moment when he'd gotten a good look at the wagon, he had seen that it would never go anywhere again, not without a lot of work, anyway. Both axles had snapped under the sudden weight of the boulder.

All twelve of the crates containing the rifles had broken open. Some of the weapons no doubt were ruined.

Most of them were still usable, though, and it would be up to Matt and Wilbur to make sure none of them wound up in the wrong hands, along with that ammunition.

Sam and Stovepipe caught the two remaining horses and swung up into the saddles they had emptied. Before they could ride off, Wilbur said, "Hey, we could unhitch a couple of horses from the wagon team—"

"No time," Sam said. "We've got to find Elizabeth."

He heeled his mount into a run toward the spot where they had left the redheaded teacher. Stovepipe was right beside him. Although Sam was trying to stay calm, worry gnawed at his guts.

As enraged as Juan Pablo was bound to be at having his plans ruined like this, there was no telling what he might do to Elizabeth to vent his anger.

Back at the wagon, Matt asked, "Did you get a good look at the hombre who was giving orders, Wilbur?"

"Pretty good, I reckon. Why?"

"You've been hangin' around the settlement for a while, according to what Sam said. Did you recognize that fella?"

"I don't know his name," Wilbur said, "but I recollect seein' him in the Buckingham a few times. You know, the way you see anybody in a saloon, drinkin' and playin' cards."

Matt nodded.

"Then we'll probably be able to find him in Flat Rock later. We've got some settlin' up to do with that hombre."

Wilbur snorted and said, "We'll be lucky to find him. He's probably takin' off for the tall and uncut right now. Won't stop until he gets to Denver or Santa Fe or El Paso."

"I think you're wrong," Matt said. "He's put a lot of time and effort into this scheme. He'll try to figure out some way to salvage it. If he could cause some trouble that he could blame on the Navajo . . . like maybe burning down the saloon or something . . . he might try it."

"You really think he'd do that?"

"Somebody who would steal a bunch of army rifles and try to turn them over to a troublemaker like Juan Pablo . . . I wouldn't put much of anything past him," Matt said.

The flame of rage burned so brightly inside Zack Jardine that it threatened to consume him. He had been close, so close, to achieving his goal . . .

And then like judgment striking literally from the heavens, that boulder had come crashing down and ruined everything.

He hadn't gotten a good look at the men who'd been shooting at him, but he was certain one of them was Sam Two Wolves. That blasted half-breed had been a thorn in his side ever since Two Wolves had shown up in Flat Rock.

Joe Hutto and Dave Snyder galloped up alongside Jardine. All the others had fallen to the volley of gunshots from the top of the bluff, including Doyle Hilliard. Jardine had seen him go down with blood spouting from a bullet hole in his chest.

"Zack, what are we gonna do now?" Hutto yelled over the pounding hoofbeats.

"It's all ruined!" Snyder added, echoing Jardine's thoughts.

But Jardine wouldn't let himself give up. He had

come too far, invested too much in this scheme. As he cudgeled his brain, an idea came to him.

"Head for Flat Rock!" he told the two men. "We're gonna grab that Englishwoman from the Buckingham Palace!"

"What good will that do?" Hutto wanted to know.

"Plenty, when Noah Reilly tells everybody that Indians carried her off! Everybody in town knows Reilly, and they'll believe him!"

The more Jardine thought about it, the more he believed the hastily formed plan stood a chance of working. Nothing stirred up frontiersmen quicker than a threat to a woman.

If the men of Flat Rock and the nearby ranches believed that Lady Augusta had been kidnapped by the Navajo, they would mount a rescue effort and go charging recklessly out to the canyon where the Navajo lived.

Juan Pablo would meet that attack with all the ferocity he and his followers could muster, even without those army rifles, and blood would be spilled on both sides.

That was all it would take, Jardine told himself.

The blood was the key to everything.

And that key would unlock the fortune that could still make Zack Jardine a rich man.

When Sam and Stovepipe reached the spot where they had left Elizabeth, they found her gone and the horses scattered, just as Sam expected.

"That was pure bad luck," he said as he brought his mount to a halt. "Juan Pablo and the others must have ridden right into her while they were trying to get away."

"You reckon they headed back to the canyon?" Stovepipe asked.

"I don't know where else they would go." Sam lifted the reins and urged the horse into a run again. Stovepipe followed suit.

The time it took to reach the canyon where Caballo Rojo's clan lived was torture to Sam. He hadn't gotten to know Elizabeth all that well before he left to search for the bushwhackers, but from what he had seen of her, she was a fine young woman.

And she had taken good care of Matt, which meant a lot, too. Sam didn't want anything bad happening to her. He doubted that Juan Pablo would kill her outright—he had expressed his intention to take her as his second wife, after all—but there was no telling what else he might do.

The eastern sky was starting to turn a faint shade of gray from the approach of dawn when Sam and Stovepipe came in sight of the cliffs where the canyon was located. They reined in to talk about their plan of action.

"If we just ride straight in," Stovepipe said, "Juan Pablo's probably left guards with a couple of those Springfields he grabbed at the mouth of the canyon to shoot anybody who shows up."

"That's the only way in there," Sam said. "We don't have any choice."

"What we need is a distraction. I'll go chargin' in to draw their fire, and you come along behind me and pick 'em off."

"That's a good way to get yourself killed," Sam protested.

"You got a better way to get in there?"

Sam had to admit that he didn't. But he said, "Why don't I go first and let you pick them off?"

Stovepipe didn't answer him. Instead, the range detective kicked his horse into a run and galloped straight at the mouth of the canyon.

Sam drew his revolver and followed. Stovepipe had a good lead on him. Sam might have been able to cut into that gap, but he knew this was their best chance of getting into the canyon.

At least one of them might make it through, he thought grimly.

As if warned by some instinct, Stovepipe abruptly pulled his horse to the right, then back to the left. Muzzle flame spurted from both sides of the canyon mouth.

That gave Sam the location of the guards, assuming that there were only two of them. The Springfields were single-shot rifles, and although someone trained in their use could reload very quickly, the Navajo would be far from expert at that.

Sam was counting on that to give him a slight advantage. While the guards were fumbling to get fresh shells into their weapons, he reached the mouth of the canyon himself. He triggered two shots toward the place where he had seen a muzzle flash on the right, then twisted in the saddle and sent two more rounds toward the guard on the left.

He didn't know if any of his bullets had found their targets, but he was in the canyon now and he could still hear the pounding hoofbeats of Stovepipe's horse, so he hoped the range detective had made it through all right, too.

What happened from here on out depended on things that were largely out of Sam's control. How many of the Navajo would support Juan Pablo now that the rifles he had promised them wouldn't be delivered after all? Would Caballo Rojo continue to step aside, or would he try to take control of the clan again?

A shape loomed up out of the darkness. Sam was reloading his Colt as he rode. He thumbed the sixth cartridge into the wheel, snapped the cylinder closed, and lifted the gun.

"Hold on," Stovepipe said. "It's just me. Were you hit, son?"

"No, I made it through all right," Sam said. "How about you?"

"Nary a scratch." Stovepipe chuckled. "I'm pretty good at ziggin' when folks think I'm gonna zag."

"Now that we're in, the guards may come after us. And the shots may have warned Juan Pablo that we're on our way."

"We best move fast, then, before the varmint has too much time to get ready for us."

They rode swiftly along the creek. When they

came to the first hogan, Sam expected shots to come from it, but the dwelling remained dark and silent.

That was a good sign, he told himself. It could mean that Juan Pablo didn't have as much support among the other Navajo as he claimed to. Maybe most of them were going to stay out of this clash.

Sam and Stovepipe left that hogan behind and headed for the next one, a couple of hundred yards along the creek. The Navajo liked their privacy and didn't live clustered up like some of the other tribes. Juan Pablo's hogan was about three-fourths of a mile into the canyon, and Caballo Rojo's was another half-mile beyond that.

After they passed two more hogans, they slowed as they approached the one belonging to Juan Pablo.

"He's gonna be waitin' for us, or for somebody to come after him, anyway," Stovepipe warned.

Sam brought his horse to a halt and swung down from the saddle.

"I'm going ahead on foot."

Stovepipe dismounted as well.

"Good idea," the range detective said. "I'll back your play, Sam, whatever it is."

"We'll need to draw him out. I know one way to do that: walk right up and challenge him."

"The ol' paint a target on your back trick, eh?"

"That's right," Sam said. "Only this time it'll be on my front. And you're going to come in from behind and get into that hogan so you can free Elizabeth while I'm dealing with Juan Pablo."

"Mighty risky tactics . . . but I don't have any better idea."

They split up, Sam going toward the front of the hogan and Stovepipe circling to the rear. Sam looked for possible cover as he approached but didn't see any. The only things he saw were the stake where Matt had been tied and the burned-out ashes of the fire nearby.

Gun in hand, he called, "Juan Pablo! Come out and face me!"

As soon as the words were out of his mouth, Sam leaped to the side. The direction he chose was a gamble. He might be jumping right into the path of a bullet.

But as one of the Springfields cracked from just inside the hogan's door, the slug whined harmlessly through the air to Sam's left. He couldn't return the fire for fear of hitting Elizabeth or Juan Pablo's wife, so he continued sprinting to the side, hoping that would draw Juan Pablo out of the earthen dwelling.

Instead the renegade called, "Leave this place, half-breed, and I will allow you to live!"

"It's over, Juan Pablo! There won't be any uprising against the whites!"

"This is Diné land! It will always be Diné land!"

"No one will take it away from you," Sam said as he crouched, out of a direct line of fire from the hogan's entrance.

"Already the white men build towns and run their cattle on it! Soon their railroad will come! The Diné will be forced to leave our homes again!"

"Don't you see that's exactly what the men who tried to give you those rifles want? They know your people can't win a war against the army. Rising up against the whites will have just the opposite effect to what you really want."

"Lies!" Juan Pablo cried. "All lies! You might as well be white!"

Sam tried another tack.

"Let Miss Fleming come out of there," he urged. "You're alone now, Juan Pablo." Sam made that guess based on the fact that no one seemed to be helping the would-be renegade anymore. "Let her go, and things don't have to get any worse than they already are."

"No! The woman is mine! I—"

Sam heard a loud thud from inside the hogan and recognized it as the unmistakable sound of something hard hitting flesh and bone. The thud was followed by a groan, and then Elizabeth called, "Sam! Sam, get in here!"

Sam dashed for the doorway. He saw Stovepipe coming around the hogan in a hurry, too, as the range detective responded to Elizabeth's summons.

Holding his Colt ready, Sam stepped into the dwelling's shadowy interior.

"I'm over here, tied up," Elizabeth went on. "Get me loose, Sam, please."

Sam could make out Juan Pablo's crumpled form lying on the ground. The man's wife stood over him, a chunk of firewood in her hand. Sam realized that the woman had clouted Juan Pablo with the wood and knocked him out.

Stooping, Sam took hold of the Springfield rifle that lay next to Juan Pablo's unconscious form and handed the weapon to Stovepipe, who had followed him into the hogan.

Then he holstered his Colt and pulled the Bowie knife from its sheath.

"Josefina saved me again," Elizabeth said as Sam knelt next to her to cut the bonds around her wrists. "Of course, she did it out of jealousy, not any great affection for me. In fact, I think she'd be pleased if I left the canyon and never came back."

"Which is exactly what you're going to do," Sam said.

Elizabeth opened her mouth as if she were going to argue with him, but then she shrugged instead.

"You're right," she said. "I can't stay here anymore. Maybe someone else can help educate these people. They deserve it."

"What happened to the men who were with Juan Pablo?" Sam asked as the cut ropes fell away from Elizabeth's wrists. She began massaging her hands to get the blood flowing again.

"They had a big argument outside after Juan Pablo forced me in here and tied me up," she said. "I couldn't follow all of it, but I'm pretty sure the other men told him they didn't want anything more to do with his uprising. He let them down when they didn't get the rifles." Elizabeth paused. "I guess you and the others were responsible for that."

Sam nodded as he helped her to her feet.

"That's right. Matt and Wilbur are standing guard over the rifles now. We need to get back to them and head on to Flat Rock as soon as possible, to make sure the gang behind all this doesn't try anything else."

Elizabeth looked down at Juan Pablo.

"What are you going to do about him?"

"I'm going to leave him for Caballo Rojo to deal with," Sam said. "And his wife. I've got a hunch she's not going to put up with much more foolishness from him."

"It's true that the women wield a great deal of power in Navajo society. And Caballo Rojo is still the headman of this clan. I think he can keep Juan Pablo in line now that all the other men have abandoned his cause." Elizabeth shook her head. "I don't think he's truly a bad man. He just has a hard time getting used to life the way it really is."

"Reckon everybody's that way sometimes," Stovepipe said.

Elizabeth started to hug Juan Pablo's wife, but the woman turned away with her face as stoic as ever.

"Thank you anyway," Elizabeth told her. "Thank you for everything. Gracias."

The woman relented in her stiffness enough to give her a curt nod.

Sam, Stovepipe, and Elizabeth stepped outside. Sam stiffened as he saw Caballo Rojo standing there with a grim look on his face.

The headman leveled an arm toward the canyon mouth.

"Go," he said simply.

"That's where we're headed," Sam said. "You won't see us again after this, Caballo Rojo."

The Navajo looked like that would be just fine with him.

Chapter 37

The more Matt thought about it, the more he knew that he had to get to Flat Rock. He couldn't afford to wait for Sam and Stovepipe to return. The ringleader of that gang was going to try something else.

"I'm gonna take one of those horses from the wagon team and head for town," he told Wilbur. "You can stay here and keep an eye on those rifles."

"You're loco," Wilbur responded heatedly. "Stovepipe and Two Wolves told us to stay here."

"Once it gets light, you can fort up in these rocks and keep anybody who comes along away from the guns," Matt argued. "My gut tells me the varmint behind all this isn't finished yet."

"Yeah, well, my gut tells me the same thing, and you're hurt worse'n I am. If anybody goes, it ought to be me."

"No offense, Wilbur, but you're not exactly a gun-fighter."

Wilbur glared at him.

"You ever notice, when somebody says 'no offense,' they're about to say somethin' damned offensive?"

Matt was already unhitching one of the horses. He didn't answer.

"Besides, you never even been to Flat Rock," Wilbur went on. "You don't even know how to get there."

"Tell me the general direction. I can find it."

"Why should I?"

Matt looked at his companion intently and said, "Because I'm the only one who stand a chance right now of stoppin' that bunch from raising more hell."

Wilbur glared, but he finally said with obvious reluctance, "Oh, all right." He told Matt how to find the settlement. "But you're gonna be outnumbered at least three to one. Don't come complainin' to me when you get yourself killed."

"Wouldn't think of it," Matt said.

He cut lengths of rein off the wagon's lines and attached them to the bit in the horse's mouth. Then he climbed onto the animal and set off bareback toward Flat Rock, steering by the stars that were still bright in the night sky.

He couldn't hope to reach the settlement before the members of the gang, since they had a good lead on him, but he pushed the horse as hard as he could so that maybe they wouldn't have time to get up to too much mischief before he got there.

After an hour or so, the eastern sky began to lighten. Matt knew dawn wasn't too far away. If he had still been a prisoner back in the canyon, the sands of his life would be running out right about now, since Juan Pablo had intended to execute all four captives when the sun came up.

But they had foiled that idea, and Matt hoped Sam and Stovepipe had been able to rescue Elizabeth as well. He was going to worry about her until he saw her again with his own eyes.

He spotted a few scattered lights up ahead. It was too early for very many people to be up and about in Flat Rock, but clearly some of the citizens were awake. Matt pushed his horse harder, anxious to get there.

He was still at least half a mile from the settlement when he spotted the three riders. They were just shadows in the graying light at first, but then he was able to make them out better.

He recognized the big, brawny shape of the man in the lead, who was carrying something draped over the saddle in front of him. Sensing that this was trouble in the offing, Matt veered his horse to intercept them.

Even over the pounding hoofbeats, he heard a shout of alarm from one of the men. They split up, the leader angling to the north, the other two charging straight at Matt with their guns spitting flame.

The big draft horse he was riding was slow and ungainly, but the animal had sand, Matt had to give it that. The horse didn't spook from the racket of gunshots and the smell of powdersmoke, even when he filled his hands with both of his irons and cut loose.

Bullets sang around his head as he thundered toward the two would-be killers. His Colts roared and bucked. One of the outlaws suddenly cried out and slewed around in the saddle before toppling off his mount. The other rocked back as one of Matt's slugs drove into his chest but stayed upright and kept firing. Matt triggered again as they swept past each other, and this time the man's head jerked as a bullet tore through his throat and angled up into his brain. He had to be dead when he hit the ground.

Matt wheeled the horse and looked after the leader. He didn't know if his horse could catch up to the man.

But then the boss outlaw's horse broke stride, and as the dawn light spread over the landscape even more, Matt realized there were two people on the horse, not one.

And those two people were engaged in a desperate struggle.

Matt started after them, urging the horse underneath him to surrender every bit of speed and strength it possessed. The animal responded gallantly. As Matt closed the gap between him and his quarry, the second figure on the other horse suddenly broke free and either fell or jumped off.

The leader of the gun-runners hauled his mount around, but instead of going after the person who had escaped from him, he drew his gun and threw a shot at Matt. As Matt leaned forward over his horse's neck, he barely took note of the fact that the person on the ground was a woman. Her long auburn hair was in disarray.

The boss outlaw fired again. Matt's horse stumbled.

He didn't know how badly the animal was wounded, but the horse didn't go down. It charged ahead, and now Matt straightened from his crouch with both Colts leveled.

The guns roared as he emptied them, and the hammerblows of the bullets striking the ringleader of the gang drove the man out of the saddle. He hit the ground hard, rolled over a couple of times, and lay still.

Using the makeshift reins, Matt pulled his horse to a stop and slid down from its back. He saw the crease on the horse's shoulder and was glad that the animal wasn't hurt any worse than that.

His right-hand Colt was empty, but the left-hand gun still had one round in it. Out of long habit, Matt had kept track of the shots he had fired. He pouched the right-hand iron but kept the other one ready as he approached the fallen ringleader.

The man wasn't a threat anymore. He had dropped his gun, and the front of his shirt was sodden with blood from several bullet wounds. He pawed feebly at the crimson flow as he gasped for breath.

The man looked up at Matt and managed to say, "Who . . . who . . . ?"

The two of them had never seen each other before close-up, Matt realized.

"I'm Matt Bodine," he said. "Who're you?"

"King . . . king . . ."

Matt thought that was the dying man's name.

But then he said, "King . . . of the . . . Four Corners . . ."

"Not hardly," Matt said as the man's final breath rattled in his throat.

Matt left the body there and turned back toward the woman. She ran to meet him, but before she could get there, his strength abruptly deserted him. His guns slipped from his fingers, and he fell to his knees.

"My God!" the woman exclaimed. "Are you hurt?"

Matt looked up at her, thinking that she was beautiful even in her disheveled state, and said, "You've got . . . a British accent."

"That's because I'm from England." She leaned over to take hold of his arm. "Let me help you, sir."

"I like the way . . . you folks talk."

"That's all well and good, but you seem to be injured—Oh!"

Her startled exclamation was the last thing he heard before the dawn light went away and darkness closed in around him.

When Sam, Stovepipe, and Elizabeth reached the wagon and found Wilbur there alone, Sam left the others behind and raced on into Flat Rock, arriving there at mid-morning.

Practically the first thing he saw was Matt sitting on a bench in front of the Buckingham Palace Saloon with Lady Augusta Winslow.

Matt grinned as Sam pulled up at the hitch rack and almost leaped from his saddle.

"Figured you'd be along directly," Matt said. "Take it easy, I'm all right."

"Yes, other than being addlepated for going off after that bunch by yourself," Sam said. He nodded to the woman. "Lady Augusta. Good morning."

"Yes, it is, thanks to your friend Matt," she told him with a smile. "He rescued me, you know. Zack Jardine and two of his henchmen had kidnapped me."

"Zack Jardine," Sam repeated. He didn't know the name.

"Big fella who was the leader of the bunch tryin' to start a new war with the Navajo," Matt explained. "Don't worry, I didn't know his name, either, until after I shot him."

"He's dead?"

Matt nodded.

"And so are the other two who got away when we busted up their attempt to deliver those rifles to the Indians." A worried look appeared on Matt's face. "You got Elizabeth away from Juan Pablo all right, didn't you?"

"She's fine," Sam assured him. "And Juan Pablo won't give any more trouble. His wife will see to that, along with Caballo Rojo."

"Can't help but think maybe it would've been better to shoot him," Matt said. "I don't cotton to somebody tellin' me I'm gonna be shot at dawn. But I guess if they can keep him settled down, that'll be all right."

"Now the only one we have to worry about is poor Noah Reilly," Lady Augusta said.

Sam's eyebrows rose in surprise.

"The little fella who runs the general store?"

"That's right," the Englishwoman said. "He was found unconscious in front of the store early this morning. I think he must have seen Jardine and his men come into town and gotten suspicious of them. He may have confronted them before they came up the back stairs of the saloon and abducted me. Mr. Reilly appears to have been struck with a pistol."

Sam shook his head.

"Poor little fella. Where is he?"

"I had him taken up to my room and put to bed there, in hopes that he'll regain consciousness and recover."

"Well, when he does wake up, he'll be in a good place," Matt said.

"Hush, Mr. Bodine," Lady Augusta said with a smile. "You're in no shape to be flirting with anyone. You only regained consciousness yourself a short time ago."

"I was just a mite tired, that's all. You said yourself those bullet holes in my side look like they're still healin' up just fine, ma'am."

"Yes, but you're going to need a great deal of rest before you're back to normal."

Matt might have had something to say about that, but before he could, one of the bartenders stepped through the batwings and told Lady Augusta, "Ma'am, that girl you had keepin' an eye on Reilly just came down and said he's awake. He's all agitated, though, so I reckon you ought to go up there."

"Of course," she said as she got to her feet.

"I'll come with you," Sam said. "Noah was one of the first folks I met here in Flat Rock."

Matt stood up.

"I'll come, too. I want to hear what he's got to say about what happened."

The three of them went upstairs to Lady Augusta's suite. They found Noah Reilly sitting up in bed, looking impatient while one of the saloon girls wiped his forehead with a wet cloth.

Reilly's eyes widened for a second when he saw Sam.

"What are you doing here?" he asked. His eyes flicked toward Matt. "And who's this?"

"Don't worry about that, Noah," Sam said. "Are you all right? You got clouted pretty hard on the head, it looks like."

Reilly closed his eyes for a second and winced.

"Yes, I . . , I'm fine. I can't believe those savages didn't scalp me, or at least cut my throat."

"Savages?" Matt repeated with a frown.

"Yes, the Indians I caught skulking around early this morning when I got to the store to open up. They looked like they were going to try to sneak into the saloon." Reilly swallowed and looked up at Lady Augusta. "Are you all right? I knew your life would be in danger when I saw those Navajo."

Matt and Sam exchanged a quick look. Sam said, "You're sure it was some Navajo you saw, Noah?"

"What? Why, of course I'm sure! I've seen plenty of them around town in the past. I know a Navajo when I see one."

Matt said, "And you got a good look at them?"

"I was close as I am to any of you. I had to be, for them to have hit me and knocked me out the way they did." Reilly lifted a hand toward Lady Augusta. "Dear lady, did they harm you? How in the world did you escape from those red savages?"

Lady Augusta looked confused.

"I don't understand, Mr. Reilly," she said. "It wasn't the Navajo who carried me off. It was Zack Jardine and two of his men."

Reilly stiffened in alarm. Matt saw him start to reach for something under his coat. One of Matt's Colts seemed to appear in his hand as if by magic.

"Whatever you're reachin' for, you'd better leave it right where it is, mister," Matt said. "And while you're at it, you can start explainin' why the story you're trying to tell us doesn't match up with any of the facts."

"Why, I . . . I . . ."

Sam sighed and shook his head. He had liked the little storekeeper.

"You should've kept your mouth shut and claimed you didn't know what happened, Noah," he said. "You probably would've gotten away with it, then. Now, though, it's pretty obvious that you cooked up this whole deal with Jardine. Were the two of you partners?"

Reilly's face hardened.

"Partners, hell!" he spat with such concentrated venom that it seemed impossible it could have come from such a mild-looking hombre. "The entire thing was my idea! And if we had pulled it off, I would have been the ruler of the whole Four Corners!"

Matt shook his head.

"This is America, mister. We don't have kings." He glanced at Lady Augusta and smiled. "No offense, Your Ladyship."

"None taken, I assure you. Why do you think I came to America in the first place? I didn't want a bloody king, either!"

By that evening, another wagon had gone out to pick up the crates of guns and returned with them. They were locked up at the moment in the back room of the now-closed general store.

Matt, Sam, Stovepipe, and Wilbur sat on the bench in front of the saloon and watched the day's light fade, taking with it some of the scorching heat.

The four of them had been over the whole thing, hashing out what they knew and what they could guess, and they were convinced that they had a pretty accurate picture. Noah Reilly hadn't offered any sort of detailed confession after the things he had said that morning, but he was locked up, too.

A rider had carried word to Fort Defiance, and Matt and Sam expected an officer and a cavalry detail to show up in a day or two and take charge of everything, including the lone surviving member of the gang.

"Here's what I can't believe about the whole thing," Wilbur said. "You weren't in on the end of it, Stovepipe. I'm used to you bein' the one who rounds up the head varmint."

"I reckon I did my share," Stovepipe said. He looked at Matt and Sam. "Couldn't interest you boys in a job, could I? You seem to be good at gettin' to the bottom of things. The Cattlemen's Protective Association could use you."

"Not a chance," Matt said with a smile and a shake of his head. "Sam and I don't cotton to workin' for wages."

"You just gonna keep on driftin' like a pair of fiddle-footed cowboys?"

"That's the plan," Sam said.

"But not just yet," Matt added. "I'm gonna go call on Miss Elizabeth Fleming and take her to supper at that café you fellas told me about."

"And I'm gonna go talk to Lady Augusta," Wilbur put in.

"You'll get so tongue-tied and start sputterin' so much she's liable to think you got the hydrophobia," Stovepipe told her partner.

"Dang it, there you go again, always tryin' to interfere in my love life!"

"I'm just tryin' to keep you from gettin' your feelin's hurt. Anyway, you can't go makin' calf-eyes at that gal. Soon as the army gets here and takes charge of them guns, you and I got more work to take care of."

"More work? Where?"

"I dunno," Stovepipe admitted. "We'll have to find us a telegraph office and check in with the boss. But you know how it is, Wilbur . . . hell's always poppin' somewhere."

That was true, Sam thought. Hell was always popping somewhere, especially wherever the blood brothers went.

But that's the way it was with brothers of the wolf.

And brothers of the gun.

Turn the page for an exciting preview of

SAVAGE TEXAS

An explosive new Western series by

William W. Johnstone
with J. A. Johnstone

*America's leading Western writer captures the most
violent chapter in frontier history—in the saga
of a Yankee with a rifle, an outlaw with a grudge,
and a little slice of hell called . . .*

SAVAGE TEXAS

For renegades and pioneers, there is no place like
Texas—as long as you have a gun and the guts to use
it. Now, the Civil War is over. Carpetbaggers and
scalawags rule Austin. Soldiers return to pillaged
homes. Longhorns roam the wilds and the state is in a
state of chaos. Especially a town called Hangtree.

Sam Heller and Johnny Cross are Hangtree's
newest citizens: Heller is a former Yankee soldier,
a deadly shot, and a believer in right from wrong.
Cross is a gun for hire with dark dreams of wealth
and power—and at any cost. Hangtree, with its rich
grazing land and nearby mineral deposits, soon
erupts in murderous violence. By fate and by
choice, these two strangers will find themselves
on the opposite side of the law.

On sale now wherever Pinnacle Books are sold!

"Texas . . . Texas . . ."

—Last words of Sam Houston,
soldier, patriot, and founder and
president of the Republic of Texas

Chapter 1

Some towns play out and fade away. Others die hard.

By midnight Midvale was ablaze. The light of its burning was a fire on a darkling plain.

It was a night in late March 1866. Early spring. The earth was quickening as Midvale was dying.

The well-watered grazing lands of Long Valley in north central Texas supported many widely scattered ranches. Midvale had come into being at a strategic site where key trails came together. The town supplied the needs of local ranchers and farmers for things they couldn't make or grow but couldn't do without.

A cluster of several square blocks of wooden frame buildings, it had a handful of shops and stores, several saloons, a small café, a boardinghouse or two, and a residential neighborhood.

Tonight Midvale had reached its end. Its passing was violent. The killers had come to usher it into extinction. Raiders they were, a band of cutthroats, savage and merciless. They came under cover of darkness and fell on the town like ravening wolves—gun wolves.

The folk of Midvale were no sheep for the slaughter. The Texas frontier is no place for weaklings. For a generation, settlers had fought Comanche, Kiowa, and Lipan Apache war parties, Mexican bandits and homegrown outlaws. The battle fury of the recent War Between the States had left this part of Texas untouched, but there was not a family in the valley that hadn't given husbands and sons to the armies of the Confederacy. Few had returned.

The folk of Midvale were not weaklings. Not fools, either. They were undone by treachery, by a vicious attack that struck without warning, like a bolt out of the blue. By the time they knew what hit them, it was too late to mount any kind of defense.

Ringing the town, the raiders swooped down on it, shooting, stabbing, and slaying. No fight, this—it was a massacre.

After the killing came the plundering. Then the burning, as Midvale was put to the torch.

The scene was an inferno, as if a vent of hell had opened up, bursting out of the dark ground in a fiery gusher. Shots rang out, shrieks sounded, and hoof-beats drummed through the red night as the killers hunted down the scant few who'd survived the initial onslaught.

All were slain outright; all but the young women and children, boys and girls. Captives are wealth.

The church was the last of Midvale to burn. It stood apart from the rest of the town, a modest distance separating it from worldlier precincts. A handful of townsfolk had fled to it, huddling together at the foot of the pulpit.

That's where the raiders found them. Their screams were silenced by hammering gunfire.

The church was set on fire, its bell tower spire a flaming dagger thrusting into night-black sky. Wooden beams gave, collapsing, sending the church bell tumbling down the shaft into the interior space.

It bounced around, clanging. Dull, heavy, leaden tones tolled Midvale's death knell.

The marauders rode out, well satisfied with this night's work. They left behind nearly a hundred dead men, women and children. It was a good start, but riper targets and richer pickings lay ahead.

The war had been over for almost a year, but there was no peace to be found on the Texas frontier. No peace short of the grave.

But for the ravagers and pillagers who scourge this earth, the mysterious and unseen workings of fate sometimes send a nemesis of righteous vengeance. . . .

Chapter 2

From out of the north came a lone rider, trailing southwest across the hill country down into the prairie. A smiling stranger mounted on a tough, scrappy steel-dust stallion.

Man and mount were covered with trail dust from long days and nights of hard riding.

Texas is big and likes bigness. The stranger was no Texan but he was big. He was six feet, two inches tall, raw-boned and long-limbed, his broad shoulders axe-handle wide. A dark brown slouch hat topped a yellow-haired head with the face of a current-day Viking. He wore his hair long, shoulder-length, scout-style, a way of putting warlike Indians on notice that its owner had no fear of losing his scalp to them. A man of many ways, he'd been a scout before and might yet be again. The iciness of his sharp blue eyes was belied by the laugh lines nestled in their corners.

No ordinary gun would do for this yellow-haired wanderer. Strapped to his right hip was a cut-down

Winchester repeating rifle with a sawed-off barrel and chopped stock: a "mule's-leg," as such a weapon was popularly known. It had a kick that could knock its recipient from this world clear into the next. It rested in a special long-sheath holster that reached from hip to below mid-thigh.

Bandoliers lined with cartridges for the sawed-off carbine were worn across the stranger's torso in an X shape. A six-gun was tucked butt-out into his waistband on his left side. A Green River knife with a foot-long blade was sheathed on his left hip.

Some time around mid-morning, the rider came down off the edge of the Edwards plateau with its wooded hills and twisty ravines. Ahead lay a vast open expanse, the rolling plains of north central Texas.

No marker, no signpost noted that he had crossed a boundary, an invisible line. But indeed he had.

Sam Heller had come to Hangtree County.

Chapter 3

Monday noon, the first day of April 1866. A hot sun topped the cloudless blue sky. Below lay empty tableland, vast, covered with the bright green grass of early spring and broken by sparsely scattered stands of timber. A line of wooded hills rose some miles to the north.

The flat was divided by a dirt road running east-west. It ran as straight as if it had been drawn by a ruler. No other sign of human habitation presented itself as far as the eye could see.

An antlike blur of motion inched with painful slowness across that wide, sprawling plain. It was a man alone, afoot on the dirt road. A lurching, ragged scarecrow of a figure.

Texas is big. Big sky, big land. And no place for a walking man. Especially if he's only got one leg.

Luke Pettigrew was that man, painfully and painstakingly making his way west along the road to Hangtown.

He was lean, weathered, with long, lank brown hair and a beard. His young-old face, carved with lines of suffering, was now stoically expressionless except for a certain grim determination.

He was dressed in gray, the gray of a soldier of the army of the Confederate States of America. The Confederacy was now defunct a few weeks short of a year ago, since General Robert E. Lee had signed the articles of surrender at the Appomatox courthouse. Texas had joined with the South in seceding from the Union, sending its sons to fight in the War Between the States. Many had fallen, never to return.

Luke Pettigrew had returned. Minus his left leg below the knee.

A crooked tree branch served him for a crutch. A stick with a Y-shaped fork at one end, said fork being jammed under his left arm and helping to keep him upright. Strips of shredded rags were wrapped around the fork to cushion it as best they could. Which wasn't much. A clawlike left hand clutched the rough-barked shaft with a white-knuckled grip.

A battered, shapeless hat covered his head. It was faded to colorlessness by time and the elements. A bullet hole showed in the top of the crown and a few nicks marked the brim.

Luke wore his uniform, what was left of it. A gray tunic, unbuttoned and open, revealed a threadbare, sun-faded red flannel shirt beneath it. Baggy gray trousers were held in place by a brown leather belt whose dulled metal buckle bore the legend: CSA.

Many extra holes had been punched in the belt to co-incide with his weight loss. He was thin, half-starved.

His garments had seen much hard use. They were worn, tattered. His left trouser leg was knotted to-gether below the knee, to keep the empty pant leg from getting in his way. His good right foot was shod by a rough, handmade rawhide moccasin.

Luke Pettigrew was unarmed, without rifle, pistol or knife. And Texas is no place for an unarmed man. But there he was, minus horse, gun—and the lower part of his left leg—doggedly closing on Hangtown.

The capital of Hangtree County is the town of Hangtree, known far and wide as Hangtown.

From head to toe, Luke was powdered with fine dust from the dirt road. Sweat cut sharp lines through the powder covering his face. Grimacing, grunting between clenched teeth, he advanced another step with the crutch.

How many hundreds, thousands of such steps had he taken on his solitary trek? How many more such steps must he take before reaching his destination? He didn't know.

He was without a canteen. He'd been a long time without water under the hot Texas sun. Somewhere beyond the western horizon lay Swift Creek with its fresh, cool waters. On the far side of the creek: Hangtown.

Neither was yet in sight. Luke trudged on ahead. One thing he had plenty of was determination. Grit. The same doggedness that had seen him through battles without number in the war, endless forced marches, hunger, privation. It had kept him alive after the wound that took off the lower half of his left leg while others, far less seriously wounded, gave up the ghost and died.

That said, he sure was almighty sick and tired of walking.

Along came a rider, out of the east.

Absorbed with his own struggles, Luke was unaware of the newcomer's approach until the other was quite near. The sound of hoofbeats gave him pause. Halting, he looked back over his shoulder.

The single rider advanced at an easy lope.

Luke walked in the middle of the road because there the danger of rocks, holes, and ditches was less than at the sidelines. A sound caught in his throat, something between a groan and a sigh, in anticipation of spending more of his meager reserves of energy in getting out of the way.

He angled toward the left-hand side of the road. It was a measure of the time and place that he unquestioningly accepted the likelihood of a perfect stranger riding down a crippled war veteran.

The rider was mounted on a chestnut horse. He slowed the animal to an easy walk, drawing abreast of Luke, keeping pace with him. Luke kept going, looking straight ahead, making a show of minding his own business in hopes that the newcomer would do the same.

"Howdy," the rider said, his voice soft-spoken, with a Texas twang.

At least he wasn't no damned Yankee, thought Luke. Not that that made much difference. His fellow Texans had given him plenty of grief lately. Luke grunted, acknowledging that the other had spoken and committing himself to no more than that acknowledgment.

"Long way to town," the rider said. He sounded friendly enough, for whatever that was worth, Luke told himself.

"Room up here for two to ride," the other said.

"I'm getting along, thanks," muttered Luke, not wanting to be beholden to anybody.

The rider laughed, laughter that was free and easy with no malice in it. Still, the sound of it raced like wildfire along Luke's strained nerves.

"You always was a hardheaded cuss, Luke Pettigrew," the rider said.

Luke, stunned, looked to see who it was that was calling out his name.

The rider was about his age, in his early twenties. He still had his youth, though, what was left of it, unlike Luke, who felt himself prematurely aged, one of the oldest men alive.

Luke peered up at him. Something familiar in the other's tone of voice . . .

A dark, flat-crowned, broad-brimmed hat with a snakeskin hatband shadowed the rider's face. The sun was behind him, in Luke's eyes. Luke squinted, peering, at first unable to make out the other's features. The rider tilted his head, causing the light to fall on his face.

"Good gawd!—Johnny Cross!" Luke's outcry was a croak, his throat parched from lack of water.

"Long time no see, Luke," Johnny Cross said.

"Well I'll be good to gawd-damned! I never expected to see you again," said Luke. "Huh! So you made it through the war."

"Looks like. And you, too."

"Mostly," Luke said, indicating with a tilt of his head and a sour twist of his mouth his missing lower leg.

"Reckon we're both going in the same direction. Climb on up," Johnny Cross said. Gripping the saddle horn with his right hand, he leaned over and down, extending his left hand.

He was lean and wiry, with strength in him. He took hold of Luke's right hand in an iron grip and hefted him up, swinging him onto the horse behind him. It helped that Luke didn't weigh much.

Luke got himself settled. "I want to keep hold of this crutch for now," he said.

"I'll tie it to the saddle, leave you with both hands free," Johnny said. He used a rawhide thong to lash the tree branch in place out of the way. A touch of Johnny's boot heels to the chestnut's flanks started the animal forward.

"Much obliged, Johnny."

"You'd do the same for me."

"What good would that do? I ain't got no horse."

"Man, things must be tough in Hangtree County."

"Like always. Only more so since the war."

They set out for Hangtown.

Johnny Cross was of medium height, compact, trim, athletic. He had black hair and clean-lined, well-formed features. His hazel eyes varied in color from brown to yellow depending on the light. He had a deep tan and a three-day beard. There was something catlike about him with his restless yellow eyes, self-contained alertness and lithe, easy way of moving.

He wore a sun-bleached maroon shirt, black jeans, and good boots. Two guns were strapped to his hips. Good guns.

Luke noticed several things right off. Johnny Cross had done some long, hard riding. His clothes were trail-worn, dusty; his guns, what Luke could see of them in their holsters, were clean, polished. Their inset dark wooden handles were smooth, well worn with use. A late-model carbine was sheathed in the saddle scabbard.

The chestnut horse was a fine-looking animal. Judging by its lines it was fast and strong, with plenty of endurance. The kind of mount favored by one on the dodge. One thing was sure: Johnny Cross was returning to Hangtree in better shape than when he'd left it.

The Cross family had always been dirt-poor, honest but penniless. Throughout his youth up till the time he went off to war, Johnny had worn mostly patched, outgrown clothes and gone shoeless for long periods of time.

Johnny Cross handed the other a canteen. "Here, Luke, cut the dust some."

"Don't mind if I do, thanks." Luke fought to still the trembling in his hands as he took hold of the canteen and fumbled open the cap. The water was as warm as blood. He took a mouthful and held it there, letting the welcome wetness refresh the dust-dry inside of his mouth.

His throat was so dry that at first he had trouble swallowing. He took a couple of mouthfuls, stopping though still thirsty. He didn't want to be a hog or show how great his need was. "Thank you kindly," he said, returning the canteen.

Johnny put it away. "Sorry I don't have something stronger."

"That's plenty fine," Luke said.

"Been back long?"

"Since last fall."

"How's your folks, Luke?"

"Pa got drowned two years ago trying to cross the Liberty River when it was running high at flood time."

"Sorry to hear that. He was a good man," Johnny said.

Luke nodded. "Hardworking and God-fearing . . . for all the good it done him."

"Your brothers?"

"Finn joined up with Ben McCullough and got kilt at Pea Ridge. Heck got it in Chicamagua."

"That's a damned shame. They was good ol' boys."

"War kilt off a lot of good ol' boys."

"Ain't it the truth."

The two were silent for a spell.

"Sue Ellen's married to a fellow over to Dennison way," Luke went on. "Got two young'uns, a boy and a girl. Named the boy after Pa. Ma's living with them."

"Imagine that! Last time I saw Sue Ellen she was a pretty little slip of a thing, and now she's got two young'uns of her own," Johnny said, shaking his head. "Time sure does fly. . . ."

"Four years is a long time, Johnny."

"How was your war, Luke?"

"I been around. I was with Hood's Brigade."

"Good outfit."

Luke nodded. "We fought our way all over the South. Reckon we was in just about every big battle there was. I was with 'em right through almost to the finish at the front lines of Richmond, till a cannonball took off the bottom part of my leg."

"That must've hurt some," Johnny said.

"It didn't tickle," Luke deadpanned. "They patched me up in a Yankee prison camp where I set for a few months until after Appomatox in April of Sixty-Five, when they set us all a-loose. I made my way back here, walking most of the way.

"What about you, Johnny? Seems I heard something about you riding with Bill Anderson."

"Did you? Well, you heard right."

Hard-riding, hard-fighting Bill Anderson had led a band of fellow Texans up into Missouri to join up with

William Clarke Quantrill, onetime schoolteacher turned leader of a ferociously effective mounted force of Confederate irregulars in the Border States. The fighting there was guerrilla warfare at its worst: an unending series of ambushes, raids, flight, pursuit, and counterattack—an ever-escalating spiral of brutalities and atrocities on both sides.

"We was with Quantrill," Johnny Cross said.

"How was it?" Luke asked.

"We gave those Yankees pure hell," Johnny said, smiling with his lips, a self-contained, secretive smile.

His alert, yellow-eyed gaze turned momentarily inward, bemused by cascading memories of hard riding and hard fighting. He tossed his head, as if physically shaking off the mood of reverie and returning to the present.

"Didn't work out too well in the end, though," Johnny said at last. "After Bill's sister got killed—she and a bunch of women, children, and old folks was being held hostage by the Yanks in a house that collapsed on 'em—Bill went off the deep end. He always had a mean streak but after that he went plumb loco, kill crazy. That's when they started calling him Bloody Bill."

"You at Lawrence?" asked Luke.

Lawrence, Kansas, longtime abolitionist center and home base for Jim Lane's Redlegs, a band of Yankee marauders who'd shot, hanged and burned their way through pro-Confederate counties in Missouri. In retaliation, Quantrill had led a raid on Lawrence that became one of the bloodiest and most notorious massacres of the war.

"It wasn't good, Luke. I came to kill Yankee soldiers. This business of shooting down unarmed men—and boys—it ain't sporting."

"No more'n what the Redlegs done to our people."

"I stuck with Quantrill until the end, long after Bill split off from him to lead his own bunch. They're both dead now, shot down by the bluebellies."

"I'd appreciate it if you'd keep that to yourself," Johnny said, after a pause. "The Federals still got a grudge on about Quantrill and ain't too keen on amnestying any of our bunch."

"You one of them pistol-fighters, Johnny?"

Johnny shrugged. "I'm like you, just another Reb looking for a place to light."

"You always was good with a gun. I see you're toting a mighty fine-looking pair of the plow handles in that gunbelt," Luke said.

"That's about all I've got after four years of war, some good guns and a horse."

Johnny cut an involuntary glance at the empty space below Luke's left knee.

"Not that I'm complaining, mind you," he added quickly.

"Hold on to them guns and keep 'em close. Now that you're back, you're gonna need 'em," Luke said.

"Yanks been throwing their weight around?" Johnny asked.

Luke shook his head. "'T'ain't the Yanks that's the problem. Not yet, anyhow. They's around some but they're stretched kind of thin. There's a company of them in Fort Pardee up in the Breaks."

"They closed that at the start of the war, along with all them forts up and down the frontier line," Johnny said.

"It's up and running now, manned by a company of bluebelly horse soldiers. But that ain't the problem—not that I got any truck with a bunch of damn Yankees," Luke said.

"'Course not."

"What with no cavalry around and most of the menfolk away during the war, no home guard and no Ranger companies, things have gone to rot and ruin hereabouts. The Indians have run wild, the Comanches and the Kiowas. Comanches, mostly. Wahtonka's been spending pretty much half the year riding the warpaths between Kansas and Mexico. Sometimes as far east as Fort Worth and even Dallas."

"Wahtonka? That ol' devil ain't dead yet?"

Luke shook his head. "Full of piss and vinegar and more ornery than ever. And then there's Red Hand."

"I recollect him. A troublemaker, a real bad 'un. He was just starting to make a name for himself when I went north."

"He's a big noise nowadays, Johnny. Got hisself a following among the young bucks of the tribe. Red Hand's been raising holy hell for the last four years with no Army or Rangers to crack down on him. There's some other smaller fry, but them two are the real hellbenders.

"But that's not the least of it. The redskins raid and move on. But the white badmen just set. The county's thick with 'em. Thicker'n flies swarming a manure pile

in a cow pasture on a hot summer day. Deserters from
both armies, renegades, outlaws. Comancheros selling
guns and whiskey to the Indians. Backshooters, women-
killers. The lowest. Bluecoats are too busy chasing the
Indians to bother with them. Folks're so broke that
there ain't hardly nothing left worth stealing any more,
but that don't matter to some hombres. They's up to all
kinds of devilments out of pure meanness.

"Hell, I got robbed right here on this road not more
than a day ago. In broad daylight. I didn't have nothing worth stealing but they took it anyhow. It'd been
different if I'd had me a six-gun. Or a good double-
barreled sawed-off."

"Who done it, Luke?"

"Well, I'll tell you. First off, I been living out at the
old family place, what's left of it," Luke said. "Somebody put the torch to it while I was away. Burned
down the ranch house and barn."

"Yanks?" Johnny asked.

Luke shook his head. "Federals never got to
Hangtree County during the war. Probably figured it
wasn't worth bothering with. No, the ranch must've
been burned by some no-goods, probably just for the
hell of it.

"Anyhow, I scrounged up enough unburnt planks
and shacks to build me a little shack; I been living
there since I come back. Place is thick with maverick
cattle—the whole range is. Strays that have been gone
wild during the war and now there's hundreds, thousands of them running around loose. Every now and

then I catch and kill me one for food. I'd've starved without.

"I had me some hides I'd cleaned and cured. I was bringing 'em into town to sell or barter at the general store. Some fishhooks, chaw of tobacco, seeds . . ."

"And whiskey," Johnny said.

"Hell, yes," Luke said. "Had my old rifled musket and mule. Never made it to Hangtown—I got held up along the way. Bunch of no-accounts come up, got the drop on me. Five of them."

"Who?"

"Strangers, I never seen 'em before. But when I seen 'em again— Well, never mind about that now. Lot of outsiders horning in around here lately. I ain't forgetting a one of 'em. Led by a mean son name of Monty."

"Monty," Johnny echoed, committing the name to memory.

"That's what they called him, Monty. Big ol' boy with a round fat face and little piggy eyes. Cornsilk hair so fine and pale it was white. Got him a gold front tooth a-shining and a-sparkling away in the middle of his mouth," Luke said. "Him and his crowd gave me a whomping. Busted my musket against a tree. Shot my poor ol' mule dead for the fun of it. Busted my crutch over my head. It hurt, too."

Luke took off his hat, pointing out a big fat lump in the middle of his crown.

"That's some goose egg. Like I said, you always was a hardheaded fellow. Lucky for you," Johnny said.

"Yeh, lucky." Luke put his hat back on, gingerly

settling it on his head. "While I was out cold they stole everything I had: my hides, my knife, even my wooden leg. Can you beat that? Stealing a man's wooden leg! Them things don't grow on trees, you know. That's what really hurt. I walked from hell to Texas on that leg. Yes, you could say I was attached to it."

"You could. I wouldn't."

"When I come to, them owlhoots was talking about if'n they should kill me or not. Only reason they didn't gun me down on the spot is 'cause Monty thought it would be funny to leave me alive to go crawling across the countryside."

"Yankees?"

"Hell no, they was Southerners just like us. Texans, some of 'em, from the way they talked," said Luke.

His face set in lines of grim determination. "I'll find 'em, I got time. When I do, I'll even up with 'em. And then some. That gold tooth of Monty's is gonna make me a good watch fob. Once I get me a watch."

He waved a hand dismissively, shooing away the topic as if it were a troublesome insect. "Not that I want to bother you with my troubles. Just giving you the lay of the land, so to speak. And you, Johnny, what're you doing back here?"

Johnny Cross shrugged. "I came home for a little peace and quiet, Luke. That's all."

"You come to the wrong place."

"And to lay low. The Border States ain't too healthy for any of Quantrill's crowd."

"You wanted, Johnny?"

"Not in Texas." After a pause, he said, "Not in this part of Texas." .

"You could do worse. Hangtree's a big county with lots of room to get lost in. The Yanks are quartered forty miles northwest at Fort Pardee in the Breaks. They don't come to Hangtown much, and when they do they's just passing through. They got their hands full chasing Indians."

"They catch any?"

Luke laughed. "From what I hear, they got to look sharp to keep the Indians from catching them."

"Good, that'll keep 'em out of my hair."

"What're your plans, Johnny?"

"One thing I know is horses. Mustangs still running at Wild Horse Gulch?"

"More now than ever, since nobody was rounding 'em up during the war."

"Figured I'd collect a string and sell 'em. Folks always need horses, even in hard times. Maybe I'll sell 'em to those bluebellies at the fort."

Luke was shocked. "You wouldn't!"

"Gold's gold and the Yanks are the ones that got it nowadays," said Johnny Cross.

Something in the air made him look back. A dust cloud showed in the distance east on the road, a brown smudge on the lip of the blue bowl of sky. Johnny reined in, turning the horse to face back the way they came. "Company's coming," he said.

"Generally that means trouble in these parts," Luke said.

"Ain't necessarily so, but that's the way to bet it," he added.

Johnny Cross unfastened the catch of the saddlebag on his right-hand side, reaching in and pulling out a revolver. A big .44 front-loading cap-and-ball six-gun like the ones worn on his hips: new, clean and potent.

"Here," he said, holding it out to Luke. "Take it," he said when the other hesitated.

Luke took it. The gun had a satisfying heft and balance in his hand. "A six-gun! One of them repeating revolvers," Luke marveled.

"Know how to use it?" Johnny asked.

"After four years with Hood's Brigade?" Luke said in disbelief.

"In that case I'd better show you how it works, then. I wouldn't want you shooting me or yourself by accident," Johnny said, straight-faced.

Luke's scowl broke into a twisted grin. "Shucks, you're joshing me," he said.

"I am? That's news to me."

"You're still doing it, dang you."

Johnny Cross flashed him a quick grin, strong white teeth gleaming, laugh-lines curling up around the corners of his hazel eyes. A boyish grin, likable somehow, with nothing mean in it.

Sure, Johnny was funning Luke. Hood's Brigade of Texans was one of the hardest-fighting outfits of the Confederacy, whose army had been distinguished by a host of fierce and valiant fighters.

Johnny turned the horse's head, pointing it west, urging it forward into a fast walk.

Luke stuck the pistol into the top of his waistband on his left side, butt-out. "It's good to have something to fill the hand with. Been feeling half-nekkid without one," he said.

"With what's left of that uniform, you are half-nekkid," Johnny said.

"How many more of them ventilators you got tucked in them saddlebags?"

"Never enough."

"You must have been traveling in some fast company, Johnny. I heard Quantrill's men rode into battle with a half-dozen guns or more. That true?"

"And more. Reloading takes time. A fellow wants a gun to hand when he wants it."

Luke was enthusiastic. "Man, what we couldn't have done with a brace of these for every man in the old outfit!"

"If only," Johnny said flatly. His eyes were hard, cold.

A couple of hundred yards farther west, a stand of timber grew on the left side of the road. A grove of cottonwood trees.

East, the brown dust cloud grew. "Fair amount of riders from the dust they're kicking up. Coming pretty fast, too," said Luke, looking back.

"Wouldn't it be something if it was that bunch who cleaned you out?"

"It sure would. Any chance it's somebody on your trail, Johnny?"

"I ain't been back long enough."

Luke laughed. "Don't feel bad about it, hoss," he said. "It's early yet."

Johnny Cross turned the horse left, off the dirt road into the cottonwood grove. The shade felt good, thin though it was. The Texas sun was plenty fierce, even at the start of spring. Sunlight shining through spaces in the canopy of trees dappled the ground with a mosaic of light and shade. A wild hare started, springing across the glade for the cover of tall grass.

Johnny took the horse in deep behind a concealing screen of brush. "We'll just let these rannies have the right of way so we can get a looksee at 'em."

Luke was serious, in dead earnest. "Johnny—if it is that pack that tore into me—Monty is mine."

"Whoa, boy. Don't go getting ahead of yourself, Luke. Even if it is your bunch—especially if it is—don't throw down on 'em without my say-so. They'll get what's coming to 'em, I promise you that. But we'll pick the time and place. Two men shooting off the back of one horse ain't the most advantageous layout for a showdown.

"I know you got a hard head, but beware a hot one. It should have cooled some after four years of war," Johnny said.

"Well—it ain't," said Luke.

Johnny grinned. "Me neither," he said.

The blur at the base of the dust cloud sweeping west along the road resolved itself into a column of riders. About a dozen men or so.

They came in tandem: four pairs in front, then the wagon, then two horsemen bringing up the rear. Hard-bitten men doing some hard traveling, as indicated by the trail dust covering them and the sweat-streaked flanks of their horses. They wore civilian clothes, broad-brimmed hats, flannel shirts, denim pants. Each rider was armed with a holstered sidearm and a carbine in a saddle-scabbard.

A team of six horses yoked in tandem drew the wagon. Two men rode up front at the head of the wagon: the driver and a shotgun messenger. A freight wagon with an oblong-shaped hopper, it was ten feet long, four feet wide, and three feet high. A canvas tarpaulin tied down over the top of the hopper concealed its contents. Crates, judging by the shape of them under the tarp.

The column came along at a brisk pace, kicking up plenty of dust. There was the pounding of hoofbeats, the hard breathing of the horses, the creak of saddle leather. Wagon wheels rumbled, clattering.

The driver wore his hat teamster-style, with the brim turned up in front. The men of the escort were hard-eyed, grim-faced, wary. They glanced at the cottonwood grove but spotted no sign of the duo on horseback.

On they rode, dragging a plume of brown dirt in their wake. It obscured the scene long after its creators had departed it. Some of the dust drifted into the glade, fine powder falling on Johnny, Luke, and the horse. Some dust got in the chestnut's nostrils and he sneezed.

Luke cleared his throat, hawked up a glob of

phlegm, and spat. Johnny took a swig from his canteen to wash the dust out out of his mouth and throat, then passed the canteen to Luke. "What do you make of that?" he asked.

"You tell me," Luke said.

"You're the one who's been back for a while."

"I never saw that bunch before. But I don't get into town much."

"I'll tell you this: they was loaded for bear."

"They must've been Yankees."

"How can you tell? They don't wear signs, Luke."

"They looked like they was doing all right. Well-fed, good guns and mounts, clothes that wasn't rags. Only folks getting along in these parts are Yankees and outlaws.

"They was escorting the wagon, doing a job of work. Outlaws don't work. So they must be Yanks, damn their eyes."

"Could be."

"They got the right idea, though. Nothing gets nowhere in Hangtree less'n it's well-guarded," said Luke. "Wonder what was in that wagon?"

"I wonder," Johnny Cross said, thoughtfully stroking his chin. A hard, predatory gleam came to his narrowed eyes as they gazed in the direction where the convoy had gone.